Latter-Day Dora

Latter-Day Dora

Jane Gillespie

PETER DAVIES : LONDON

Peter Davies Limited
15 Queen Street, Mayfair, London W1X 8BE
LONDON MELBOURNE TORONTO
JOHANNESBURG AUCKLAND

Printed in Great Britain by
Northumberland Press Limited
Gateshead

I

No one who had ever seen Deborah Dring in her childhood would have supposed her destined, in the terms of her generation, to be a heroine. Her parents were affectionate and enlightened and had fed and housed her most adequately; she had attended a progressively liberal school, where she had worked quite hard and gained four A-levels; she had good health, good looks and a normally amiable temper. Yet with all these disadvantages, she had not been five months in London on her university course before she had appeared once at a VD clinic and twice in court.

The first of these occasions turned out to be a false alarm. The second, on a charge of possession of drugs, resulted in a discharge with a warning. But on the third occasion, after Deborah had assaulted a policeman, a more serious view was taken by everyone except, apparently, Deborah.

Her parents were, this time, apprised of their daughter's adventure, and her mother travelled down to London to attend the court and to discuss the situation with everyone except Deborah, who maintained a silence—lofty, or sullen—that insulated her effectively.

All she said was: 'They can send me to prison if they must.'

Her mother suspected that Deborah was, if anything, simply exhausted. She had not seen her since the beginning of her London career, since Deborah had not been home for Christmas. The excitements of London had already changed her; she looked grey all over, as if shrivelled from within and grubby without. The latter was understandable since she was

[5]

living at present in a squat in Maida Vale, along with about twelve friends, deprived of running water and electricity.

What she had been doing with herself, apart from throwing home-made bombs at policemen, Deborah did not relate; evidently, she hadn't been going to any university classes.

'*That* crap,' she said, distantly, when her course of study was mentioned; it was clear that she had already dismissed if not forgotten it.

Her mother, alone among Deborah's immediate well-wishers, did not press her to explain herself. That could keep. Consulting all the relevant officials, she was persuaded by them—as much as she persuaded them—that Deborah's offence was not grievous nor her character irredeemable. Probably she had been carried away by the excitement of the political protest during which she had hurled the bomb, which, anyway, according to witnesses, had been thrust into her hand by a fellow-protester; the policeman, whom she had anyway missed by a couple of feet, had had the misfortune to come round a corner untimely. Generally, Deborah could be blamed only for being young and excitable and for keeping bad company. Even this blame was laid on obliquely; everyone conspired to excuse her; if Deborah were conscious of her good luck, she gave no sign of it. Throughout all the proceedings and discussions she manifested an increasing boredom.

It was decided that Deborah might be taken home, where care and supervision should be the best in her present circumstances. The various authorities agreed that the girl's mother seemed a responsible and intelligent woman; of her father, as the author of *Ebb Tide* and *The Summit*, some of them had heard; *that* Alan Dring...? It was as if a writer, possibly bohemian but still liberal and regenerative, must necessarily exert a positive influence. Both Dring parents, the authorities learnt, had started life as schoolteachers; they lived nowadays in beautiful rural surroundings; all in all, Deborah would be better off there, and less of a charge on public funds besides, than under any more formal detention.

'Her own home will do more for her than anything just now,' they told the mother.

It didn't seem to have done much for Deborah so far, judging from this situation; but in view of everything, Judy Dring didn't bother to point that out to them.

Late at night on Euston station, when mother and daughter were for virtually the first time alone together, Judy was merely as bored with the whole issue as Deborah still appeared; she felt, anyhow, quite as exhausted as Deborah looked. There would be so much to discuss and reflect on and plan, arising out of the débâcle, but, for God's sake, not *yet*.

Also from the look of Deborah, Judy was not in for any immediate unbosomings, but she did not doubt they would come; she had always been on such terms with Debby. Meanwhile there was the journey to be endured by both of them.

She had not expected to be able to bring Deborah back with her. The wonder was that she'd brought enough money for another ticket. As it was, they had had only enough for a sandwich at the buffet, after telephoning Alan—repellent sandwiches, too, but Judy had finally eaten Deborah's as well as her own, not to waste anything. The food had warmed her a little, and so had changing back into trousers and duffel coat. Her go-to-town suit, which she had thought called for by the occasion, was now in her suitcase, on which she perched, waiting for the train. She indicated the other corner of the case to Deborah, who glanced at it but took no further notice. All the February winds from the far north whistled along the platform, drifting grit.

'You're going to be cold,' remarked Judy. 'I can get out my red sweater for you.' And, after a moment: 'Are you sure you haven't got any luggage at *all*?'

This, almost above all else, gave Deborah an air of more than poverty—of inhumanity. Rather than a ghost of herself,

[7]

she was to Judy's eyes just now a corpse of herself. Ghosts, necessarily haunting, imply even by that some sense of attachment; it didn't seem to Judy human to leave a city where one has lived, empty-handed. She thought, not of toothbrushes and necessities, but of books for instance—trinkets—surely a young girl must ... Well, if not, there was an adjustment to be made that was just now beyond Judy. She stared for a moment quite detachedly at this skinny stranger, knowing herself excluded, as it were by the death of a problem. Her tiredness beaten back by Deborah's unresponsiveness accepted a truce. So that, on the train, as the rhythm of motion began to tick her mind over a little, maternal anxiety remained numb —after all, here Debby safely was, imprisoned and in transit, even asleep?—and Judy pondered the problem in general, or, deprived of Debby's personality, let the problem attach itself to her own. She thought: I simply don't understand what goes on nowadays; what gets *into* them...?

Judy, and Alan—their ages were about the same—had been young during the passive-resistance era. Deborah had been on an Aldermaston march in her pram. Judy's dedication to non-violence had been total but she hadn't, she was pretty sure, preached it to her children in such a way as to force a reaction. So what the hell had made this next generation violence-crazy? Judy couldn't see. She hitched herself up and slid down again uncomfortably. Leaning across Deborah in her corner, she wiped the steamy pane with her sleeve; outside, the lights from the train flickered across an embankment, with scabs of snow on dead grass. One supposed there were swings of pendulums, but this one had overswung; there was no correspondence at all between *that* ideal and *this* barbarism ... What Judy, especially in the nonplussedness of this moment, could not conceive of, was that her own principles could prove ineffective. So she came up against this blank; she had knelt in the snow outside nuclear weapons bases and been douched with cold water from the deck of a nuclear submarine, and something of those experiences had remained precious; she would have deeply resented anyone who asked: But what *good* did it all do?

Her own father, on an escapade with a band of 'irregulars', had slit the throat of a German sentry. An uncle had taken part in saturation bombing raids. Judy, ten years after the end of the war, had asked them vehemently: 'But what *good* did it all do?' They had scowled at her but given her no satisfactory answer.

And twenty years later, of her own daughter she thought: There can't ever have been *such* a gap between one generation and the next as there is now— The whole lot of them seem to have gone underground ... And she felt finally out of touch with Deborah inert there, strands of greasy hair hiding her impenetrable face.

Judy, on a train at night, alone, unoccupied and overtired —all unusual to her—saw the gap opening between herself and the world. Imposed vacancy threw up: What's the *point*? ... If one's values are superseded, how can anything make sense?

Her education, and nature, wouldn't let her at any rate deny those values. Thinking, as education conditions one to, from the inside outwards, she could not impose the world on herself. Identified with truth, how could Judy essentially change? The train's jolting, and its brackish light, made her look all of her forty-five and scraggy and bitter with it, but a part of her was always the Judy, aged ten, being told by her brother about the extermination camps of Poland. Some moments were, in revelation, eternal—

The train stopped at a station; Crewe, or somewhere. Judy felt Deborah stir and heard her drily yawning. Bodies barged along the aisle and cold air slid along the floor. Deborah asked her first and only question of the week:

'Why did you come down, and not Daddy?'

Judy opened her eyes, astonished by a reminder of blessed normal nowadays-life; in fact she could hardly remember it— but towards it, inconceivable as tomorrow's dawn, this train was carrying them. She said, confused: '... I don't know ...' and as she drew in a breath to start explaining, saw that Deborah had lost interest and hunched herself into her corner again.

The train dragged itself on, into darker night concealing wilder country. Towns fell behind and moorland stretched towards the rising hills and the dawn and the promise of peace and home.

There was yet no sign of dawn when the alarm clock began to ring in the back bedroom of Broom Cottage. It began only, because at the first chink of its bell Alan Dring's hand shot out and whammed down its button. The icy rural silence of the night closed in again.

In it, Dring sat up, looking towards the open window and thinking briefly of Judy rattling along in some stuffy train— Where, by now? Lumbering over Shap...? He switched on the lamp and reached for his clothes, making with them for the comparative warmth of the bathroom. Then for the welcoming warmth of the kitchen, where he riddled the Rayburn, filled a kettle and stood yawning, watching it.

It was six years since he had had to get up early in the mornings. It was pleasant to know that, if he had to now, he still could. Dring liked, without seeking, these little reassurances. It was positively pleasant from this distance to remember the daily scramble with collar and bus and books and razor ... He absently ran his fingers through his beard— But while the kettle boiled, he ought to be making sure the car would start.

Outside he said: '*Whooo* ...' aloud as the cold enveloped him. He kicked at the byre door to free it of ice and rammed it back against the yard wall. The car started; only the surrounding silence made it sound querulous, noisier than usual. Dring ran it into the lane and came indoors to a kitchen full of steam. Lydia in her pyjamas was scratching her head in the doorway. 'You might', pointed out her father, 'have taken that kettle off.'

She looked at it. 'You woke me up, starting the car.'

'D'you want to come with me?' Dring asked, hefting the kettle.

'Where?'

Impatiently, he reminded her: 'To meet Mummy and Deb.'

'Oh,' she registered, flumping into a chair by the table. 'Where?' she added, scratching a foot.

Since she knew perfectly well where, Dring did not reply. Lydia irritated him nowadays; he made no allowance for her being still half asleep. Besides he was hunting about for the tea caddy, forgetting for the hundredth time about the tea dispenser his sister-in-law had given them for Christmas ... 'Carlisle?' Lydia presently suggested, and then, after slow and anxious thought: 'Would I be late for school?'

'I shouldn't think so. D'you want some tea?' He had punched a lavish amount into the pot, which he stirred with the handle of a fork. Lydia stared at him, weighing his assurance about school, then sighed and said gloomily:

'It'll be nice when Mummy's back.'

Dring, who thought so too, did not agree. That Lydia was now staring at the sink where last night's slightly burnt casserole was soaking, he took as a reflection on his housekeeping; though he had coped perfectly well. Only, the absence of Judy gave an expectation of dishevelment that denied the house's tidiness. 'Get dressed, if you're coming,' he said, curtly. 'I'm going in five minutes.'

'Oh all right ... What shall I wear?'

Consoled by a sip of hot tea Dring said in a milder tone: 'Anything warm. And hurry up.' She had not waited for an answer but was on her way upstairs, ignoring her mug of tea. Dring leaned on the stove with his, relaxing and beginning himself to wake up.

Or resuming, more exactly, his own life, which nowadays was deeply channelled in that area of his sub-being that dealt with his work. Propped against the stove with both hands round his mug and eyelids drooping he was more evidently going back to sleep. For these blessed five minutes he might brood over the abyss, calmed by the prospect of having Judy back and having more chance of settling down to writing. Perhaps, even, the domestic interruptions of the last few days had provided a fertile pause. Once he started again, he'd find it was all going better than before ... In which case, urgency could slacken; he thought of nothing but the aroma of tea.

'Loafing about,' his father would have said. If Dring had recollected this now, it would have been merely with amusement.

Dring's father had thought it right at all times to control the circumstances of his children for their own good. To this end he had concealed from them his own financial position, lest they suppose they had expectations; which, as it turned out on his sudden death, they might well have had. His death came as a happy surprise, not entirely, it must be candidly admitted, for financial reasons.

Philip Dring had been particularly apprehensive of the effect of independent means on his elder son Alan, who, as a young man, had wanted to be a writer. Given the chance he might throw up his safe and useful career in teaching for such a whim. In the event, that is just what Alan Dring did on receiving his patrimony, although he had by then, he thought, abandoned the idea.

Alan Dring was thirty-eight when his father died and beginning to resign himself to middle age. If he had never chucked teaching for writing it was because he didn't think he would be a good enough writer, and not because he didn't think he would earn enough money by it. It was Judy's expressed wish for a country life that first tempted him. Couldn't they, she said, 'get right away'— What about the Lake District, where he'd had such marvellous holidays...? She tackled agents and found Broom Cottage and they began to calculate possibilities. If they sold out all his father's shares or whatevers, and bought the cottage outright, and made some insurance for Deborah's school fees (she was about to start at Mede Hall and they saw that as a priority) and budgeted for fairly simple housekeeping, they ought to be all right for two to three years. Lydia was then not quite four; her education was surely tomorrow's worry.

'After all,' said Dring, 'we're not committing ourselves ... I could always get a job again.'

'Or, *I* could,' said Judy, heroically. She had already gone back to teaching for a year after Deborah first started school, and had hated every minute of it. That wasn't surprising, since she'd taken the job on the advice of her doctor because she had been suffering from depression, brought on by various strains in her marriage; teaching had set up more strains in every direction, and altogether that had been a bad patch, patched over in turn by the birth of Lydia a year or so later. What surprised both Alan and Judy on their removal to Broom Cottage was the rebirth of their marriage. They seemed to turn to each other in delighted recognition. For that alone, it was worth the upheaval and the share-selling fuss.

'But for God's sake,' said Alan's brother Michael, inheritor of their father's business acumen, 'those are *investments*— you can't just realize the lot—'

Judy's mother remarked: 'And now, I suppose, Alan will just sit down and try to write.'

That was the last thing Alan intended, because he had, and secretly knew he had, deny it as he might and had, the spirit of a writer. To 'try to write' would stifle that. So he busied himself about the cottage till his freedom worked on him inwardly and he felt himself rising to a surface; then one day he threw down his screwdriver and found a pencil and began *Ebb Tide*.

From that point, if he looked back, it was not to reflect that he'd wasted his life so far, but to see it as no sort of a life at all.

'Do you really,' said Michael Dring's wife Fiona, with some

deference, after she had read what 'they' said in *The Sunday Times* and *Observer* about *Ebb Tide*, 'think now, it was worth giving up so much for ... this?'

Alan and Judy merely laughed. They couldn't remember giving up anything.

They weren't short of critics of their new style of life; unless it was that, in their very happiness, there was a quality that made them over-aware of disapproval. Perhaps this helped to make them more self-sufficient, which was as well, considering they had left friends and social life behind in the London area. (Miss Mitchell in the village told Judy: 'Be sure not to have a spare bedroom, or you'll find all your friends are terribly anxious to come and stay, when you live in a place like this!') Dring found himself highly sensitive to criticism of *Ebb Tide*, but that was because he'd never before exposed such a tender and undeniable part of himself to public scrutiny. So he was not attracted to literary or London company; in any case, criticism of *Ebb Tide* was far more favourable than not, and already he was burgeoning with another creation. When his agent wrote to hope Dring would not have 'second-novel trouble' Dring had no idea what he meant; his second novel *The Summit* sailed off as smoothly as *Ebb Tide* and was almost as well received. Reviewers habitually compared it with *Ebb Tide*, having some second-novel trouble themselves, but by then Dring was forming a protective shell against them. He felt he was only beginning to draw on his inner resources. All his life, ideas had been pent up in him; now he was free to produce them; he was turning to poetry, conscious of progress. He knew just what Keats meant by a 'teeming brain'.

Incidentally the two novels sold fairly well; it was no fault of Dring's that prices during those years were rising so fast.

Social life, the Drings felt little need of, which was also as well, because the neighbourhood was small. Locally they ranked as 'off-comers', somewhere between natives and visitors, and were left by both groups to pursue their own affairs.

Lydia began to attend the village school but the Drings were not churchgoers and Judy did not feel obliged to join the W.I. Broom Cottage stood apart up its stony lane so they had no popping-in neighbours. They could, by putting Deborah and Lydia in the same bedroom, entertain staying guests, and sometimes did, especially relatives who announced their arrival as if by right, and who, observed Judy, ate a great deal, complained a great deal of bad weather as if the Drings had laid it on for them, and came through with a potted plant or box of chocolates for the children on departure. When Deborah's Mede Hall cronies reached hitch-hiking age, bevies of them descended in the holidays, but often they pitched tents in the garden and were satisfied with baked beans. The Drings had no television but listened to the radio and took in the *Guardian* and *New Statesman*; Cockermouth library was helpful in finding books; Dring did not consider himself a recluse. In touch with the weather of fells and dales he felt himself, too, vitally in touch with the essential world. Poetically brooding over his mug of tea, he wondered only hazily what effect it might have on life when Deborah was brought home in disgrace.

2

THE DRINGS, reassembling at this unusual hour in the gloom of Carlisle station, felt in any case rather strange to each other. It wasn't till full daybreak, as they bowled along the hog's-back road towards Cockermouth, that normality began to dawn. Here they were again, going somewhere, packed into their own little world-on-wheels like any other family nowadays.

Judy said, surprised: 'It's going to be a nice day.'

She ran her fingers through the hair she had combed before she left the train, as if settling it into a more comfortable untidiness. The smell of train still clung to her but the sight of this landscape visibly refreshed her; she no longer looked scraggy and bitter, but wiry and intelligent. 'Look,' she pointed, 'Criffel—'

'M'm,' agreed Dring, indulging her sense of novelty; envying it, for a moment: It must be wonderful to come *back* here.

To their right, the Solway and even the Scottish hills were appearing; left, the lakeland fells' covering of snow took on the glister of freshly ironed damask. Judy wound her window down further.

Lydia turned to stare at Deborah, whose eyes were shut. She prodded Deborah's elbow and said: 'Hey *Deb* ...' And as the eyes foggily opened: 'You might *look*. You haven't been home for ages.'

Deborah looked, foggily, ahead over Dring's shoulder.

Lydia pursued: 'What've you come home for anyway? Are you pregnant or what?'

Judy said: 'Don't bother her, Lyddie. She's tired.'

'Well,' said Lydia, sitting forward with a bounce, 'nobody ever tells *me* anything. I only wondered—'

Lydia, just eleven, was approaching the adult world in a series of in-and-out bounces. Lately she had displayed a talent for saying the wrong thing and taking offence when she failed to see why it was. Now she changed tack and went straight on: 'But you know Mummy, I told you didn't I, Susan Martin said she was getting a pony, well, she hasn't, *yet*, so that shows she's only a great big liar ...'

Judy turned round to listen, glancing incidentally at Deborah, who in this cleaner light looked even dingier and more shrivelled, in contrast perhaps to Lydia. The two daughters resembled each other and their father—fair, square-nosed, dimple-chinned—leaving Judy alone in being dark and slightly beaky. This morning, Dring in his guernsey, Lydia in her quilted anorak, looked immensely solid and well-fed, scrubbed to a polished glow by the winter winds; Judy stretched back to put her hand on Deborah's knee:

'Nearly home, darling.'

Deborah did not respond; Dring glanced at her in his driving mirror. 'She all right?' he asked Judy aside.

'Well ... We'll have to see ...' she murmured.

'Not going to be sick or anything, I meant?'

'Oh no.'

He nodded, returning his attention to the road as they came to the half-awake town. Through it, they shot on south, faster, as if the car were a horse recollecting its stable. It left the main road, climbed, twisted through a couple of hamlets, and crunched up their lane to stop, when Dring had snapped on the handbrake, in total silence and the first of the sunlight.

It seemed to Judy that the kitchen woke up as she entered it, the blue-striped plates and some oranges in a bowl opening like eyes. 'Let's', she said on a long breath, 'all have a *big* breakfast.'

'Excellent idea,' said Dring, who at first, coming in behind

her, had looked round too, but doubtfully, not quite es-
tablishing contact. Now he relaxed, sitting down to pull on
his slippers.

'I'll be late for school if you start *cooking* things—' protested
Lydia, kicking off her gumboots on the doorstep.

'You won't— It won't take long ... Have we got any
bacon?' said Judy with the frying pan in her hand. She had
thrust her suitcase and coat into the passage and was so much
back in command that she added apologetically: 'It seems
funny, not to know—'

'I think you'll find', Dring told her, coolly, 'that the
domestic scene is adequately maintained—'

'Yes, I can see, everything's fine— But don't take that tone;
it's your own house, to muck up if you want to ... Oh yes,
here's bacon. Where did you get it? It looks rather bony ...
Anyway, I can go into town later, because I did order the
bread last week, didn't I ... It seems so long ago— And I'll
be able to go in tonight, too, after all—'

'Tonight? Oh God yes,' said Dring. 'That class.'

'Friday ... I warned them I might not be back; I'd better
ring.' She had laid the bony bacon in the pan and went to the
pantry for eggs, adding over her shoulder: 'Lyddie, lay the
table, please?'

'But I've got to do my *hair*—'

'Darling, it's only *ten past*.'

Dring was brooding with his elbows on the table. He'd forgotten that it was Friday, which meant that Judy would be
going to take her evening class, which meant that the other
end of this day would be bunged up too; its middle,
threatened, now dwindled; he'd probably get nothing at all
done ... He regretted, as he'd known he would, letting Judy
do that class. Not that he could have prevented her, and not
that he could deny the money was useful; besides, she enjoyed
it; but it was odd how, when something happened 'only one
evening in the week', it always was that evening; Fridays
came round thick and fast— It was odd too how tiresome he

[18]

found them, when all that was required of him was to be in the house and simply tell Lydia to go to bed if she didn't, which in fact she almost always did. He sighed, looking forward in his dwindled day no further than to the immediately cheering prospect of breakfast.

Lydia started slamming cutlery and bread-board on the table. In the commotion of arrival, no one had noticed that Deborah, the central cause of it, had been ignored. She was standing inside the door, shoulders sagging, hands in the pockets of her jeans. Lydia barged past her to get mugs from the shelf and said: 'Why don't you sit down or something?'

Judy turned, looked at Deborah thoughtfully and said: 'What you need is a bath, don't you think?'

Dring looked up at her frowning, puzzled by something about her but unable to see what that was. As he said nothing, and Deborah still said nothing, and Judy waited to be answered, Lydia too paused to stare at Deborah, this curious core of uncertainty—of nonentity—suddenly planted in the middle of their house.

Then Judy said, over-brightly: 'Come on; let's eat.'

Broom Cottage did not rise to a 'study' for its literary owner. He worked in the largest—or least small—bedroom, his and Judy's. This morning, serene with food, he threw the continental quilt over the bed, put away his pyjamas, straightened the rug, and sat down at his table in the window ready for what he disliked calling 'work'. His eyes traced habitually the lines of the view: one tall sycamore, a group of alders, the beck tumbling past them, then upward to bracken and rushes on either side of the gill that presently flattened into dull grass and the skyline of the fellside. He found this outlook, he said, less distracting than the wider views from the other sides of the cottage. At present the trees were bare, the beck ice-fringed, bracken rusty-dead, and thin snow swept up to the rim of a sky already blue. For six years now Dring had more or less absently gazed at all this, in all seasons and weathers, and it was more or less a state of his own mind to him.

He had begun to notice that when he glanced up in the middle of a productive train of ideas, he dwelt on the lower part of the gill where water showed. Stuck, he stared at the bouldery section among the bracken. When he'd completed a stint, he rested his vision on the smooth grass of the upland. Satisfied with it, he detached his mind by looking right up at that narrow strip of sky.

He hoped this was no sort of a superstition with him, especially as, recently, he'd found himself fixing his half-attention more and more on that upper grass where the gill had dried up. Dring was sure he himself was nowhere near 'drying up'. Still, once or twice he'd fancied the view was getting too much of a habit and he might move to another room for work—or would that be a superstition?

Delightfully difficult, this tuning-in to the creative spirit. Like, Dring imagined, prayer. A tremendous negative effort; a submission. He sighed, fiddling with sheets of paper, beset by the usual excuses and distractions—he was too full of bacon and egg, almost sleepy; he ought really to verify those references about Engels before even considering the next section of his novel; he couldn't settle to that before he'd re-drafted the 'autumn' poem ... Nor had he remembered to buy cartridges for his pen— Hadn't Judy said she was going shopping...? Besides, he couldn't help thinking about Deb.

Of whom he had expected such great things. But, for heaven's sake, the girl was barely nineteen; this dark consternation in himself that he had hesitated to examine couldn't be labelled as disappointment. Probing at it, Dring still couldn't identify it. He couldn't identify, perhaps, this glum, dingy creature Judy had brought home with his brilliant, golden little girl. Nor could he remember quite what he had expected—hysterics, rebellion, attitudes; argument and scenes? Deprived of which, he had simply found the glumness infectious; he sighed more heavily, spreading his elbows on the table.

Deborah had always been a surprise to him. Fatherhood had kept him marvelling, from the first appearance of such a miniature creature complete with fingernails, to the development of a being so different from his, though presumably his own. He had admired her respectfully, marvelling at so analytical an intelligence, such intuitive political grasp, such quickness in mental arithmetic, such deftness with the workings of cameras and tents. Admiration of all the qualities in her that he had not— Had that, he now wondered, set him too far apart from her? When she was little she wanted to be with him more than anything in the world. At thirteenish— approaching adolescence—she had drifted off rather; which Dring had tried not to let her know he minded (telling himself that independence was bound to be a feature of her age, it was a recognized fact; like many who fancy themselves original thinkers, he fell back on the thoughts of others when discomfited). Though, looking back from this point of uncertainty, *should* he have tried to keep her...? Oh, but now he was getting morbid. The two of them had always had a lot in common. For instance, it was he who had introduced her to, and shared with her, the fells ...

He was slumped over the table, lost in the mist on Eel Crag, Deb's hair soaked, her cheeks pink, her high, resolute voice telling him: '... A hundred paces due east from here ought to bring us just about to the trig stone ...' as she bent over the compass in his cold hand— When he managed to remind himself that he had slid into daydream. Hoisting himself upright he began to shuffle his papers again. It was—what time? Time to be getting something done, anyhow.

The house was quiet. The racket of Lydia's departure for school had ended some while ago. Taps had been running, the fire-door of the Rayburn banging, but now, emptiness ... Into which a sharp recollection stabbed: Coke. He hadn't told Judy ... Oh damn.

Yes, but a pretext for going downstairs at least got him moving and allowed him to see Judy again. She looked as if she'd never been away, sitting at the kitchen table in her yellow overall, apparently writing a shopping list while washing soaked in the sink, warmly steaming the window and closing off the chilly outdoors. 'I forgot to tell you,' began Dring, '... I could do with some coffee.' He went for the kettle, easing it clear of the washing to fit it under the tap. '—Joe Rigg rang; they haven't got the coke in yet. So he won't be delivering it before the weekend at best. I think', he added vaguely, 'somebody's on strike ...'

Judy said in her oblique fashion: 'As it is, I'll have to buy *some* clothes for Debby. She's brought literally nothing but what she stands up in, and that'll fall to bits in the wash from the look of it.'

Dring thought that over, running his hands over his face. On a yawn he asked: 'Did you have enough with you?'

'Yes, but I've brought none of it back.'

'... I'm beginning to feel as if I got up too early.'

'So you did,' she said, glancing up, solicitous.

'But *you*; why not go to bed for a bit, now?'

'I'm not tired. Being home's enough.'

'What was it like?' he asked suddenly, dropping his hands to study her with more alertness. 'Being in town again, apart from anything else?' They had slid away from the topic of money, on which they never dwelt; sliding away from that topic usually gave Dring more interest in the next, but he did want to know what poor Judy had been going through while he languished here using up the coke.

'Well, it mostly was anything else, if you see what I mean ... I didn't notice. Oh, Stella sends her love. And Richard. They wouldn't let me pay them, which was just as well.'

'We'll send them something ... Coffee, yourself?' he asked, going for mugs. 'I expect it was as hellish cold as ever in their flat. But you must have done a good job on all those police and people. More than *I* could ...'

Judy looked up again, as if wondering at something in his tone. They were talking in the lower-key voices of intimates;

on his last remark Dring had raised his voice slightly, and he was making a business of filling the mugs. He pushed Judy's towards her with some ceremony. 'There you are,' he said, unnecessarily.

'I've mucked up your day,' she admitted. 'As well as the last several ... Has Lyddie been good?'

'I suppose so. Yes. I daresay I'm just having a stagnant phase.'

After a pause Judy said: 'Oh well ...' with so little expression that one could not have called the comment as much as tactful. She was stirring her coffee, very slowly.

She did not need, explicitly, to encourage Dring in his writing. She valued his work with a sincerity that she did not need to make evident, and in the pattern of their marriage they talked about that even less than about money. According to pattern they discussed topics only when they were not fully in sympathy on them; sex, for instance, between them, they had rarely had occasion to mention. Possibly for this reason they had not yet, even now they were apart from her, mentioned Deborah. Yet, as they silently drank their coffee, the quiet of the rest of the house began to echo Dring's confessed stagnation. Glancing from side to side, aware of something missing, he presently asked: 'Where *is* she?'

'I sent her to bed,' Judy told him, soothingly; she didn't really want to start up the Deborah-question while he was in this mood, half in and half out of his work. All the same she couldn't help adding: 'I can't think quite how to approach her—'

'*You* can't?'

She bent her head, fidgeting with her shopping list. Before seeing Deborah she had fixed on no attitude; she had waited to see whether compassion or reproach would be more in order. Since meeting her, Judy had had to admit that nothing, where Deborah was concerned, was in order; unevoked reactions cancelled each other out; she had, on the train, begun to hope only that getting home would rouse Deborah to life;

and, since getting home, that perhaps ... 'I wondered,' she said helplessly, 'whether *you* ...'

'She hasn't even looked at me yet,' said Dring angrily.

'Well— Nor at me. I do hope,' Judy went on, sitting up, 'they won't want us to pay back her grant for this term—'

'The things you think of,' said Dring, turning away to clap down his mug by the sink. 'Why the hell should they? If she hasn't been to any classes or anything they ought not to be out of pocket on her—'

'I don't really know how it works,' Judy said, dismissing that; but as he turned to go: '—Oh and, by the way, she's got to report to the probation officer or somebody, in Workington, I expect it will be—'

'*God,*' said Dring in final disgust. He spun round from the door as if all exits were denied him. 'Bloody impertinence— Do "they" suppose we can't keep her in order ourselves?'

Judy said nothing. She rose, and went to peer at her washing. If Alan could only get down to work he'd take everything else a lot more calmly; 'off' work, he seemed to go off life in general, she'd noticed. Saying nothing was at such moments her most valuable contribution. Over his writing they were in their closest accord; from the outset she'd known better than to come out with; 'How's it going, dear?' or any such inanities. Whether they could or could not keep Deborah in order, Judy would rather not enter on with him at the moment.

And Dring, scowling, did not pursue his question. He found himself thinking only about lunch— How long till...? But after a large breakfast he couldn't be hungry. This was just a kind of nervous dissatisfaction. All *right*, so the day was already wasted; admitting which, he was weighed down intolerably by the very idea of finding something *else* to do; the hours ahead of him were solid and grey as porridge, through which he must somehow shove his way, all incentive gone. Ought he, for instance, he wondered, to offer to go and do the shopping, since Judy was busy here and would have to drive into town later to her class? Yes, he ought. It was a good idea, a useful and helpful idea, and the more he tried to admire it the more loathsome it became. Inertia increased, in inverse proportion to his active intention. He leaned on the doorpost and stared at the steamed-up window, imprisoned in his own fogged-up mind, waiting for energy to show just a flicker, show him he was still alive.

Deborah stood staring out of her bedroom window in the gable end of the cottage. This was the finest view from the place; between tipsy old larches she looked down a slope of fields to the fells beyond Loweswater and, when the trees were bare, to a glimmer of the lake itself. The sky was magnificent, with slate-dark clouds piled in the clear blue, and gold-and-indigo patches splashed across the high snow. Her pet fell, Mellbreak, glowered northwards with its dark, dead-heather face. And it was all quite, quite unreal. Deborah just stared, only faintly surprised by this continuing unreality of everything, because nothing so unreal could seriously matter.

Life had snapped off as suddenly as a dream, only it was the dream that was real. Since the climax of events, at the demo, she had been in a wonderland where everybody else was crazy. She knew herself a heroine; if nobody else recognized this, it was too bad for them. Deborah couldn't be expected to enlighten them. Besides, they were barmy; they got it all wrong.

You mightn't expect them to grant the principle, but they could at least have tried to get the facts right, Deborah reflected, observing them from her distance. Even Mummy— or Ma, as Deborah had more recently taken to calling her— had gone along with the tale that Deborah was just a simple country girl exposed for the first time to the perils of London life. Phooey. God knew (and Ma knew) she'd spent weeks in and out of London in school holidays, and spent a couple of summers hitching round Europe and the Balkans, and been introduced to pot by the maths master at Mede Hall who

[25]

thought it ought to be legalized, and— Oh hell; all the rest of it. They all talked as if Deb had been swept away from herself in the adventures of the last few months when as a matter of sober fact she'd been fully herself for the first time. She'd been *living* her principles, in which case they ceased to be theoretical; identified with truth, one was *alive*. No wonder nothing had mattered, since. Since some sweaty cop had dragged her into a van— And there again: What was she supposed to have done? They hadn't bothered to find out that the 'bomb' had been only a noise-maker, or that the whole demo had been originally Deb's idea, or that those smug brutes inside the Embassy were the worst kind of criminal. Nobody knew, or even cared, what went on in that country, or anywhere else apart from *their* own safe little circle ...

But even indignation had died in her. She was too suddenly here, in the oblivious calm of the cold landscape, all silent except for the placid mutter of her parents' voices somewhere downstairs. She was all alone; Mike and Simon and Lesley and all of them had vanished so abruptly that it was pointless to wonder what had become of them. More pointless to wonder what would become of herself; in such a totally unreal world, what could? Chilly after her bath, she wound her arms round herself automatically but didn't bother to move; a few tears sliding on to her cheeks felt as cold as the ice outside.

Deborah had been educated, after the style of her time, to believe herself potentially capable of simply anything; she had never been repressed into limits less than hers and been forced to establish the boundaries of selfhood; this had remained fluid. Her sense of reality remained subjective. She had never consciously depended on someone else to 'understand', but, at present, a consciousness that was lacking was not entirely her own. She had imagined vaguely, when she was arrested, that somebody—Daddy?—might come and rescue her and explain her to 'them'. But anyway; it didn't matter now. It had all fizzled out, leaving this meaningless winter landscape that she so dimly recognized.

Mummy—Ma—came in, saying: 'Darling, I thought you were *asleep* ...' Murmurings and fussing, Deborah being hoisted on to the bed, having her feet rubbed; would she like some coffee, she mustn't be miserable, she was at home now and nobody was going to be cross with her ... God almighty, thought Deborah remotely, there was no need to treat her like a *child* ... Tucked up, her forehead kissed, she lay limp, gazing towards the window, bearing the insult passively.

She opened her eyes as a blaze of sunlight filled the room. She might have been asleep; the sky was a deeper blue and the icicle above the window was dripping. She got up, standing again to stare out, as blank as if she were trying to remember something. But, no use; it had gone—

A thump at the door; Daddy—Pa—looked in, then opened the door wider to say:

'Oh; if you're awake— Feeling better? What about coming out for half an hour? We might go up on the fell while it's sunny?'

She winced at this breezy brutality. *God*— Couldn't he see she was just too ... fizzled-out to do anything? Least, be dragged into that glaring unreal landscape—

'We might talk,' he bullied on. 'I want to hear your story, you know, about all this.'

All what? Couldn't people see that there was nothing to say— That what she needed was a bit of gentleness and cherishing, not to be shoved around ... She closed her eyes.

He had gone, and presently the day began to fizzle out too, dull pink flooding the sky, and lake and fells dissolving into a limbo of twilight.

3

BY THE TIME Judy had to drag herself out into the twilight, ice crackling under the tyres, she was, as she admitted to herself though not to Alan, pooped. If she'd let herself lie down this afternoon she would never have woken again, but now she wished she had, and hadn't.

So she was agreeably surprised, halfway through her class, to find herself laughing at something some idiot had said, and to admit: Good heavens; I'm waking up.

Everybody was laughing. Well, the idea that an 'impatient hen' was waiting for the king to arrive, had an appealing absurdity. 'No, *Une foule*, Mr Wilson, *avec "f"*,' she protested. *'Une poule, ce n'est pas du tout la même chose ...'*

Quite cheerfully, she set out on the drive home. It seemed less cold. Rimed twigs danced in the headlights. She reflected: I like adult students. They don't take it all so seriously ... Then she reconsidered: Maybe I mean, they don't take *me* so seriously?

She gave her attention to a road junction, preferring not to let it wander back to her schoolteaching career. But the stimulus of this evening's class had worn off and her attention drifted to the subject that, when she was alone nowadays, more and more seemed to absorb her: Money.

Alone, often meant while she was driving to and from town. Various trees and signposts, variously lit, marked points in the circular argument, which she always abandoned. It was a solitary circuit because, as she put it to herself, she didn't want to bother Alan about it. As she did not put it, Alan didn't want to bother himself about it.

Still, she reminded the thorn hedge on the long bend of the main road, things were a bit more urgent with all this about Debby cropping up. Apart from food, and clothes (and it was grim if you couldn't have your own daughter at home for a while without counting the cost)—what were they going to do with her after this? 'This' was a blank, to be filled in later. Immediately, there was the coke bill and they still hadn't paid the garage for the new clutch. *Ebb Tide* and *The Summit* had sold fairly well, as books did sell, but ... It would be nice, pondered Judy, if he sold the film rights for a massive sum. But she could see that the books weren't really filmable. And the third novel was evidently going to be of the same kind. They were solid, scholarly works, based on the fall of the British Empire, and on its high point—Alan hadn't been a history master for nothing—and the third, from what Judy could gather, was to be about the emancipation of the working class up to the present day.

Meanwhile, let's face it, they were drifting. Alan was having trouble of some sort with the work. They paid bills when they really had to and, hand-to-mouth, kept themselves fed and the house more or less in repair. But the car was rickety and nothing had been said, somehow, about Lydia's going to Mede Hall. Of course, she wasn't as bright academically as Deb had been ...

At which point, Judy turned off the main road. Usually, heartened as she neared home, she broke off from Lydia's education to tomorrow's meals. And then back to Alan's poetry. But tonight—perhaps tiredness, not shaken off, was waiting for her here—she lapsed into a thoughtless gloom and said: 'Oh God ...' aloud; and then, harking back to the jollity of the French class, unexpectedly: I *could* get a full-time teaching job.

Astonished by the idea she put her foot down and zoomed wildly up the narrow road past Martins'.—Well, so she could. She tested the idea and it held. It wasn't just a freak of tiredness or a whim of desperation. She was pleased with herself. Dropping into low gear for their stony lane turning, she smiled. She must tell Alan.

And if she told him, she might be able to talk at last about the fiasco of her earlier teaching. Poor Alan. She owed him more than that. She hadn't been able to confess to—so, less, able to explain or apologize for—her complicated horrors and failures. In fact she'd been a tiresome neurotic bitch and heaven knew how he'd put up with it. Ever since, trying to make it up to him, she'd known she was avoiding the issue. Which had probably been just as well; because, like this, out of nothing, a form of confidence or whatever it was had come back. So, perhaps, all she had needed was a few years' quiet life in the country to let the whole turmoil die down of itself.

The door of the byre-garage was open. She edged the car in beside the wheelbarrow and stepped out into the welcoming icy silence. Hard old snow made the planks of the door shudder as she slammed them. She dashed for the cottage, bursting blurry-eyed into the warmth of the kitchen.

The light was on, but nobody here. Often, Alan would be waiting for her, written-out, making toast or soup; they enjoyed these little reunion suppers on Fridays. Struck by an emptiness in the house Judy paused in closing the draught of the extravagantly-hot Rayburn; her face altered. Her self-colloquy in the car had had a neurotic element, isolating her; now reassociated, but blankly, she thought: There's something wrong ... Without consciously wondering what, she ran up the stairs and opened the door of Deborah's room. But Deborah was asleep, stretched out with face tilted to the ceiling. Judy bent over the bed, pulling up the covers, biting her lip and peering down at the inscrutable, doubly inscrutable, sleeper. Then, giving it up, she went back into the passage. Lydia's door was open and she was asleep too, curled up, flushed and grumpy in the passage light. Judy drew her hair off her face and half-closed the door. In their room, Alan was

[30]

asleep too, the lamp on, one arm over his face— No; as Judy came in he said: 'Hullo...?'

'Are you all right?'

'Yes?'

'Gone to bed?' she suggested, sitting down beside him, unknotting her headscarf, clawing at her hair till it stood out in dark spikes.

'More or less ... You, too? You must be bushed.'

'Not too bad. What's Debby been doing?'

'Nothing,' he said, faintly surprised. He lowered the arm from his face and added: 'And that seems to be what she's set on doing.'

'Well— So far. But give her a chance.'

'I tried to, today,' he said gloomily.

'I know. But it may take time—'

'Today was a washout in any case. What the hell does she expect of us?'

'I wish I knew. But don't let it worry you,' she said, in a tone of uncertain politeness, since they both felt they might both well worry. And Dring, grunting, in irony or protest, rolled over with his back to Judy, '... bound to be a bit disrupting,' he muttered, or so it sounded.

'You mustn't let it ...' she said, still uncertainly. 'I mean— not so that it distracts you from work— Oh listen,' she said, reminded, brightening, 'I had such a good idea on the way home. Suddenly I thought, I could get a full-time teaching job—'

'Oh Christ,' said Dring at once. 'Then I'd *never* get any work done—'

He rolled over again, crooked the arm over his face and watched her from under it. She couldn't make out his expression. Disappointment hit her with one sharp chop, and thereby chopped itself off, and she was back to normal, as if she had just woken to the familiar room, the green-daisy pattern of the quilt, the low beam, the stacked papers on the table under the window ... 'No,' she said. 'All right.'

[31]

Because she knew she had to *be* here, it was part of the whole thing and it had for six years been enough. She hadn't felt idle; if anyone asked her what she did with her time, she herself rather wondered. What she wondered just now was, how she could possibly have thought of deserting him.

'Unless you *want* to?' Dring persisted, courteously.

'Oh no.' She began to unbutton her coat. 'Only, you see, it came to me, that I *could* ...' But that wasn't important. Now she considered it again, she hated the whole idea—turning out in the mornings, timetables, corrections, staff-room life—she must have been crazy.

'Would you', she asked standing up, 'like some coffee if I made it—or a piece of toast?'

'Saturday. Cheers,' announced Lydia when Judy woke her in the morning.

'I'm glad,' remarked Judy, 'somebody's cheerful about it.'

The sun was breaking through the muggy-violet mist; it might be another fine day. But in the small hours Alan had fumbled for a notebook on his table and gone prowling down-stairs with it, and now he was back in bed, scowlingly asleep. And Deborah, slightly smoothed out by rest, was still icy-eyed. In a sweater of her mother's, too long for her, she looked like a shipwreck victim—fished out of the lake, not, perhaps, in time.

Judy had made porridge, which would have to represent today's 'big' breakfast. 'Ugh,' said Lydia, smacking at it with a spoon.

'Get it down,' ordered Judy tersely. 'It'll keep you warm.'

Deborah stirred hers about, head bent. Lydia said: 'Well can I have syrup on it?' and went for the tin. 'Want some?' she asked her sister, who did not answer. '... All right,' snapped Lydia, *'don't.'*

'Don't bother her, Lyddie—'

'I simply politely *asked* her—'

[32]

'Yes. I know. Well, have two spoonfuls yourself, then, hers as well.'

'I was going to.' She did; spider-trails wrote spirit messages between her bowl and the tin. She tackled her improved porridge with more zeal. 'Going into town?' she asked.

'Not really; do you want to?'

'We never do when *I* want to ... Anyway I'm going to Susan's.' She flounced to the sink to dump her empty bowl, tossing back hair that, if not stringy like Deb's, could still do with a good brush; her backside strained the seams of her tartan trousers. 'What are *you* going to do?' she challenged Deborah in passing. And receiving again no reply: 'Look, you can't just go on saying nothing for the rest of your life.'

'Why not?' said Deborah in a coldly reasonable tone.

'Well, it's just dippy, for one thing—'

Unthinkingly Judy intervened: 'Darling, I must see if I can let out the waist of those pants. Does the button meet at the front? Turn round ...' And, reminded: 'We'll have to get new ones for Debby, though, first— If we can make these last—'

Snatching herself back from Judy's measuring fingers, Lydia said: 'Oh yes, *she'll* have to have new clothes but it doesn't matter about *me*.'

Judy glanced up at her in dismay. That had held as much rancour as injury. Awkward Lydia might be, but not ill-natured. Not as a rule. Now, as she hacked herself a slice of bread, face flushed and underlip stuck out, she was all aggrieved womanhood. The phrase 'to be reckoned with' came, along with foreboding, to Judy's mind. This morning and in this mood Lydia was so large and positive in contrast to Deb; Judy quailed a little before her, while still saying: 'Cut it *straight*, please, darling ...'

'Nag, nag,' muttered Lydia, flumping down with the vast wedge of bread in her hand. Judy ignored the comment and restrained herself from commenting in turn on the size of the wedge. Too much carbohydrate, that was probably why

Lydia burst out of her clothes, though heaven knew she was growing upwards too, fast enough, and one did begin to wonder, into what? Difficult, for the baby of the family to establish itself as a personality; if anything, Lydia seemed to be asserting herself nowadays as the family anti-intellectual.

Which supposition reminded Judy again of the education question. This autumn, suddenly, Lydia would be starting at secondary school, and was the local one the best that should have been done for her? But one couldn't go into all that at this time of day. 'Before you go to Susan's,' began Judy taking her own porridge bowl to the sink, 'you might do your bedroom floor, properly, and hadn't you better go down to Miss Mitchell's too?'

'Oh *her*,' said Lydia with her mouth full.

When Lydia with puffing and groaning had done her perfunctory chores, and stepped out into the sunshine, she forgot her woes at once and became child-happy, caught up in the moment. She stood for a while with mouth wide open under an icicle that hung from the house gutter, but it didn't drip. So she bounded across the yard, clumping with both gumboots on the thin-glazed puddles, and cantered down the field path to the lower lane, gid-upping to an imaginary pony. Her nose and cheeks flamed in the keen air.

She had begun to notice that Mummy was making a 'thing' of Lydia's going down to Miss Mitchell's, but she minded this only when with Mummy, as a matter of form. Once on her way, she accepted this chore more readily than most, because as a matter of fact she didn't see it as a chore (or, as Judy expressed it, a 'little practice in social service and neighbourliness'). Miss Mitchell was taking on a new significance as somebody of Lydia's own. No one else in the family was welcomed in that cottage.

Lydia herself wasn't so much welcomed as put up with, but even so, that went for very few people in the district. A sense of privilege has its own value, irrespective of the privilege's. In

[34]

the first place Lydia had barged her way into Miss Mitchell's as no one else dared to, because at the time she had been at the pre-school roaming age and not responsive to discouragement. So she had appeared, gaping, to stroll about the garden and indoors, taking it all as an extension of this new place they'd come to live in. Miss Mitchell, who did not care for children, had tolerated the first incursions as a mere politeness to the new neighbours; if the child were any sort of a nuisance she would be dragged home soon enough. But by chance Lydia was not a nuisance; she was marble-eyed at the fascinating treasures this house contained; she hardly needed the sharp command not to touch anything. Then, relenting, as a reward for good conduct Miss Mitchell showed her the kaleidoscope, and Lydia was hooked.

After six years the acquaintanceship still continued; though each found the other rather a nuisance, each was beginning to feel the other might have her uses.

Prunella Mitchell would not for a moment allow that she needed any 'help'. She allowed the best of intentions to the kind people who came babbling of home helps and Meals on Wheels, but let them know by her cold firmness that she still considered them impertinent. Her manner retained its authority acquired during thirty years as a senior Civil Servant; keeping her hands, whose fingers arthritis had rendered to a fixed right-angle to her palms, tidily folded, she stared down offers of assistance with her formidable polite stare. However, it was different with the little Dring girl; children ought to run errands, it was good for the child to make herself useful. 'I may be nearly eighty,' Prunella would say icily, smiling (and with some inexactness, because she was already eighty-four), 'but I'm not *ninety*. I can perfectly well manage, thank you.' And, so far, she had seen to it that she did. It was a question, she told herself, of keeping life down to its essentials. If she had to rely on other people, she would consider herself finished. She had always liked solitude and by now positively disliked strangers, not realizing herself that this was

[35]

largely because she was deafer than she admitted. Over her, as the unentertained and ultimate horror, was the Old People's Home that her nephew so strongly recommended. '... But they'd take such good care of you there ...' 'My dear Charles, if I needed to be taken *care* of I'd be better off dead and very soon should be.'

Besides—and most of all—Prunella just could not contemplate being separated from her cottage and her possessions. The dream of retirement to a cottage in the Lake District, where she could assemble her own belongings, had sustained her through her working life and never faded since. She had been brought up to believe that one should not lay up treasures on earth, but the older she grew, the more her own treasures took on a quality of the heavenly. This life, achieved, was the ultimate; she would, and by now could, envisage no other.

What had first softened her towards the little Dring girl was the respect the child had shown for the objects in the cottage. Even Prunella sometimes needed an audience, and in Lydia she found the same one over and over again, willing to be shown the Felix Pratt autograph on the jug and the hallmark on the George the First ladle. If Prunella always wound up these sessions by letting Lydia play with the kaleidoscope, and suspected that Lydia endured the sessions only for that reward, she was not less grateful. In some ways they understood each other sufficiently to make allowances.

But this morning Prunella, feeling the cold, wanting to wear her thick blue cardigan, was depressed to find that, in the first place, she simply could not manage the buttons; and in the second place, to find herself wondering if Lydia would come, in which case Prunella might ask her to do the buttons up. She sat with the cardigan on her knee, weighing with some detachment, in spite of her depression, whether this might not be a sign of defeat, 'asking for help' at last. At any rate, she couldn't wear the cardigan without fastening up the buttons, eight of them right to the throat. She had her standards. The cottage, for instance, was always spick and span for as far as anyone could see; or as far as anyone, under Prunella's gaze, was likely to look. She disarranged things as little as possible, to avoid the effort of tidying up. And she took sensible care of herself. If that included drinking cold milk all the time rather than grappling with the electric kettle (a present from kind Charles) and, for the same reason, shivering in bed rather than try to fill a hot-water bottle, that was no one's affair but Prunella's. Her hair, cut short for convenience, was always combed and her rough tweed skirt, sagging away from her bony hips, showed no marks. Thank goodness for tights, which meant no struggling with suspenders. However, she would not slop about in an unbuttoned cardigan. Yet obstinately she had decided to wear it. She was still pondering when Lydia thumped at the door and came in.

'Oh,' said Prunella coolly. 'Good morning.'

'Hullo,' said Lydia, sitting down on her usual ladder-backed chair against the wall and continuing to shred with her thumb nails the hazel catkin she had picked from the hedge.

'Don't *please* scatter that on my clean floor.'

'I'll sweep it up if I do ... D'you want anything?'

'Let me think.' Shopping arrangements had altered a great deal since Prunella came to live here. Everybody nowadays had a car; the vans that used to travel round were disappearing. 'I think I have enough food for the weekend,' said Prunella at last, after a decent appearance of reflection. 'I had thought of a chicken, but then I changed my mind.' Quite often she did ask Lydia to bring shopping, not wanting people to think she starved herself. Quite often Lydia forgot what she'd been asked to bring, but so did Prunella. 'Did you close that door?' queried Prunella, shivering. Lydia got up and gave the door a testing kick with her gum-boot.

'Yes— Are you cold? Put your cardigan on.'

Prunella raised her eyebrows at the presumptuous tone. 'It

is a cold morning, but the sun's getting stronger every day. Would you like a cup of coffee?'

'No thanks,' said Lydia, as Prunella had hoped and known she would. There was a pause, wherein Lydia reflectively ate her catkin and stared across at the picture on the wall opposite her. This wide, stone-flagged room was the only one Prunella used now; if sometimes she even slept here on the couch rather than climb to her bedroom, or used the same plate and cup several times rather than go out to the sink in the chilly little scullery, that was a private matter. In here, she had assembled her favourite possessions, relegating the second-favourite to the dust-sheeted front room. Occasionally she thought of changing some of them round, but was increasingly nervous of touching breakables. Certainly she would never ask Lydia to do anything like that; it had taken her five years to trust the child to hold the kaleidoscope in her own hands. Now, as she half lifted the cardigan, still hesitating, she looked at Lydia and smiled, relaxing:

'You like that picture, don't you?'

'Yes; I do,' said Lydia gravely. Since she could remember, she had sat on this chair and stared at the picture; it was a habit of mind, as well as an object that grew along with her consciousness. She said now: 'You kind of go into the middle of it, and I like that bit of blue.'

'It's an *early* Hugh Mostyn,' said Prunella not for the first time. 'One of what he used to call his dark phase. He gave it to my mother, whom he knew—as he knew all of us—intimately ...'

'I used to think it was bears going into a cave,' remarked Lydia. 'But now I can see, it's trees. A kind of a wood.'

'He was quite a young man then,' went on Prunella not listening. 'His style changed considerably but I never feel it developed much beyond this phase ... I even heard he took a dislike to these "dark" paintings and destroyed most of them. He was always impetuous.'

'Has he been dead a long time?' asked Lydia doubtfully.

[38]

'Oh I expect so. He was—' She had been going to say, older than I. But not much older. Indeed they must both have been in their mid-twenties when he spent that summer near Prunella's native village in Norfolk. '... So expressive,' mused Prunella, looking at the picture but seeing Hugh Mostyn, seeing the paint-stained smock and smelling turpentine. More and more, her treasures stood for their place in her life; Lydia, though she hadn't noticed it, was treated to far more anecdote than critical explanation. 'I had been ill,' explained Prunella, 'and the doctor ordered me home for a month's rest.' Her thin, mauve-veined face went slack as she read into the picture the whole boring prospect of a month at home, and then the sudden lightening— 'There are people staying at the Manor cottage, Pruey—an artist ...' And his second wife—if wife she were ... Of course, he had given the picture to Mother, or so he said, but Prunella had often imagined—was it imagination?—that it was only because he hadn't dared ... Dared offend Mother; and of course, Prunella had given him no encouragement ... one didn't, in those days ... The vicar's daughter was still in a different class from an itinerant painter ... She sighed, turning to look at the sampler at this side of the hearth, consoling herself by remembering *that* summer, at Grandmama's, Prunella twelve, in a sunbonnet, cutting the roses— Noticing Lydia again, she returned to the present, finding it colder and wuzzier than ever, as she seemed to nowadays. She made an effort and said brightly:

'So, what's the news of your big sister?'

'Oh; she came home yesterday,' said Lydia without interest.

'From what I hear,' pronounced Prunella, 'she's a very naughty girl.'

'June Croasdell says she ought to have gone to prison.'

'Really? I can't imagine what June Croasdell knows about it.' One might not have imagined that Prunella, seeing, by her own account, no one from one week's end to another, would know much about it either. But by some natural law of rural Britain, news travelled from cottage to cottage under

[39]

its own impetus, like thistle-seed on the wind. 'I expect,' Prunella added disdainfully, 'she's no worse than other girls as they're brought up now. Or educated, rather. It's only as a student that she's turned out so difficult, isn't it. Quite possibly you'll be the same at that stage.'

'I won't. I'm not going to be a student anyway.'

'Oh really? No, you're going to be a real Cumbrian at this rate. No ambition at all.'

Lydia, considering that, said: 'Oh I dunno. Look at Joss Naylor.'

'You might equally well say,' appended Prunella, 'look at William Wordsworth. I'm erratic in my facts.' She shook her head, tutting at herself, and lifted the cardigan again, holding its warmth against her cheek. Her attention faded; she murmured: 'Well, I mustn't keep you ...' wanting to be alone, to sit peacefully looking at things. Lydia stood up.

'Ta-ra, then.'

'Oh, Lydia; before you go, I wonder if you'd do one little thing? There's a tin of meat in the pantry and I can't seem to get the hang of that new tin-opener *yet*. So awkward of me—but *would* you just open it for me?'

'Okay.' The tin-opener wasn't very new and was a quite simple piece of mechanism, but Lydia always took this request at face value. At a similar value she took the pantry, which led off the scullery, and was as usual all muddly and rather stinky, with mouse-tuppences all over everything and shreds of paper mouldering on the stone floor. On the slate slab, a tin of luncheon meat waited beside a half-packet of Ryvita and a saucer smeared with rancid butter. Opening the tin, Lydia left it where it was and came out again. She viewed Miss Mitchell's backstage arrangements with disgust but no contempt; she had enough respect for Miss Mitchell to allow her to live as she liked, and was besides young enough—just —to regard other people in general with an uncritical indifference. So, saying: 'Seeing you—' she went out, firmly pulling the latch shut behind her, into the clean young day.

Halfway up the field she remembered: Oh blast, I didn't have a go with the kaleidoscope. Never mind, I might go down again tomorrow.

By the time Dring reawoke at nine, his porridge had stewed and thickened till it was irresistible, but heavy to the mind. So was the baked potato that Judy produced at midday, accompanied by spring onion and a little cheese. It had occurred to him lately that their meals were increasingly stodgy, and so was his waistline. He uttered no complaint of either; he knew Judy was rightly trying to economize on housekeeping; now and then, he practised heaving in his tummy muscles, but as soon as he forgot again, he forgot.

The ideas he had conceived during the night hadn't, with one thing and another, taken on the substance he had; he decided to walk it off while the sun shone, and then get down to work this evening. Saying so to Judy, he laced on his boots.

'... Are you going to ask Debby to come out with you?'

After yesterday's reception of his invitation he hardly felt obliged to. He compromised by calling upstairs: 'Coming up the fell, Deb?' and, unanswered, leaving without further appeal.

What the Drings called 'the fell' was the rolling sprawl of sheep-pasture behind the cottage. It wasn't distinguished by heights or crags but its own viewpoints were no less distinguished, and it was quiet.

Well, usually. He had forgotten that this was a weekend. As he topped the first rise he saw a trio of walkers approaching, in bright anoraks, accompanied by a frolicking dog. 'Hullo!' they greeted Dring jovially; he nodded with reticent civility.

Not too long ago he had been a holidaymaker here himself but he looked back on that self from another life, out of which he had as it were grown, shedding for ever that childlike silliness—or gaiety? To live here was to be, at first, eternally on holiday but, with time, something was lost and gained; as,

Dring thought, in marriage; the romance wore off, the relationship strengthened; to 'take for granted' was fully to accept.

All the same, from long habit, he glanced at his watch as he reached the summit of Low Fell. Not bad. The uphill stint done, he went on at a stroll. One more walker passed, a veteran in drab colours, whose nod was sourer than Dring's; then the landscape was empty, scoured for thought. At which moment, Dring noticed that the sun had gone in.

He had intended to do his usual circle—the mile or so to the next summit, and back round by the lane—but now he found himself saying to himself: Oh, that'll do.

As if coming out had been a duty. He stood still for a minute, gazing broodily at the greyish snow at his feet and the dun vale below. Colour drained out, the surroundings were sour as that solitary who had passed him. Besides, there was work to be done. Winter seemed to close down as he turned back. From the coast a solid wall of grey was moving in; raindrops spattered his forehead; the wind had changed. Dring found himself saying to himself: That's all it needed: For the weather to change.

As if this gloom in the elements accounted for his own. He hurried, loping zigzag down from snow to grass. At any rate, he told himself, now you'll be able to settle down to work ... He began to look forward to the warmth of the house, perhaps coffee—

When he turned the last bend of the track and the gable end of the cottage met him, Deborah was standing at her window, looking out, with so little expression on her face that she might have been a ghost, haunting the place. She showed no recognition of her approaching father, whose gloom, on observing this, darkened finally.

'Oh *God*,' he muttered, dragging himself indoors. 'Couldn't you', he said tersely to Judy who was ironing, 'put a *light* on?'

Equally tersely Judy said: 'I can see perfectly well to *iron*.'

[42]

And then they exchanged a look of equal surprise, Dring pausing with his half-unfastened zip in his hand and Judy with the iron in hers; they might not till now have realized to whom they were speaking; and they looked away from each other again quickly, both at a loss, till Dring said vaguely: 'It's raining.' To which Judy said as vaguely: 'And Lyddie didn't take her anorak.' She began to iron again and Dring pulled down his zip. They had disconcerted not each other but themselves.

The unsayable, the obverse of domestic peace, had been contained in what each did not say. (Dring: Can't you keep the house bright and welcoming? Judy: I've got to save money whenever I can.) They understood each other well enough for each to have heard the undertone. The unthinkable had risen closer to the surface than ever before. They did not look at each other again, as Dring put on a kettle for his coffee and Judy applied herself to the collar of Lydia's school blouse. When there was a sudden streak of drops down the window, Judy said: 'Yes, it *is* raining,' as if she only now believed him.

Dragging himself upstairs Dring regarded the mug of coffee and large slice of cake in his hands and thought, still gloomy: It'll be drink, next.

Unexpectedly his gloom, reduced to absurdity by this, and filled in with chocolate cake, dispersed into a resigned blank that presently began to yield the promise of a quite new idea ... for a poem. Dring did not even know he had been 'at work' till the phase drew to an end, yielding consciousness of house-noises, darkness outside the window, smells of cooking ... Tiredness and hunger. He stretched, switched off the table lamp, went downstairs. Lydia in pants and vest, cleaning her teeth, looked round at him without interest as he passed the bathroom door.

Judy, at the kitchen table with French textbooks, rose saying: 'Sausage and bacon? Won't be a minute—'

'No; I'll do it.' He was glad of the occupation for his

[43]

hands in this unwinding-pause. He decided to have an egg too, and stood idly trimming it with a spatula as it whitened in the pan.

'. . . She didn't want any supper, but I didn't insist,' Judy said.

'Who?'

'Debby. She still seems so . . .' Running a red pencil through her hair Judy hunted for a word, frowned, and said: 'Darling, I do wish, when you aren't busy, you'd have a go at her.'

'I will, yes,' said Dring readily. When he was afloat on creative work, everything else became similarly buoyant. He pictured with far more sensitivity, and sympathy, that wan face at the window. 'She's not *with* us at all is she,' he murmured, tipping his egg on to his plate.

'I do think, we've got to make contact—'

'M'm,' he agreed, eating. He was, however, busy; Deborah hovered like the next idea. Judy looked at him, assessing his preoccupation and its consequent calm, and decided to unload her next tidings on to what she had of his attention:

'That was Fiona on the telephone, about half an hour ago.'

'M'm?'

'I said I'd ring her back. The point being, it's half term all over the place, and they thought they'd come up— '

'They did, did they,' said Dring in vague foreboding. 'Who?'

'Well, evidently Cathy's going skiing, from school, so it would be those two and Shaun— She said Shaun could bring his tent.'

'She did, did she.' Dring, turning to cut more bread, raised one eyebrow at the streaming windowpane.

'I told her Deb was at home but she merrily said we'll all manage somehow . . .' They both laughed, almost as much amused as annoyed. The Michael Drings had the idea that relatives in the Lake District lived in a constant state of YHA slap-happy pack-'em-all-in piggery; they treated Broom Cottage rather as a climbing hut. Judy, cheered by

[44]

Dring's reaction, added: 'If they come now they might not come at Easter.'

' 'Strue. Well then, they may as well come. —When?'

'At the end of next week, this would be.'

'Oh well then,' said Dring, comfortably shelving it. He went back upstairs, this threat taking its place in his general contented fulness that lasted until he searched out the draft of his frost-on-ferns poem and discovered that it was better than the one he'd been engaged on since afternoon. At once his day's achievement vanished like a blown-out flame.

Or was it better. The language was over-elaborate, now he read it again; possibly the second had more impact ... Possibly neither of them was any bloody good at all. He threw down the papers and rubbed his hands over his face.

He'd go to bed. Look at them both again in the morning. When he turned round he saw that Judy had come to bed already. The room felt quiet; he had no idea of the time. Stiffly, he stood up and walked round the curtain by the bed's head (a mere formality; Judy never disturbed him and the curtain was permanently tied back) to peer at her face.

She was reading the *New Statesman*, sleek-headed, propped on one elbow. She looked back at him over her reading-glasses, which caught the reflection of the bedside lamp; above them her eyes were blank. She said nothing, as if waiting; he sat down beside her, rubbed his face again, and then asked confidentially:

'What *was* all that about a full-time job?'

'That was all,' she said after a moment. 'It was only a thought.'

'Still, it must have *been* a thought. What occasioned it?'

'Why', she countered, 'bring it up now?'

Because he was chilly and disconsolate and his gloom, returning, had brought this buried dissatisfaction with it. 'I meant to ask, earlier ... Thoughts don't just pop up out of nothing.'

'You should know.'

[45]

He frowned to himself and amended: 'Ideas may, I suppose.'

'Then, this was only an idea.'

She smiled, on that, but Dring's frown did not yield. 'It's that evening class,' he pronounced, pondering. 'It's given you confidence?'

'Yes. I suppose it must have.' Gaining animation, Judy pulled off her glasses. 'It was on my way home, you see, when the class bucked me up although I'd thought I was so tired. It was quite a surprise, but I suddenly saw it as *possible* again. After so long.'

He nodded, elbows on knees, listening. She threw aside the *New Statesman* and sat up to lean on his shoulder. 'D'you know, as if a fog had cleared off. It all looked really quite simple. Such a *relief*. Of course, it might not be as simple in practice, but I think so. I should never be so idiotic again— Shouldn't make such a *thing* about it. Or about anything, really. Do *you* think I'm changing at last? Settling down? Getting middle-aged?'

'Hardly that. But settling down doesn't exactly seem to be what you have in mind.'

'In myself, I meant. You ought to be pleased, if I'm turning out a well-integrated sort of person ...'

'I am pleased,' said Dring, and he smiled as she slid round to look into his face. Judy returned the smile rather weakly; his expression had distracted her from self-analysis ... 'But you don't want me actually to go and get a job.'

'You admitted, it was only an idea— Yes,' he added, carefully, 'you must do just what you like.' He rubbed his forehead again and insisted: 'Of course, you must. There's no need at all for you to hang about here waiting on me all day.'

'I don't do that,' she said, absently, remembering his first reaction to her idea, last night—when he had, probably, been half asleep. 'It's just,' she broke out, 'the money—'

'Oh God.'

'I know, darling. Never mind. Anyway we don't need to worry about it yet.'

'We don't need to *worry* about it at all,' he said loudly.

'No. I know. I won't. *We* won't. Would you like a drink or—'

'Since you raised it, we might as well be clear: If I finish this bloody novel I'll get a pretty substantial advance right away. They've said so. So if that amounts to—'

'All right, my dear. Not sums, at this time of night. You just', she said in a soothing tone, 'get it finished, in peace.'

He drew in a breath, shot her a furious glance, and let out the breath again. Heaving himself to his feet he began to pull off his sweater. As he moved away from the bed, the space between him and Judy felt cold and midnight; a sudden gust of wind thudded at the window, the panes creaking.

Peace, Dring echoed silently; what with the weather and Deborah and visitors coming, and now Judy ... It all seemed to crowd into him as if a vacuum had been made.

On the easterly side of the cottage in the lee of the wind Deborah still stood at her window, listening to the noises of the night, rain slapping from gutter to cobbles and larches whirring; it made her feel dead-quiet inside, a vacuum. Or, 'feel' wasn't apt; all sensation was still fizzled-out. Her astonishment, that it went *on* like this—that nobody recognized her—was a numb astonishment. The spark of glory that was real-Deborah would never, at this rate, be re-ignited. She didn't positively blame her family—she was in no way, now, positive—but she didn't realize either that, to test them, she was receding from them. She couldn't see how they couldn't *see* ...

Wind and rain swept over the valley while sheep huddled by the bare hedges and cottages huddled among their stone walls. Prunella Mitchell, reminded by some reference during today, had taken Wordsworth's *Prelude* from her bookcase and was absorbed. She had put a Shetland rug round her

[47]

shoulders and pulled the electric fire close to the couch. After sniffing at that luncheon meat, or whatever it called itself, she'd recoiled, and decided to have a good meal tomorrow to make up for it. One had to be sensible. Meanwhile she had occupation enough to see her through this stormy night:

> *'Me hath such deep entrancement half-possess'd,*
> *When I have held a volume in my hand,*
> *Poor earthly casket of immortal Verse! . . .'*

She smiled to herself, pulling out a handkerchief to mop at the dewdrop on her nose. She did hate the wind. Everything banged and rattled so . . . Meanwhile again, the piece of cardboard she had jammed into the broken pane of her pantry window popped out and let in a blast of air that lifted even the rag rugs on the kitchen floor. Oh dear, but one really couldn't cope with that sort of thing in the middle of the night . . . She turned the pages:

> *' . . . and the midnight storm*
> *Grew darker in the presence of my eye . . .'*

Very amusing. Her hands, awkward anyway, were too cold now to cope with pages. She might memorize the passage she was reading, to fill in the time as she waited for dawn.

4

'BUT IF YOU simply don't say anything,' said Judy, reasonably and persuasively, 'how can I understand you?'

Deborah stretched herself stiffly along her bed, closing her eyes and clenching her fists.

Outside, the larches whipped their twigs through cascades of rain. Sunday morning was darkly stormy like the night. Judy was sorting through Deborah's drawers to assess her garments; Deborah, who was normally strict about her privacy, lay there and let her mother do it. Judy, sitting down with a crumpled cotton frock in her hands on the low windowsill, glanced dismally at the weather, stared at Deborah and said in a brisker voice:

'One thing, I'm sure you need a couple of Senokot.'

At that, Deborah emitted a snort of laughter. She couldn't help thinking: God; mothers. As if constipation accounted for everything . . .

Judy's stare sharpened. 'Is all this', she inquired, 'some sort of an act?' But Deborah had gone totally limp, her face turned away. There was silence. Downstairs, a rhythmic bumping indicated some activity of Lydia's. Alan, as far as Judy knew, was still in bed. She shook out the cotton frock and folded it ready to put away. 'I hoped, when you'd had a day or two . . .' she began. Then: 'Well, you know I'm always *ready* to listen . . .'

Turning back from the chest of drawers she noticed that Deborah's lips were pursed, to a grim refusal. In spite of her principles Judy had a strong impulse to slap that rigid face and scream: *Say something!*

[49]

Deborah might have welcomed such a sign of enthusiasm. But as it was, Judy, on her way out of the room with an old matted sweater she might as well try to wash, said: 'Honestly, you're as bad as Alan.'

'How?'

The question—so unexpected—took Judy by surprise; she didn't know what she had meant ... 'Oh, you know, all this *inner* life ...' she half-explained. 'But his does come out through his writing.' She lingered, but Deborah had no comment.

Lydia was chasing a toy football round and round the kitchen, belabouring it with the rolling-pin. 'We're going', announced Judy, 'to have a proper Sunday lunch today.' She swerved as the ball flew at her. 'With Yorkshire pudding,' she added, restrainedly. But as Lydia blundered past again, bumping into her, she pursued: '—So would you *please* come out of this second infancy and peel some potatoes for me?'

'No,' said Lydia on the rebound, 'I'm busy and anyhow I'm going down to Miss Mitchell's in a minute.' The rolling-pin caught Judy a really painful crack on the ankle. She grabbed a handful of Lydia's hair and pulled her upright.

'Look, this is no time for you to start being tiresome. Why happen to think of going to Miss Mitchell's just when the weather's too foul to go out and I want you to do a job for me?'

Lydia, who privately agreed about the weather, bawled with anguish at having her hair pulled, but, released, went to get the potatoes, dropping several and kicking them across the floor towards the sink. By the time she had peeled enough, they had to be put to boil, and then the 'proper lunch' was on the way; which was how it happened that Charles Mitchell, paying one of his duty visits to his aunt, was the first visitor to her cottage on that day. He arrived at two o'clock, slithering up the cobbled path in the rain, and pounded on the door to receive no answer; which was as usual; also as usual, he went to attract his aunt's attention by waving at the various windows; squinting in, he saw her huddled on the couch in a stiffly tipsy attitude, her eyes shut and face as white as bone. Charles, a vigorous and decisive character (manager of a chain of breweries in the north-west), rapidly found the broken pantry pane, opened the window and climbed in. She was alive—he thought, barely. The cottage was as coldly dank as the outdoors. She might have been trying to pull the electric fire closer to the couch: its plug had come out of the wall socket; one warped blue hand hung between the fire and the copy of Wordsworth's *Prelude* face down on the rag rug. Charles wrapped her up, plugged in the fire, dosed her with whisky from his flask and dashed for his car to make for the nearest telephone—Martins'. Within an hour an ambulance came nudging up the streaming lane.

'All this commotion,' said Prunella thinly but firmly, 'is quite unnecessary.'

'We'll see about that,' remarked Charles Mitchell to Mrs Martin as the stretcher sailed down the cobbled path; it was flat as a baking-tray; there was no weight on it at all. Gwen Martin, noticing that, shook her head.

'She shouldn't't've been on her own here like this—'

'She won't be again,' promised Charles, flicking back his sodden hair, 'if *I* can help it.'

He and Gwen went perfunctorily round the cottage before leaving it empty, Gwen tutting and Charles scowling at the pathetic state of things they discovered. People, Charles felt, would say all this was *his* fault; he'd a damn good mind to get the old girl put away for good and all—supposing, of course, she survived, but he didn't underestimate her stamina. He left the keys with Gwen and chased off after the ambulance still scowling. Gwen took the luncheon meat home for the farm cats.

The news that Miss Mitchell had been carried off to hospital did nothing to brighten the week's beginning at Broom Cottage, where already the family was in unprecedented disarray. Dring, deciding that the best he could do for everybody was to apply himself to his writing, did so to no great effect, and was restlessly about the house making coffee and hunting for books. Lydia, on half term from school, bumped about the place finding nothing to do. Deborah, to a degree emerging from her immobility, took to appearing at odd moments, blank-faced, tenser. Judy kept beginning the sort of household chore that creates muddle, such as tidying out a cupboard, and then abandoning it half-finished because the prevailing confusion denied her the patience. The weather, even for this area, excelled itself; the whole cottage shuddered at the blasts of wind and the view was greyed-out by rain.

'Darling, you aren't sad about Miss Mitchell, are you? She'll be well looked after in hospital,' Judy persuaded Lydia. 'I'll take you in to see her—'

'I don't want to.'

'But I'm sure she'd like you to. You could take some flowers—'

'No, she wouldn't,' Lydia interrupted, her face shutting up into a grumpy version of Deborah's impenetrability.

Nobody could understand anybody; it was Deborah's defection that drove this widening wedge of silence among them.

When Judy complained to Alan, in bed: 'Lyddie's being bloody-minded about poor Miss Mitchell ...' he replied with evident non-interest: 'Oh; why?'

'That's what I can't understand ...' And she sighed, wondering whether she need bother. '—Oh; I put the coke bill with the others, in the green folder,' she remembered; whereat Alan sighed, offering no more comment.

Deborah, growing a little more aware, noticed the unusualness of the others, and related it, like everything else, to herself, without ascribing to herself the power of causing it. *They* began to seem unreal, as she began to need them. What Ma had said—that Deborah had an 'inner life'—had, after a delay, caught Deborah's attention. So, Mummy *knew*. So, people knew there was something, extinguished but vital; in

[52]

which case, why didn't they do anything to help? Because, clearly, they were all too much wrapped up in themselves.

Nobody cared. Consigned to deadness she still began to wait about, displaying her wall of glass; nobody took any notice. They couldn't see that she couldn't be expected to eat, or chat, or read, like a substantial being. She began to feel they resented her.

Still, she couldn't possibly pretend to be alive, just to please them. As a matter of fact, she couldn't pretend to life in any case; she couldn't, even if she did try, live ... Dimly realizing this, she began, far inside herself, to be afraid.

If the Michael Drings conducted a visit to Broom Cottage with some informality, it could well have been because they found conditions of life there informal, not to say primitive, in comparison with their own life-style in commuters' Warwickshire. Getting there, in the first place, Michael usually found the worst part of it. The motorways shot you north quickly enough, but it took as long again to zigzag along narrowing roads and lanes to the cottage, and his nerves didn't necessarily slow down to match. 'Anyhow,' he remarked in this Thursday's tangerine-tinted sunset, 'it looks as if the weather's going to be better.' The fells, approaching, approachable, were demure under balls of harmless cloud, with merest flecks of snow. 'We'll be able to get a couple of decent walks in. Pillar, maybe.'

His wife Fiona said nothing, because she was admittedly not a walker. His son Shaun, lolling in the back seat, gave a faintly enthusiastic grunt for form's sake, while wishing the rain would return. He was a gentle, idle, overgrown creature of thirteen whose idea of pleasure at Broom Cottage was to muck about on the lower slopes with his cousin Lyddie, damming little becks and looking for larks' nests.

'*This* the way?' queried Michael, crossly, knowing the way quite well, but cross because he'd changed his car since he was last here in the autumn and didn't look forward to fiddling the present one in and out of the cottage yard. 'How long,' he added, 'have they been here now?'— As if things had gone on long enough.

'... Six years, isn't it?' said Fiona after reckoning.

'Good Lord; it must be, yes,' he admitted, marvelling, perhaps at his brother's staying power, and not unadmiring. He had a great respect for Alan's mind, if not for his brains. The two brothers' careers had followed such disparate courses that they might well not have kept in touch. But they had, maintaining a closeness—of hit-and-miss anxiety, rivalry, possibly some affection—formed in childhood; their mother had died when they were fairly small; whatever they had then looked to each other for, they had never quite stopped looking for, out of habit. Each thought he put up with the other pretty graciously, considering. It was usually Michael who made any overtures.

'Doesn't the time fly,' said Fiona, who was not much given to inanities, but who was reorientating herself to visitorhood after this cosy interlude of the journey. She would much rather have stayed at a hotel but wouldn't have dreamt of saying so.

'Wonder,' muttered Michael in the tone of one who doesn't in fact wonder at all, 'what line they're taking with Deb.'

'Judy didn't exactly say. Well, she just said Deb was tired and coming home for a bit of peace—'

'*I* wouldn't give her much if she were mine. Good God.' He did not enlarge on this, because he was drawing up outside the cottage yard, in which a long pool lapped at the cobbles in the spring-like evening breeze. 'Gate, Shaun, please. Wake up ... Or maybe he'll want me to shove her up under that damned scratchy thorn hedge—' He sounded his horn. For several moments, as the three gazed towards the cottage, there was no reaction. Then the back door opened and Alan came out, lifting a hand, barely smiling, paddling unhurriedly through the pool in his gumboots.

'I bet,' said Michael, 'they're taking no line at all and

everything's going on here exactly as usual.'

If it were not, the arrival of the Michael Drings disguised the fact. Their cocktail-party-trained social manners made any arrival an affair of glad cries and profuse speech. Besides, change was the last thing Michael would have looked for here; the household should of its nature blend into the countryside; once he had bestowed his car, he was ready to relax and adapt himself, taking what came.

What immediately did was a splendid supper already prepared by Judy. Even without a preliminary drink this went down well, the crowd round the table giving a convivial atmosphere—

'. . . Sorry, Michael, could I just get into that drawer for a spoon— Lyddie, move your chair a bit this way, would you? It's rather congested in here, isn't it—'

'That's okay; we eat in the kitchen ourselves mostly nowadays,' said Fiona. So they did, but in a dining recess that had room for two rubber plants and newspaper rack as well as the table. Broom Cottage's sitting-room was smaller than the kitchen, and anyway Shaun's camp bed had been put up in there; Fiona had had no intention of letting him sleep out of doors at this time of year.

'Well, what've you been up to since we last saw you?' Michael kindly asked Deborah. She merely looked at him in a foggy fashion. He began to wonder if maybe her parents were for once showing disapproval; they appeared to ignore her as steadily as she ignored everyone else. It was rather rough on the girl, who was looking thoroughly washed-out and younger than one remembered; she was, after all, only a couple of years older than his own Cathy.

Upheaval broke out again as apple pie was produced, and then over the making of coffee. The meal seemed to take a long time; Michael's face was scarlet with the warmth of the kitchen and his thick Lake District sweater; Shaun was yawning his head off. Fiona told him to go straight to bed, which meant there would be nowhere for anyone else to sit

[55]

in what was left of the evening. Michael went up to unpack, bumbling round the tiny bedroom, finding nowhere to put anything. Fiona helped Judy wash up. Apparently, Deborah and Lyddie were not expected to. Lyddie had been sulky, not a bit her usual rosebud self; she was getting to the awkward age.

'... They do grow up, don't they,' Fiona observed as she dried a handful of assorted spoons. 'Cathy's frightfully difficult about helping round the house nowadays.' Cathy did, however, always fill and empty the dishwasher, as a regular job.

'I hope the snow's good this week at Davos,' said Judy. Fiona talked about Cathy as she wiped plates. '... Girls are a problem ...' She let that hang, knowing Judy must want more than anything else to talk about Deborah, not knowing what she herself would find to say on that topic. That one must have an opinion on every topic, Fiona was media-minded enough to believe; that Judy would not necessarily value her opinion did not occur to her, not through vanity, because Fiona placed no great value on her own opinions; she just uttered them. Nor did she much listen to anyone else's; to communicate, that was the thing.

The sisters-in-law had, on these terms, communicated fairly readily without making significant contact. Judy thought Fiona was a rather dim goose but meant no harm; Fiona, thinking Judy 'clever', felt that was all right as long as Judy kept it to herself in the interests of friendly relations. This evening, as Judy wrung out the dishcloth and turned from the sink, Fiona unconsciously began to wrap herself in a caddis-case of bright platitudes against the threat of profound analysis of Deborah.

'I like those shoes,' Judy remarked. 'I saw a lot of people wearing them in town. But are they comfortable?'

'What? Oh, these?' said Fiona, surprised. 'Yes—they're all right when you get used to them. Everybody's wearing them.'

[56]

'I'm not,' said Judy without emphasis. She supposed Fiona meant by 'everybody', the layer of provincial society that constituted her own circle. 'I wonder', she said, pursuing the thought, 'what the average time-lag is in fashion: Paris to London, one year, then London to Cockermouth, two years. . . ?'

'I daresay,' said Fiona, not caring about the fashions of Cockermouth, if any. 'But I shouldn't have thought it mattered to you.'

'Me? Why not?'

'Oh well,' said Fiona, recognizing *faux pas*, 'I meant . . . You know; clothes don't matter so much in a place like this . . . And you've got better things to worry about,' she added generously.

'That,' said Judy raising her brows and slamming a saucepan up on to its shelf, 'is just *it*.'

'Just what?' asked Fiona, cautiously interested.

'Oh, I think, when I was in town, and had to spend all the time interviewing officials when I wanted to look at the shops— Though that was pure escapism, of course—' She remembered: it wasn't the officials who had provoked the desire for escape, it was Debby. Now, as Judy gazed through Fiona leaning on the table, the dark night of the train came back: dashing down to London full of maternal fear for Deborah she had been rebuffed, and thrown back on a distraught self that looked about wildly—but with startled honesty—for refuge. Since London, Judy hadn't been the same; she'd forgotten why; and why, since she'd achieved nothing, had she gone? Because Alan had been busy writing and she had had nothing particular to do. Debby had asked something about that—

'Were they difficult?' Fiona asked politely.

'Who?'

'The—er—officials?'

'Oh. No; very kind, actually. But I just wish I had a *lot* of new clothes.'

Fiona laughed, puzzled by the *non sequitur* and Judy's harassed expression, but relieved by the introduction of such a safe topic. 'You're lucky, you can wear simply anything, though, with your nice slim figure. I'm having the hell of a time with my hips ...' She patted them ruefully. 'I really look like nothing on earth in trousers, but I couldn't come here in anything decent—I mean, a skirt would look rather— What I mean is,' she said valiantly, 'I look too fat in skirts as well.'

Judy studied her. 'Don't be silly, you aren't at all fat.'

'Well—plump,' said Fiona gratefully. 'You know, I never thought you were interested in clothes at all. We never seem to talk about them—'

Judy said, with a sigh like relief: 'It's marvellous to have somebody here who'll talk to me at all.'

Dring meanwhile was resigning himself to being talked to for a couple of days, which he could surely spare at the end of this wet, washed-out week. Michael and family would have to start home on Sunday morning, so when Friday dawned clear, it was decided that this was the day for a decent walk. Passive during the preparations for that, preparing himself inwardly for the worst possible, Dring came down from ostensible writing again at ten o'clock to find the worst indeed had after the usual delay been arranged. Only he and Michael were to walk; the women wanted to go shopping, Shaun was threatened with earache, his own daughters were nowhere. And Michael, who had talked of Pillar, now talked of Great Gable. Not that Alan Dring had anything against that noble pile as such; only, he thought as he pulled on his boots, even the untrodden forests of Ennerdale as an approach were to be denied him.

Well, all right; this was Michael's holiday. Very holiday-ish Michael looked too, accoutring himself in scarlet socks, britches, gaudy anorak, woolly cap with pompon, and rucksack checked over for map, compass, whistle, exposure bag, glucose tablets, flask ... Alan, resolving that he was going to bear this whole expedition with unruffled temper, did not inquire whether his brother had included the kitchen stove. Michael could—a survival of childhood squabbles—drive him, as nobody else could, to petty exasperation. Controlling which, Alan noted the more irritably that as they drove the length of Crummock Water in the limpid morning, Michael talked about nothing but this new car and its price and performance.

The car park at the top of Honister Pass was milling with gaily-clad figures hauling on bootlaces. 'Quite busy,' said Michael, locking his car. 'Where do they all *come* from?'

'School half-term, I suppose ... But as soon as the sun shines, they pop up in their thousands nowadays.'

'It's those damned motorways. The whole world can pile into the district in an hour or two,' said Michael, apparently forgetting he'd done just that himself only yesterday. Alan, still forbearing, did not point this out. What he did say, as they left the car park, was: 'I'm not too sure about this weather, you know. There's some cloud forming towards the coast—'

'Oh, there can't be,' asserted Michael with conviction.

All right, there can't. Probably Alan had been seeking excuses because of the school party (wasn't this supposed to be half-*term?*) setting out alongside them up the derelict quarry tramway that formed the first section of the path. Of all obstructions to peaceful fell-walking Alan found school parties the worst, and this one promised to be a horror; already half a dozen eager sprinters were ahead and the leader was bellowing from the rear for them to wait. Puffing and blaspheming emulators of the half-dozen jostled past the Dring brothers as they began to climb. 'The weather can't change as quickly as *that,*' Michael was pronouncing, 'even in this part of the country.'

All right, it can't. In any case Alan had to withhold contradiction because of the pace Michael set; opening his throat lest he audibly pant, Alan reminded himself: He won't be able to keep *this* up long ... Sweat trickled between his shoulder-blades.

'One thing about squash,' remarked Michael presently, 'it does keep you in trim for this sort of thing.' He halted to take off his anorak and roll it up. Alan moved a few paces ahead, miming reluctance to pause. 'You're putting it on a bit, aren't you?' added Michael.

'Putting what?'

'Tummy.'

Obviously, this was going to be one of those occasions whereon Michael unfailingly said the wrong thing. Alan governed himself to a non-committal 'M'm?' At the top of the tramway the van of the school party waited, yelling derision at their slower comrades. A female teacher was screaming admonitions at them from a quarter of a mile back. Ahead, the long cairned track levelled a little, dotted with walkers and dogs. Alan noticed a trail of mist lapping at the far skyline but did not draw attention to it. He felt rather sick with exertion.

'How's the writing going?' asked Michael, affably.

'So-so.'

'When's the next book coming out?'

The forerunners of the school party barged by, but after that, it seemed Michael was waiting for a reply; Alan said shortly: 'No date.'

'Well, I suppose you're bound to run out of ideas sooner or later. After all, you've been at this lark—what—five years?'

Alan had the less defence against all this, in that he had very little idea of Michael's own work, so couldn't issue retaliatory questions. He asked, dodging as the second wave of the school party trod on his heels: 'You getting another promotion soon?'

'Not yet, good Lord. As it is, I'm the youngest senior exec. in the whole outfit. Money getting a bit tight?'

'Nobody can't complain of that, nowadays.'

'Oh I don't know,' said Michael after sorting out the negatives. 'I'm due to be upped another thou. in March. More or less keeps up with rising prices. But I bet they don't up your royalties in proportion. What're they giving you now?'

Thirty years ago Alan would simply have said: None of your bloody business. At that time he had been used to despising Michael just a little, for being amiable but thick, a rugger-player who collected photographs of topless girls and thought Rilke was a type of German aircraft. The attitude had persisted when Michael became a rising young business executive who went water-skiing and thought Saint-Saëns wrote a piece of music called 'The Dying Swan'. Lately —since the move to Broom Cottage—Michael had taken on a more menacing image; it was against Michael that many of Alan's inner arguments were directed; Michael threatened to be some sort of unacknowledged conscience-figure. All the same, Alan was not sufficiently spiritless in the face of his own conscience to feel obliged to explain the details of his finances to Michael. He said coldly: 'They're fairly generous,' and looked aside, waiting for the point in the path that would show the long sweep of ground down to the length of Buttermere and Crummock and home. The lakes shone gauzy-blue, but the gauze thickened beyond them and a puff of solid grey closed off the far distance. At any rate, he was breathing more easily now, settling to his stride. Michael's breath was fully equal to conversation at all times:

'What are you going to do about Deb, by the way? Has she quit the university?'

'That remains, so far, to be seen.'

'Well, I'd see pretty quick, if I were you. You don't want her hanging about the house like an invalid for ever. —Good view,' he threw in, turning his head to glance down towards Lorton Vale as if, Alan thought, he were glancing aside from the wheel of his car. 'She could always get some kind of a job locally and help fill the kitty,' drove on Michael, performing a nimble leap over a boulder.

'H'm.'

Three youths in blue cagouls bounded towards them. 'Hullo,' 'Hullo,' 'Hullo,' they exclaimed in succession. Michael said 'Hullo' back, and Alan called after them:

'Misty on top?'

'Gonna be, yeah,' called back the hindmost. 'Just blowing up Wasdale.'

'Now, what did you want to ask them that for?' grumbled Michael. 'You always were a pessimist.'

Receiving no answer to that he looked at Alan and was surprised by the buttoned-up scowl on his face. What have I said? wondered Michael without trying to remember what he'd said. Altogether, old Alan wasn't being a sunbeam today. He was making heavy weather of this walk, in both senses. Maybe he'd rather have stayed at home and got on with his work? Though how anyone could want to waste a day like this, indoors ...

Michael had always entertained some private contempt for Alan, who was a haphazard shot with an airgun and didn't know the difference between a crankshaft and a gasket. This had lingered on when Alan became a rather scruffily dressed schoolmaster who hadn't the dimmest idea of the value of money. As for this writing lark ... Respect had suspended Michael's judgement; one never knew, Alan might easily come up with a best-seller, turn into a TV personality ... Only after five years did Michael faintly begin to wonder: Might Alan, when it came to the crunch, not make it? This suspicion brought with it a new affection for his brother; pity, admitted for the first time, floods in warmly. '—Not,' Michael said, with sudden diffidence, 'that you've got anything to be pessimistic about really.'

'Thanks.'

Askance, Michael turned to him; but the male school-teacher at that moment overtook them, breathlessly roaring at the dwindling figures ahead. Alan and Michael both watched his floundering progress. 'Bet you're glad to be out of that job, all the same,' remarked Michael after a while.

'Yes,' agreed Alan, retrieving dignity and temper; which observing, Michael said:

'Things aren't too sticky, though, are they?'

Alan could guess what was implied by 'things': Money. He couldn't quite guess what made Michael assume this anxiously benign—not to say patronizing—tone. 'We'll manage,' he said, looking now ahead for the first sight of their objective. Great Gable loomed round the corner, or part of it did; a blanket of cloud was trailing down its north face.

'Well, I'd like to think you could do more than *that*, by now—'

'Look: mist,' pointed out Alan grimly.

'Oh hell. Never mind. It may clear again. Let's press on. You've got waterproofs with you?' He glanced doubtfully at Alan's dingy little rucksack and worn grey corduroys; surely the bloke, living here, wasn't too poor to equip himself decently for fellwalking? Once that pedestal on which an elder and brainier brother stood had shown a sign of tottering, one's angle of vision altered; old Alan did look a bit seedy; he hadn't the sprucely trimmed beard that one associated with a successful writer; he might even, when one thought of it, be unsuccessful as a father too, judging by Deborah's capers ... 'I hope you did the right thing,' said Michael, depressed, 'bringing your family here, and all the rest of it—'

'I hope I did,' said Alan with unfriendly irony.

'Well, but I only meant ...'

'Oh God, let's not go into what you meant.'

'Just as you like,' said Michael stiffly. They went, at increased speed, down into the dip before Green Gable, where the school party waited for its laggards, whooping and guffawing and throwing boulders into the tarn. The brothers, passing them with averted eyes, could ignore the fact that they had also averted their eyes from each other. In silence they strode up to the summit of Green Gable, where a mixed party was eating sandwiches against a background of heaping cloud

[63]

where the Scafells should have been. A few drops of rain spat out of a gust of wind. Michael, without slackening his pace, swung off his rucksack and pulled out his anorak. As they slithered down the gravelly slope he tried to struggle into his anorak, but Alan slid to a halt in the depression to wait for him.

'Does *that* thing keep the wet out?' Michael asked, jerking his head at Alan's drab covering. Now the mist engulfed them; they were suddenly alone together in the dank lee of Gable itself.

'Near enough. You want to go on up?'

'Lord, yes. I enjoy this sort of thing.' He slung on his rucksack again, bracing himself. 'Got to get to the top now ... I don't want to sound like Father, you know. Just don't like to think of you all starving.'

On an impulse Alan said: 'Judy's talking about getting a full-time teaching job.'

'Now *that's* a bright idea. Why not?'

Recoiling slightly, Alan half turned to move on. 'I can think of various reasons why not.'

'Well, *I* can't. It might be the answer. After all, she's nothing much to keep her busy, running a house *that* size, and you can't be much company for her either, buried in your writing all day. And you can't have scruples about living on your wife; nobody has, nowadays. Women's Lib, and all that—'

Alan said, to himself: 'Oh God ...' and then reminded himself that he was going to make this Michael's day and suffer all things. 'I grant you that,' he said dully. The concession inspired him to add: 'But the point has always been, between Judy and me—'

But here came the sprinters of the school party, looming and swerving through the mist to hurl themselves in final assault. The female teacher could be heard peahenning in the murk behind. Alan and Michael waited till the first wave had passed, then Michael asked:

[64]

'You were saying—Judy and you. . . ?'

'I've forgotten what,' said Alan, impatient. 'Let's get on.'

'As you like.'

This last half-mile of path was familiar to them both, besides being cairned, and trodden to knobbly pavement by legions of boots. The rain turned to sleet and the wind strengthened till they could hardly have heard each other speak. But neither spoke; Michael in an Oh-well-then indifference had applied himself to reaching the summit; Alan had to apply himself to keeping up with Michael, for whom, under these conditions, he rapidly conceived a murderous hatred. Nobody in any case is as loathsome as the person whose spry figure is disappearing ahead over slippery loose rock in sleet, mist and gale. Cheeks numb, eyes stinging, chest pounding, stomach heaving, Alan stumbled on. On the summit plateau, the wind choked the breath out of him and the sleet skimmed horizontally. It was dark as twilight. A few reeling bodies passed them but no one had the leisure to say Hullo. Alan thought remotely: Of all the damn silly ways to waste a day . . . He threw himself forward, welcoming oblivion, and came up against the cluster of rocks at the top. A few huddled creatures in the crevices could have been the school-party valiants, about whom he had quite forgotten; but one of them was recognizably Michael, legs sprawled, face crimson, beaming.

'Well,' Michael said with asinine smugness, 'we made it.'

5

WITH THE CAMP COT jammed against Lydia's bed there was no floor space in the room. All afternoon Deborah huddled on the cot, trying to think. *Supposing I . . . Or what if I . . . Or, I might . . .*

But her thoughts had no ends and no beginnings. What she was trying to find was not so much a thought as an idea; an impulse; *anything* to do. If only she could remember how to begin; but she'd forgotten everything. She'd forgotten her *self*. Without initiative, what was she? Nothing.

Several miles away, Prunella Mitchell lay on her back in a hospital bed, staring at the ceiling, indifferent to everything. She understood perfectly well where she was and why; they had explained: exposure, malnutrition, nothing organically wrong; but what did it matter when, transposed from familiar surroundings, she necessarily became unreal? She put up passively with all this—injections, tests, mounds of stodgy food, nothing to read—but would care about nothing till they took her home again; without the treasures of earth, she was virtually nothing.

'Oh, was it misty on top?' asked Fiona gaily. '*We* had quite a nice day.' The wives both seemed pleased with themselves. They had been over to Keswick and had a look round the shops and: '—We went to Curiosity Court and I bought Judy a present,' announced Fiona. 'I mean, something for herself, for once, and not for the house—I always do seem to give her things for the house, but I suppose it's because you *need* so much in this house . . .'

[66]

This present was no tea dispenser, but a figurine—Edwardian Worcester?—of a little girl in blue bodice and ringlets. 'I'm going to put it on the shelf here, I think, where I can look at it,' said Judy, shifting a ball of string, several dried-up biros and paperback cookery books. They all looked at it.

'H'm,' said Michael, twisting his eyebrows. 'Pretty, if you like that kind of thing.'

'I wouldn't have thought it was Judy's kind of thing, actually, but she chose it,' explained Fiona.

Alan, Deborah and Lydia, having looked at the figurine, all gave Judy the same glance of uneasy inquiry; porcelain in the kitchen...? The three of them reacted as members of a family, among whom the mother is the last to be allowed to act out of character. More individually, Alan thought the figurine Fiona-ish, Deborah failed to identify it, Lydia thought it was awfully pretty but wasn't going to say so; she had squabbled with Shaun all day and had had enough of the visitors.

Out of routine, if not of character, Judy was practically dishing up supper when Alan and Michael came in; they had stopped off at the Fish and were beginning to find their socks damp, but apparently there would be no time for a bath; the table was laid—'Friday,' Judy reminded Alan, catching his glance. 'I thought, I could leave you eating, but don't wash up or anything— If you don't mind having it a bit early?'

'What if we did?' said Alan, in very much Lydia's tone.

Fiona gaped at him, naïvely amazed; she'd never thought Alan minded at all, the casual way meals turned up here ... As she opened her mouth, Michael cut in:

'Well, I'm ready for it, myself. Nice of you to cook for us if you're going out—we'd have coped. What is this, your evening class?'

'I don't have to leave till about half past six— Yes, I didn't really think I could cut it—'

'Certainly not, just for us. Alan says, by the way, you want to take a full-time job?'

'I'd thought of it,' said Judy, offhandedly, reaching for the oven cloth. 'But it depends on Alan really.'

'The money'd be useful?'

'Well, it would, but it's more important not to throw out his routine . . .'

'H'm. He always was a selfish bastard.'

Alan felt that uncalled for. He'd put in a hard day on Michael, who had insisted on driving over to 'have a look at Borrowdale' after the Gable excursion, and then squelching up round Dock Tarn. It came to him now that, given an hour's peace upstairs, he could really settle the 1848 section of the novel. He'd counted at least on having Judy to take over the conversation at supper. Ignoring the immediate conversation he dragged off his second boot and went up to change his trousers, looking wistfully meanwhile at the papers laid out on his table. Tomorrow, he'd get down to it, visitors or not; writing was, after all, as Michael ought to agree, his livelihood.

Tomorrow, Saturday, dawned wet. He was awake before Judy who, opening her eyes, peered at once at the window and asked: 'What *shall* we do with them?'

In maintained resolution Dring said: 'Let them do what they like. I'm going to work.'

The use of that word was enough to set up immediate inhibition, and when Judy at once said 'Oh, good,' he was ready to wonder what she meant by that: good, that he was going to (a) exert himself, (b) earn some money, (c) spare the rest of them his society? He didn't ask. When after a quick breakfast he was established at his table in the bedroom window, he stared for a long time at the top of the gill—the snow washed away, all sombrely colourless, grass as grey as the sky —and surprised himself by thinking: I've never descended to this before.

He decided that by that he meant, never used writing as an excuse to avoid social commitments. Though in what way was old Michael a 'commitment', for God's sake, and hadn't Alan anyway done enough committing in that direction yesterday? He recollected that one didn't need any excuse to pursue one's vocation, and busily laid out the notes on the 1848 section. Meanwhile, the house below grew quiet. The others must have gone, as they had been proposing to, to the coast. Shaun wanted to collect pebbles from Fleswick Bay, for something to do with school. It pleased Dring that Shaun should be getting his own mild way for once, instead of being flogged up fells by his hearty Papa. Not that even Michael could have called this a climbing day ...

Dring stared again at the sky, his imagination now wandering and choosing to follow the party on its way through the little West Cumbrian towns with their bravely painted terraced houses and grassy slag heaps ... the sea would be rough at St Bees, and white against the dunes of Ravenglass, and this south-west wind would wash up the sea coal at Whitehaven ... Not to have gone with them gave him a calming sense of self-denial, and a satisfaction in solitude. He'd be able to settle to concentration now. With, perhaps, some coffee to help.

In the kitchen he remembered his perfunctory breakfast—had he been trying to act the preoccupied genius in front of Michael, or something? Amused by that notion he cut a thick slice of the fresh brown bread the rest of them had been tucking into, and buttered it liberally. He heard the kettle begin to boil, and, turning to it, saw Deborah in the kitchen doorway watching him.

He started—not only in surprise; he hadn't imagined she had gone out with the others—but almost in guilt, as if she had caught him robbing the pantry. The hand holding the bread involuntarily lowered itself, but he said composedly: 'Hullo. Want some coffee?'

She drew in a breath, wrinkled her brow, and then appeared to give it up and gazed at him with a sleepwalker's blankness. She was wearing a crumpled cotton kaftan and her hair was tousled. Relaxed by the quiet of the house, Dring felt freshly alone with her; her tension jarred on his mood. He asked, persuasive: 'What's the matter, old lady?'

Again, the pucker of a frown, vanishing like the ripple of a gust of breeze. Deborah held on to the doorpost, eyes unfocusing.

'Not feeling too well?'

The kettle's plume of steam swelled up between them, Dring lifted the kettle and looked about for the coffee jar—yes; he'd put it on the table. '*Do* you want some?'

She shook her head slightly, so he made some for himself, took a bite of his bread, looked up to find her still hazily staring in his direction, and said through his mouthful: 'Look, Deb, how long is this going on?'

No response. As if retaining some initiative, he hardly waited for one: 'You've been home for over a week and you're looking better. You've had a rest and time to sort yourself out. What's the outcome?' About to take a second bite, he hesitated and put the bread down beside his coffee. 'It isn't that we want you to explain yourself or make out a case to us. I'm beginning to feel you aren't making out much of a case to yourself, either. You're just mooching about like a lost soul,' he added, rather irritated now by her withdrawnness. '... I'm not trying to force your confidence. But, my dear, do *utter*.'

She didn't. He sat down, to show himself prepared to wait, and took another bite of bread. It wasn't as fresh as it had looked; honey might improve it. In a way it seemed hardly fitting to eat honey in the middle of his earnest appeal to his daughter, and in another way he resented her turning up like a spook to mar his innocent dissipation. 'At least,' he suggested at a tangent, 'couldn't you do something to show our relatives that you aren't entirely not-with-us?'

The frown lingered this time, and she ran a hand unsteadily through her hair, tangles snarling round her shaky fingers.

'... M'm?' prompted Dring. He tried not to remember that he'd been about to settle to 1848. '—Honestly, my dear,

[70]

you're putting us all in rather a fidget, aren't you. Is that what you want? Because you know you don't need to put on any sort of an act to get our attention. Mummy and I'—he used the childhood title automatically—'are simply waiting for you to . . . come *to*.' And, as she drooped there: 'Nobody else can really help you in that, you know. You have to have the guts to be yourself in this world, and sometimes it takes a bit of doing . . .'

He put the last chunk of bread in his mouth and meanwhile caught a glint of animation from her half-raised eyes. Had he sounded pompous? The implication of 'guts' when used by a middle-aged Papa solitarily feeding in the middle of the morning might be— But for God's sake, why should he fall into, or avoid, self-scrutiny? It was Deborah they should both be scrutinizing . . . 'I just want to assure you,' he said, reaching for the bread knife, 'that I'm willing to be as patient with you as you can possibly wish, but that *I* wish you'd make a bit of a gesture from your side. Till you do, nobody can take you very seriously in spite of all this broody act.' He sawed through the loaf and challenged her suddenly: '*Is* it an act?'

He could well believe that she was confused by recent events, and in general; but he couldn't believe, when it came to it, that she could withhold herself completely from him . . . He banged the handle of the bread knife on the table and shouted: '*Say something for God's sake!*'

That brought a reaction: she fled, dashing for the stairs, where he heard her stumbling over the skirt of her kaftan, tumbling her way to the top and banging a door behind her. He considered going after her but decided not. On the showing so far, he wouldn't thereby do her much good. He could only hope he'd had some effect; any effect could only be beneficial, he told himself as he scooped honey on to his second slice of bread.

And, anyhow, the interview had effectively shattered concentration for the present. Taking it all round, he decided he'd better do some useful tedious job to fill in time till his mood revived.

He went out into the grey wind and mended—with posts and wire—the gap in the back wall that admitted sheep. After that he warmed himself up with soup, then wrote two letters, then got out the green folder, studied the accumulated bills, compared them with the latest bank statement, did some arithmetic and wrote a cheque for the coke. All this diligence put him into a serene temper; when, before four o'clock, he heard Michael's car pussying up the lane, he was glad to hear it, and went down to put on the kettle for the homecomers.

Because of Alan's welcome, or because of the bracing sea air, or because the Michael Drings were going away tomorrow, or because, on the other hand, they were all more used to each other by now, the party assembled in the kitchen very amiably. They'd all, they said, had a lovely day. Alan said, yes, he'd got a lot done; Michael said there was something fascinating about that bleak coastline; Shaun said he and Lyddie had collected some fab pebbles; these were heaped on the table beside the confectioner's boxes— Yes, they'd come round by Cocker-mouth and been to Bryson's and Fiona had thought cream cakes would cheer them all up and do her figure no harm just for once. She laid out éclairs on mixed dinner plates, licking her fingers, her cheeks shiny and hair moppy with sea wind.

Outside, the air darkened and the second rain of the day clattered on the window. Inside, cosiness solidified. Shaun, animated, explained his stones to Michael who lounged across the table, a blob of cream on the end of his nose. Deborah came in, or as far as the doorway, where she contrived by her stare to make the room seem empty. Dring said, in a warm but cautionary tone: 'Come on, Deb. We're all having a tea party— Look, Auntie Fiona brought cakes ...' Whereupon she advanced as far as the stool by the Rayburn and crouched there, her hair and kaftan even more rumpled as if she had been rolling about, her face pinched into faint perturbation.

Perturbation was stirring in her. She had been terrified and wounded by her father's—as she saw it—attack; he might have kicked her on the very spot whereat a limb was broken. But the terror had simmered on into some promise of activity ... If she could hold on to this impulse she might see something to *do* ... Outwardly she was a little more aware, but only of the over-quietness of this place, where people ate cream cakes and beamed and chatted and it was all so *deadly* ... She recoiled from the plate of squishy objects waved under her nose by her Auntie Fiona.

'Oh, go on ... You need something to build your strength up before you go back to London—' From Alan's tone, Fiona had caught that Deborah was somehow, now, more includable, and she gladly took the opportunity; she liked Deb, who, yielding to the friendly insistence, took a vanilla slice.

'We don't know yet,' remarked Alan, 'that she's going back.'

'Oh but surely. What else could she do?'

'She's thinking of something,' said Alan, rather ominously, though he intended it to sound warningly. Michael at that looked across:

'Aren't you going to go on and get a degree, then, Deb? If you'd listen to me, you would. Plenty of time after that to start mixing yourself up in politics.'

'It isn't politics that's been her worry so far,' Judy put in, on some undirected defensive, and leaving Deb exposed to:

'Well—what has, then?' from her kind uncle.

He and Fiona gave their attention to Deborah, encouraged at last to show an interest in her. Deborah gave her attention to her vanilla slice, licking its end and frowning. It seemed to her that the room darkened as if a storm were gathering.

'I think, it's the general injustice of the world,' Judy said. 'More tea, Michael?'

'Well, that bothers as all, but we don't all— No, thanks,'

[73]

as Judy waved the pot under his nose, on which she simultaneously noticed the blob of cream. '—We don't all go to such lengths—'

'Most of us are too old and cautious— Keep still a moment—' She grabbed the dishcloth and applied it to his nose, which silenced him but allowed Fiona to take up:

'We don't know yet exactly what Deb *has* been doing, do we?'

'She hasn't felt like talking about it yet.'

'But surely, to *us*—'

'*No,*' said Lydia. 'That's *mine.*'

'But you said *I* could have it—'

Strife was breaking out between the stone-collectors. The raised voices distracted the rest of the party. Shaun had arranged before himself the little glossy Fleswick Bay pebbles with their stripes, spots and whorls; Lydia had admitted she'd already got hundreds of those. Now at issue was the haul of large, sea-smoothed trophies from St Bees, roc's-eggs in buffs, blues and pinks. Lydia held between her hands a huge white orb speckled with black and bronze, over which she was glaring at Shaun. 'I didn't. Anyhow I've changed my mind. *I* found it—'

'I know, but I'd have found another if I hadn't thought I was having that one ... Daddy,' he appealed, 'didn't Lyddie say I could have the Skiddaw granite one? Because it goes with this, the Eskdale pink—'

'I don't know what you both said. Don't let's have a childish fuss about it.'

'*He's* being childish,' said Lydia virtuously. 'All about a silly old lump of stone—'

'But I want it for our project—'

'Yes, Lyddie,' said Alan magisterially. 'If Shaun wants it for school, let him have it.'

Lydia bent over the pebble, pressing it between hands and forehead. 'But I *want* it ...' she murmured, demonstrating deep affection.

[74]

'We'll be going to the coast again,' pointed out Judy. 'But Shaun won't have another chance—'

'*Please*, Lyddie,' intoned Fiona, widening her eyes. 'Shaun, say *please* to her, and maybe . . .'

'What*ever* he says,' persisted Lydia. 'It's *mine*.'

'Oh come on,' ordered Alan, impatient. 'You can find a dozen more like that.'

'No, I want *this* one.'

'Listen, Lyddie,' Judy said stroking back Lydia's hair, 'Shaun's your guest, and—'

'He isn't. He's only bloody old Shaun—'

'*Lydia*. That's enough,' her father said. 'Give him the pebble and stop this performance.'

Lydia shook off her mother's hand and sat up with the pebble clutched to her breast and scarlet face lowered. Everyone waited; even Deborah had laid her vanilla slice on top of the Rayburn and was watching hollow-eyed. (What might Lyddie *do*. . .?) What Lydia did was to burst into tears and splutter: 'Okay *have* the bloody thing—' and hurl the stone —not, exactly, at Shaun, but just past him, so that it cracked a tile above the Rayburn, bounced ringingly against the lid of the hotplate, skimmed to the floor with a force that might have broken the stone flag, spun against the table leg with a clonk that shook the teacups, and came to rest on the mat at Deborah's feet.

Everyone had followed the stone's progress in stunned trepidation. Before anyone reacted, Deborah moved, before even she herself had reacted— She saw now what had been missing, that there had to be *violent* action, to break out of deadness and *break* something . . . She leapt up, seized the porcelain figurine from the shelf behind her and flung it clear across the kitchen, so that it hit the back door, rebounded clear of the doormat and shattered on the stone flags there, bursting in a tinkling shower of shrapnel.

All the heads turned; amazement let the crash fade into

complete silence; then Deborah broke into breathless crying and ran shakily out of the room.

Judy exclaimed: 'Thank God for that!' and hurried after her.

Fiona, looking at the fragments, said dazedly: 'Oh, what a pity . . . What made her do that. . .?'

'One wonders . . .' said Alan.

Michael said, rather grimly: 'Well, one had better find out.'

If Deborah had been trying to show her uncle and aunt that she was with them, she had at least made an impression; but as she clung weeping round her mother's neck upstairs, neither thought at all of the Michael Drings. Deborah cried because her gesture had torn her own understrung nerves; bewildered, she let Mummy fuss and comfort her . . .

'. . . and it doesn't matter about that statue, darling, I didn't like it much anyway . . .'

. . . And Judy was ready to suppose the gesture had at last struck a spark and restored Deb to animation. Why, of course, Fiona's present—aggression against her, or against Judy?—could wait. At the moment she herself felt soothed and restored. Leaving Deb wept out, she came downstairs into revived day; pale sunlight shone on Lydia who was crossing the yard kicking a paint tin before her. In the kitchen, Shaun had gathered up his pebbles and gone; the other three sat round the table. Michael's elbows were squarely on this, and Fiona's arms were folded; evidently they were in the middle of earnest discussion, whose effect on Alan appeared negative; he was slouching back in his chair sleepily; as Judy came in he looked up:

'She all right?'

'Yes, I think so.' As the other two watched her inquiringly, she added: 'It was the kind of thing I'd been hoping for— But I'm sorry it had to be my statue.' No one had thought of sweeping up the pieces; she brought the dustpan.

[76]

'I was telling Alan,' Michael began. 'Obviously this is more than just nervous exhaustion or whatever you've been telling me. The girl's in a pathological state.'

'M'm?' from Alan, whose head had drooped again.

'All right, I'm no expert,' conceded Michael, testily, 'but I'm trying to tell you who is. Foster.' He turned to Judy. 'You've heard of him, surely? The useful thing is, his place isn't far from here. Well, near Dumfries. In my opinion, if you want to do the best thing for Deb, you'll get her to him. Fast.'

So like Michael, Judy told herself, kneeling with the dustpan. Once he's in possession of all the facts he's quite sure about what's to be done, and fast. But can't he see how he puts Alan's back up by at the same time suggesting that we've been hiding the facts from him, that we don't want to do our best for Deb, and that we *want* to have his advice on how to put things right . . . 'Who's Foster?' she asked politely.

'Oh, surely even people round here have heard about him. He was on TV a month or two ago, in a programme about adolescent problems. Anyhow, he's *the* man nowadays in that field. He runs this therapy centre—doesn't call it a bin, or clinic, or anything—more or less on natural lines. Great on diet, and the patients work out of doors, and they have animals and all that. He's had tremendous success with mixed-up youngsters. Bloke in the office had a boy who'd tried suicide four times, but Foster straightened him out and now he's happy as a lark, working for his accountancy exams.'

'Deb isn't suicidal—yet,' remarked Judy, picking up a stray sliver of porcelain.

'Nor's she too keen on accountancy,' muttered Alan.

'Christ, you know what I mean. That was just an instance. Of course his fees are steepish; not the kind of thing you get on the National Health. But he's well qualified—consultant psychiatrist to half a dozen big hospitals—he's no quack— Well, maybe it'd be beyond your means, as things are, but no harm in telling you. I'd bear it in mind.'

[77]

'We'll do that,' said Judy. As Alan said nothing, she began to feel some resentment on her own account. Did Michael imagine she had no understanding of her own child and would want to hand her over to experts who made her hoe turnips? 'But I think Deb'll be better now.' She put the dustpan back in its corner, adding: 'It might be having you here that's helped her. Woken her up ...' She felt she owed them something, anyway, Fiona, for the statue.

'Actually,' Alan said offhandedly, 'I had a word with her myself today while you were all out. She seemed to be a bit more alive after that.'

'Oh marvellous,' said Judy. 'I knew that'd do it— If anybody can help Deb out of this,' she cheerfully told Michael, '*he* can.'

'If you say so,' replied Michael, audibly sceptical.

'Well, what about supper?' Judy hastened on. 'Shall we—'

Alan stood up and shoved his chair briskly into the table. 'Thanks for the tea. I'd better get back to work,' he said, departing.

6

THE MICHAEL DRINGS, who had intended to make an early start home on Sunday, finally drove off a few minutes before noon; they had been hanging about, somehow; the smiles with which Michael and Fiona lit their last backward glances were, somehow, anxious. Alan and Judy waved from the yard gate, and remained there, looking down the empty lane. He put his arm round her and she fitted her head into the angle of his neck.

'Debby,' she said after a peaceful pause, 'now she is more or less talking to me ... She seems awfully muddled ...'

The soft wind blowing up the lane was springlike. 'What', asked Dring, looking over the matter calmly, 'have we done wrong, in our dealings with her? Can *you* see?— Why she should end up behaving like this...?'

'Oh, not quite *ended* ... What I do see is, *she* doesn't think she's done anything wrong, at all.'

'Oh? ... Oh. Then, no wonder she's muddled.'

They were talking, in this posture, as they did when they lay like this in bed. 'Well,' said Judy, 'how can we judge her? Our standards could be quite different. We could be out of touch—'

'It's seemed, *she* is.'

'Only with *us* ... I mean, it could be *us*?'

'We don't throw china about and refuse to eat or speak—'

'No really, darling— It is a worry.'

He comforted her with a pressure of his arm. 'Anyway, our visitors have gone. Perhaps she'll emerge now. We'll see.'

'I'll tell you what I thought you and I might do this after-noon,' said Judy remembering, 'since Lyddie won't— Go and see poor Miss Mitchell in hospital.'

'What fun.'

'No darling— She can't have many visitors. I do feel some-body should— And you know she likes you.'

'I like her,' he agreed. Then, waking up, giving Judy a rallying squeeze and releasing her: 'I'll tell you what I ab-solutely *must* do, after the last few days, and that's get out on the tops on my own for an hour or two.' The balminess of the air was disturbing a dusty surface on his brain. He went for his boots, stuffing an apple in his pocket, deciding on Ennerdale; Michael had done him out of Pillar and he felt it was owed to him.

'If you're taking the car,' said Judy without complaint when she heard this, 'I shan't be able to go to the hospital either.'

It was, of course, Sunday, and fine; cars abounded; lonely Ennerdale was being turned by the Forestry Commission into a well-regulated playground, with attractive little painted signposts to tell people where they should walk; the bridge into the plantations, once a precarious single plank, was now a solid construction of local slate steps and handrails; but after that, Dring found it still possible to escape into solitude, even by choosing a pathless route through long heather and boulders. He slogged uphill in a concentrated trance, inci-dentally making better speed than he had when chasing his brother up Gable, and emerged on the broad ridge, sweating, alone, his brain scoured, to turn and plod happily alongside the wall over Haycock.

When he had crossed that and was settled into his stride towards Pillar he was exchanging affable Hullos with other walkers and thinking of nothing but the dappling of hazy sun-patches that broke through the cloud rolling in from the coast. On the top of Pillar he barely noticed the Coke tins and scampering dogs; he gazed at the lavender outlines below

him to the west and yielded to the equipoise of achievement—
tiredness, revival, empty satisfaction. He said to himself sar-
donically: Quite like old times ... And was too much taken
up with his sardonicism to wonder why he need have thought
of 'old' times at all.

Downhill was a self-perpetuating rhythm, like flight. Cloud
was thickening, and the air among the plantations was dank,
but Dring wished the winding forest road from Black Sail
would go on for ever; the broadening of the valley and the
gleam of the lake had an element of unwelcome dawn. It was,
however, almost twilight when he got back to the car; a day,
he told himself, well spent—invested; by the time he got
home: supper. He was hungry.

Since he had been brought up to believe it indelicate to
think too much about food, he thought of nothing at all on his
homeward drive, food being his only immediate interest.
When, turning into his yard, he saw Deborah wandering
round the side of the cottage, he called to her gaily:

'It was marvellous on Pillar this afternoon, you know. You
should have come.'

On that Sunday afternoon Charles Mitchell drove north again
to visit his Aunt Pruey. He told his wife: 'I won't take you.
I want to talk to the old dear rather seriously. But it shouldn't
take long.' This was not because he would easily persuade
his aunt to be moved into an old people's home, but because
his aunt was not likely to detain him with a long argument of
the subject. Her mind, as he had been aware from his boy-
hood, was invariably pre-made-up. He had suffered under her
merciless, and often just, criticism; that he used to be afraid
of her gave the more warmth to the tenderness he felt for her
now, as she lay so small and desiccated and alone in her
hospital bed.

As he had expected, as soon as he had brought himself to
refer at all directly to his aunt's destination on being discharged
from hospital, she said simply:

[81]

'I suppose you want to put me in a home? If so, let me assure you you'll have no success.'

He laid himself out to assure her, on the contrary, that it was not like that at all; nobody wanted to 'put' her anywhere; furthermore, 'homes' nowadays were nothing like she imagined ...

Prunella did not need to imagine; she had visited, fairly recently, acquaintances in those places with colour TV, bright fitted carpets, shining modern equipment, constant attention from doctors, constant flow of visitors, and everything else that her fastidious soul did not so much abhor as refuse to entertain. 'Impossible,' she said, staring fixedly at the ceiling.

'What is? I'm only trying to explain— You must see, it would be so much the best thing—'

'Do you know, Charles, I find I'm getting quite *deaf* lately.'

'But you must see,' he pressed on dejectedly, 'you aren't fit to go back to that house all on your own—'

'I hope somebody's keeping it aired,' remarked Prunella.

'I'm sure somebody's keeping an eye on it. Don't worry.' Charles's own soul shuddered at the idea of that cottage with its load of junk and smell of moss and mice. It was to him so obvious that Aunt Pruey would be better off simply anywhere else. She needed—everybody needed, in Charles's kind humanistic philosophy—warmth, security, companionship. He had expected her to be difficult but he was finding her perverse; almost, he suspected she might be going a little potty.

These suspicions might have been confirmed, had Prunella bothered to expound her thoughts to him. Throughout her life, her ideas had been clear-cut and so necessarily discrete. She laid aside, rather than summarily rejecting, alternatives, but held them in reserve. Religion had never been to her, daughter of the vicarage, a matter of emotion; if she had appeared to neglect it, it was by calculation; she had seen no reason to reject God, but had reasonably sold her soul on a sale-or-return basis. She had known perfectly well that—especially of late—she had laid too much value on the treasures of this world. Were these to be taken from her, it would be justly; therefore, by God; whose mercy was infinite; therefore, the alternative was not a cosy old people's home, which was irrelevant to the whole issue, and so, ungodly, didn't exist. As an adolescent frustrated, Prunella had seen exactly what Job had meant by his intention to 'curse God and die'. In old age, she saw that cursing didn't enter into it; quite the contrary.

'... But you must see,' persisted Charles, scarlet-faced in the heat of the ward, 'how *I'd* worry about you, if I let you go back to that house ...'

'Yes; I expect you would,' agreed Prunella, crisply and without much sympathy.

Deborah had known, as soon as she did it, that smashing the figurine had no point. She had known even as she clung to Mum, that this was no use. Failure swept her into its backwash; but there had all the same been *some* impulse and its effect was: she had woken up, from a dream that she couldn't remember but that she'd have to remember before anything made sense. Meanwhile she went on helplessly hanging around Mum, in bewildered dependence. Thank God, anyhow, Uncle Mike and Co. had gone. Thank God, Lyddie went back to school next morning and Dad was hidden away writing.

But the quiet of the day weighed. After she and Mum had lunch, soup and apples, she helped Mum bring in the washing; the visitors' towels were dry already in the primrosy breeze. Deborah dropped a pillowcase— 'Never mind, darling, I'll soon rinse it through again ...' It was too much like being three years old again; Deborah felt three feet high. '... I must go down to the post office; d'you want to come?'

Shaking her head, Deborah went into the sitting-room and switched on the radio. There was some sort of a concert, that went droning on ... Nobody was here, except Dad, who wouldn't know whether nobody was here or not ... Then Lydia was here, walloping through the back door and across the passage, chucking her anorak all over the table and bawling:

'What are *you* doing?'

She was eating an apple; grabbing a ball from the window-sill she began to throw it against the wall over the fireplace. Deborah said:

'I *was* listening to this music.'

'I bet you weren't. Where's Mum?'

'Out.'

'We had stinking-awful stew for dinner,' recounted Lydia. 'And Tom Barker fell off his bike in the road and bloodied his hands.' Jamming the apple between her teeth, to free both hands for her ball, she meanwhile sniffed long and damply. The ball struck a corner of a picture frame and shot aside to bounce off Deborah's arm. 'Christ,' said Deborah faintly.

'Get out of the way then. You've had the whole house to yourself all day ...' Pouncing after the ball, Lydia tripped over Deborah's foot. '*Dripping* about,' muttered Lydia, beginning her game again.

'Oh Lyddie, piss off—'

'Why don't *you*. Dripping about. Nobody wants you,' retorted Lydia with vehemence— Well, it was a bit boring, the way Deb was being babied and petted by Mum since Saturday; anybody'd think it was *clever* to go smashing presents people had given to people ... Sniffing, Lydia dropped her apple and grovelled for it— Dripping about, she said to herself again, denying a certain pathos in Deb huddled palely indoors on such a bright day. She almost threw her ball straight at the radio but caution intervened. Slightly muddled by this she threw her apple at the wall instead and took a bite of the ball; the apple split and spattered into the fireplace and Lydia fell backwards shrieking with laughter, legs in the air.

'Go *away*,' said Deborah fretfully. 'Go and see Miss Mitchell or something—'

'She's in *hospital*, don't you know that, or don't you care

[84]

about anybody except your drippy self,' hectored Lydia, sitting up.

'Nor do you. You won't even go to see her,' said Deborah with more energy.

'Nor will Dad. *So.*' Lydia pulled down her sweater over her round midriff, musing: 'What a lot of selfish people in this house.'

Deborah, beginning to shiver in the cold draught that Lydia had let into the room, sighed too; she'd had enough. Hauling herself off the couch she went through to the kitchen and rummaged lethargically in the cupboard under the stairs. Lydia followed, to stand sniffing and watching. Deborah pulled out a boot and, after further search, another; she hadn't had them on since last summer and hadn't cleaned or dubbined them then; they looked dry and bent.

'They're no use,' commented Lydia. 'That sole's coming loose.'

'Doesn't matter. I'm only going on Mellbreak.'

Lydia's valedictory sniff lasted till she was back in the sitting-room, where she turned up the radio full blast. Deborah, pulling on an anorak of Judy's from behind the back door, left the house pursued by strains of Mendelssohn. She went down the field path, past Miss Mitchell's, and dropped on to the road, turning left towards Loweswater. Her boots creaked and her legs felt stiff, but the sun glinted on catkins and wispy clouds.

Where had Mum said she was going? She might be coming back along this way. When she heard a car, Deborah slid into a gateway and crossed a couple of fields. This way, she could hit the lane into Holme Wood. The terrain unrolled itself, as if under her hand, familiarly. What if she went up by the waterfall and round to High Nook tarn? No; it had to be Mellbreak, because she'd named it to Lyddie, and she had been trained to state her destination whenever she went on the fells alone.

So telling herself, Deborah did not admit further reasons.

[85]

(It had to be Mellbreak, her mountainous friend—because 'Nobody wants you', flung even like a half-eaten apple by a peevish child, can wound the unsuspecting heart unbearably.) She trudged on over soggy tussocks, aware only that it was a hell of a long way, coming round like this, and that her legs ached; and that being out, by herself, felt queer; it made her head rather swimmy. But now she'd come, she'd better keep on. And anyhow, it slowly began to come through to her again—the mouldy smell of the woods and the lurid green streaks on tree trunks— In a way, she belonged here. It was all right; like old times.

Finally at the foot of her ascent she even felt her spirits lift a little, as they always had— '*Now* we're off!' She was warm enough to pull off her anorak and knot the sleeves round her waist. Only as she set herself to the steep grass slope did she find herself puffing and wilting. She looked upward; the beginning of the scree was miles above. And that was only the beginning of the climb. She thought: But my God, I used to race Dad up this bit ...

Only because there was no point in turning back, she dragged herself slowly on, zigzagging; pausing for breath, looking back to see the edge of the wood dropping below, she addressed herself: Well, what d'you expect, you haven't walked uphill for ages—and good God, it's only old Mellbreak, you can't come to any harm on him.— No, don't sit down, keep moving; you aren't tired, you'll get your second puff any minute.

But here was the scree slope, discouraging at the best of times. Deborah took three strides up it, slithered, and threw her hands forward to catch her weight. An edge of slate cut into her palm. *Damn*. Wobbling, she stood upright to lick at the blood, then, annoyed enough to persevere, shoved herself on again. Then a tough heather stem caught itself inside the loose sole of her boot and ripped the sole half off. Damn and *damn*. She sat, on sharp slate, to inspect the damage.

Already, at seven hundred feet, it was colder than it had

been by the lake. She unknotted the anorak and put it on again with stiff fingers tugging at the zip. Looking back now, she noticed a layer of thin haze sliding down the vale. She felt a long way from home. She thought: All right, if they don't *want* me ... and began to cry, and found this oddly consoling, so went on crying, as loudly as she wanted to, because what did it matter; there was nobody to hear and that was just what the matter was. She rolled over and laid her face on Mellbreak, his sharp slate against her cheek and his peaty smell under her nose. And in a way things began to make sense.

What was, largely, the matter with Deborah was a delayed adolescence. So far she had developed from within herself, like an onion. What she still found quite unimaginable was that she might not, after all, be someone quite outstanding—a heroine. She had never needed an audience till a treacherous self-uncertainty made her look round, to see—what? She wasn't at all used to judging herself by other people's standards, since in any case these had never been thrust on her. To need people suddenly and vitally is, of a consequence, to find them inadequate. One would have had to be a mountain, to reassure Deborah at this juncture.

Possibly because she had never as an infant thrown herself howling and frustrated flat on the ground, she acted out the gesture now with abandon. Yet the abandon, flooding itself away, left her more desolate than before. She sat up, wiping her nose miserably on her sleeve, and poked a cold finger at her boot sole. But there was a new energy somewhere—inspiring: It's their fault ... They don't want me ... Nobody loves me ... I might as well die ...

This seriously occurred to her; if she just stayed here, lying all night on the fellside, she jolly well would die. Serve them right. Yet, enough of the heroine remained; she felt this would be a bit feeble. It would be better to die on top, at least. Or anyhow, to make a more positive thing of it ... She looked upward at the scree and the tufty rocks beyond, where the heather began and the path to the summit. She looked back down, and noticed a light pricking out somewhere from a farmhouse window and wondered what time it was, and whether that haziness spreading below was going to merge into twilight; it must have taken her the hell of a time to get here. At home, they would be putting lights on, and kettles, and missing her. Maybe.— Come to think, she'd told Lyddie where she was coming. Which was annoying. Somehow, that muddled things.

It gave her impetus, at least; she'd put herself out of reach— She might go and chuck herself off Pillar Rake ... She might do simply anything, up on old Mellbreak in the dark. There was no knowing. Daring and tempting, she thought, herself, she began to clamber up the scree again, her boot sole dragging and flapping, her legs and arms all over the place like an unstrung puppet's.

Deborah, whose presence had been anyway so haphazard, was not immediately missed at Broom Cottage. Judy came back with a packet of Lyons jam tarts, for 'the children'—she sensed that Deborah was feeling three years old, and Lydia was certainly behaving it, and a little treat might cheer them up. Dring coming down to make coffee said: 'What hideous things.'

'They weren't for you, don't worry,' said Judy waspishly. Lydia's comment on the tarts was: 'Huh.' But she ate three.

Dring soon came down again, not explaining why, and went to crash about in the byre; work was, in one way or another, over for the day. Back in the kitchen he sat at the table fiddling with insulating tape, mending something. 'What's for supper?'

'I thought, bubble and squeak, with that cheese flan.'

He mumbled: 'No wonder I feel a bit warmed-up myself— Lyd, must you make so much racket?' he added loudly to the sitting-room.

'I'm practising my skipping. What are we having for supper?'

Judy called: 'What do you want, Deb? ... Isn't she in there, Lyddie?'

'No. She's gone up Mellbreak,' came huffing back between the thumping skips.

'She's gone *where*...? She might have said so—'

'She did. To me.'

'*Lyddie*, go outside if you want to skip, for heaven's sake—'

'I can't skip in gumboots and you won't let me go outside without—'

'Oh Lord— D'you think she's all right?' Judy asked Alan.

'Lyd?— Oh; Deb. Yes, why not. Do her good to get out—'

'But she left it so late—'

'It's daylight till seven or so, now.'

'I suppose so ...' But twilight mistily filled the window and the bubble and squeak was browning in the pan, and no Deborah. 'Which way will she have gone?' worried Judy.

'Up from Kirkstile and down to Scale Force, usually, unless she fancies Pillar Rake,' Dring told her nonchalantly. 'She knows that heap like the back of her hand, remember.'

It wasn't till they were halfway through supper that Lydia thought to remark: 'Serve Deb right for not dubbining her boots, the sole was splitting right off one of them.'

'Oh Lord ...'

As she stacked the plates, Judy said: 'What time do we ring the police?' And catching Dring's frown: 'Supposing her boot came to bits, she'd be pretty well stuck, wouldn't she ...' She knew that to Dring as a seasoned fell-walker, the calling out of police and Mountain Rescue was an ultimate ignominy. '... And she really isn't very fit. She'd soon be overtired ... I expect, it's no use going to look for her, ourselves?'

'Presently we'd better,' he agreed. 'With which in view, I wish we hadn't had that fry-up supper. Give me a few minutes ...'

'Take an Alka-Seltzer,' said Judy anxiously. 'Anyway, I'm

going to take the car as far as Kirkstile. At any rate that'll save her the last two miles of road.'

'Unless she comes back by Watergate and you miss her,' Dring pointed out. Judy turned her back on him saying, high-pitched: 'Damn, where's my yellow anorak— Lyddie, coming with me?'

'*She* took it. Okay, might as well.'

Dring said: 'Well, the yellow anorak should be a help if we have to search. If you don't meet her on the road, come straight back and you can take me as far as Kirkstile then when I've got my boots on.'

'We won't be long—' Nor were they; Judy didn't hang about at Kirkstile except to rush into the inn and ask whether anybody had seen Debbie today; nobody had. She didn't linger for questions but rushed back to the car:

'We'll get Daddy, right away—'

They flew back along the road; they bucked and skewed up the back lane as they had bounced down it; this was the way a walker would have come. Lydia, lounging in her seat, said: 'Mind your springs.'

'Oh don't be silly.'

Dring, still alone, reached for his boots when he heard their tale. He looked resigned and pallid; indigestion had indeed set in. Judy said: 'But you can't go up alone— Who shall we ring? You won't let *me* come, I bet?'

'With respect, my dear, it won't be that sort of picnic. Have we got a decent torch with a decent battery?'

Lydia, sniffing after her encounter with the outside air, watched him curiously. 'Are you really going all the way up Mellbreak in the dark, Daddy?'

'If I must, yes.'

'Gosh. But honestly, you know, you don't have to. She isn't up there.'

'How d'you know?' snapped Judy.

'Because I saw her. In the doorway of the barn on the road, as we came past just now.'

'In— Why didn't you *say* so?'

'I thought she was hiding,' explained Lydia. 'I saw the yellow anorak and then she popped back behind the ivy on the wall.'

'All the same you might have *told* me. You are maddening. And you were going to let Daddy go out and—'

'No I didn't. I *did* tell you.' The issue was simple enough to Lydia: if Deb wanted to hide, that was Deb's affair; Lydia took no sides in the matter. But she resented her mother's tone. 'I shan't next time,' she said darkly, clumping off upstairs.

Dring and Judy eyed each other. 'Hiding— From us?' asked Judy at last. She sat down as if forcing herself to reconsider. 'Anyhow, she isn't lost on the tops, so that's all right.'

'It occurs to me—as it must to you,' he said, 'that that's what she wants us to think?'

'She might. But how cruel of her ... Why should she?'

'You were saying yourself that she's muddled,' he said, without offering an answer.

'Yes, but *why*?' And as he straightened in his chair, pressing one first to his diaphragm, she abandoned the theoretical to hurry on: 'So you needn't put your boots on, or do you think you'd better?'

'Better?'

'Is it you she wants to go and get her?'

'From what Lyddie says, she's nearly home.'

They both listened briefly to the silence outside. 'Not', said Judy, 'if she's really hiding, down there. I wonder if she knows Lyddie saw her. If *I* went, she'd maybe think I was just fussing. —'

'You are, rather, aren't you.'

'Well for heaven's sake, couldn't *you*, a bit?'

He leaned back, drew a long breath, belched softly, and then said in a reasonable voice: 'I'm not altogether sure that that would help. If she's staging some kind of a drama, it may be more helpful to her not to take part in it. What do you think?'

What Judy thought, she did not appear to know. She stared at him baffled for some moments. 'The thing is,' she resumed, impatiently, 'she's out there in the cold and if she won't come in she'll have to be fetched. Apart from anything else she's had nothing to eat since midday. If you've got a pain and I'm in a fuss, or whatever, why don't we do neither— Just, send Lyddie down to call her?'

He nodded. 'That would be solicitous without being dramatic?'

Lyddie, summoned, thought it would be merely tiresome. 'I was counting my *pebbles* ...'

'Look, darling, you know Debby isn't awfully well, really. Won't you be just a little bit kind to her?'

'Why shouldn't *she* be kind to *me*?' But under the stern regard of both parents, she shoved on her gumboots and took the torch. Normally Lydia enjoyed going out in the dark with the big torch, throwing searchlight-beams up into trees and sky. Tonight she pounded straight down the back track, so that she would the sooner be back with her pebbles. Behind the torch's beam she was unidentifiable to Deborah, who had advanced as far as the track's foot, and stepped out of the hedge to reveal herself.

'Come on, they sent me to find you,' panted Lydia.

Deborah's disappointment made her face in the torchlight go white and thin. Exhaustion in any case had dwindled her; it had been killing, getting back here on a boot and a half; she hadn't got anywhere near the top of Mellbreak and was disappointed already in herself and it; she'd forgotten quite what she'd been hoping for, and hearing Lydia's voice said only:

'*You*? That was no bloody use.'

'Well,' said Lydia, 'I *did* find you, didn't I? Come on.'

And she set off back uphill, using the torch to light only her own way. Deborah, seeing nothing else for it, followed,

[92]

limping. At the yard gate she stopped to pull off her useless boot, and went into the house with it in her hand. The light of the kitchen blinded her.

'Oh darling—' began Mum.

'You all right?' asked Dad.

'Where were you? We've been worried stiff— Are you cold? You'd better have a bath right away—'

Deborah, ignoring her, said to her father: 'Thanks for coming to rescue me.'

'Oh darling, he *was* just putting his boots on, and I've been out in the car to—'

'Thank *you*,' said Dring, 'for finding your own way home in familiar country when you'd set out too late in the day with faulty equipment.'

'You righteous sod,' said Deborah, throwing the split boot into a corner. 'I daresay you were just too busy *writing* to bother, if you were honest.'

'I do have certain other commitments, yes, that keep me too busy to rush up Mellbreak at a moment's notice—'

'Oh yes. But you can rush up Pillar to please yourself, at a moment's notice,' she observed, giving him hardly a glance as she crossed to the passage door, but conveying in it a depth of contempt.

Upstairs, Lydia, lying before her outspread pebbles on her bedroom floor, turned to poke her head round the door as Deborah passed:

'What's the matter with you? Are you potty or what?' she inquired with curiosity.

'*I'm* not the potty one,' Deborah said, and banged her door shut.

7

'IT'S TAKEN ALL THIS,' Deborah stated, 'to show me how utterly useless he is.'

Even Judy did not come of the generation that would have said: You mustn't speak like that of your father. Her grandmother might have said it to her mother. Judy, covertly studying her daughter across the kitchen scales, listened without comment.

'... In fact, he's absolutely selfish. Through and through. He never bothers at all about anybody else at all. Let alone me ...'

Tipping the weighed flour into her mixing-bowl, Judy thought better of asking Deborah to bring the currants from the pantry. Obviously the phase of Listen-with-Mother companionableness was over. Judy told herself she hadn't expected it to last and that anyway it hadn't been healthy, but all the same she had enjoyed it while it lasted, and this new bitter distance—for Deborah, if communicative, was not confidential—left her deprived and restless.

'... He expects the world to revolve round him and his precious *work* ...'

Judy went for the currants before rubbing in the fat, for an interval's solitude; she thought: Debby never did criticize Alan before—so, this is a backlog ... We brought her up so well, really, that she never had to rebel against us.

This she would normally have noted with pride, and even now she did not wonder what might have been lost when Deb drifted so easily off on her own ploys. She didn't suppose she was expected to say anything in answer to the harangue, but coming back to the table she murmured:

'But you know, darling, he *does* love you—'

'*Love*.' Deborah tossed the word aside. 'What's the *use* of that? It gratifies him but doesn't help *me*.'

'I don't think', said Judy sententiously, 'one can ask for more than love.'

Deborah, sprawling across the table, dropped her head on her arms and groaned: '*God*.' Her hair fell in the greased baking tins. Judy flicked it out with the handle of her wooden spoon. 'One shouldn't have to *ask*, in any case. Anybody as intelligent as he pretends to be should bloody well *know* ...'

'Know what?'

'You see, you don't, either, but *he's* the one who's supposed to show such understanding of human nature. So he might, when it suits him, but only in his own pompous books—'

'They're not pompous. Be fair,' said Judy on firmer ground. But Deborah, not interested in that, sighed and began eating currants.

Later, Judy reported much of the conversation to Dring. She was in bed and he was at his table tidying away papers for the night. With his back to her, he listened.

'... So the idea seems to be, you're a totally selfish beast and no use to her at all ...'

Tearing a scrap of paper in half and dropping it on to a pile of similar scraps, Dring remarked: 'It seems, then, that I was right about the lost-on-the-fells drama last night.'

Judy's head turned sharply. 'Well, yes. In a way. But *in* a way, I can see what she means about you. Can't you?'

His hands stopped but he did not turn round. For a moment he looked as if Judy had shot him in the back; and that was how he felt. It was impossible that *Judy* should judge him as he was secretly afraid the world (for instance, his brother Michael) might and as Dring was secretly afraid of judging himself— That is: by the outward appearance.

That Judy was at the moment picturing Deborah's judgement, rather than voicing her own, escaped him; he was, at the moment, over-susceptible. Obviously, in pampering his genius he gave every outward appearance of pampering merely himself; and, should genius dry up, he would be nothing but a self-indulgent wreck. Dring would very much rather not be forced to reflect upon his own character, which he had subordinated to his genius, his one egg which he had put in a basket whose security he would very much rather not be forced to doubt. It was all unfair; Judy's potential treachery was the *end*. Fighting back against the inconceivable, he said furiously:

'No, I do not see what she means *at all*.'

He slammed two books together and slammed them into a drawer of the table, slamming that till the table rocked. When the noise stopped, Judy said hesitantly:

'I only meant—'

'I don't care what you meant. And I'm sick of all this nagging. How can I get anything done if I never get any *peace* ...' He stood up, switched off the table lamp and turned, towering in the middle of the room. Judy stared up from the bed open-mouthed. '... I can't see why *I* have to be surrounded by hysterical women— Why other people's affairs are so much more important than *mine*— Wordsworth, for instance—' he insisted, raising his voice, glaring not at Judy but at the wall beyond her, because he was throwing up a barrier between them that he had never needed before, a barrier that would stand against her accusations (feeling she had accused him baldly of being a selfish beast, whereas to Judy that was a Deborah-inspired hypothesis; it was Dring himself who admitted its truth)— 'Wordsworth had a household of women who valued his writing and took care to see he had peace of mind to work in ...' He angrily shook his head, not adding: How am I so different from Wordsworth? And Judy, not seeing that he necessarily was, was distracted and a little amused by the comparison:

'Yes, they did dance attendance, didn't they. But don't you think they were exceptional women, Mary and Dorothy?

Anyway in those days women were *supposed* to be subservient to men. And I can't see Debby as any kind of a latter-day Dora—'

'That's all beside the point,' he interrupted, not listening. He swept out of the room and downstairs, where he evidently put on the kettle and looked in the pantry for food, making enough racket to wake the house, which, no doubt, he took to be his male prerogative? Judy, who had been about to remark that Wordsworth had been a horribly selfish character anyway, left with the idea on her hands, for the first time turned it towards Alan; for the first time, unwillingly, she began to wonder.

The constraint that this encounter set up between Judy and Dring precluded, unfortunately, any further discussion of Deborah. When Dring came to bed after a random snack, Judy appeared to be asleep and he did not speak to her. Neither, indeed, had any idea what to say; as if they entertained unnameable suspicions of each other, each was at a pause in thought; they could not help each other.

In the middle of that night Judy was woken by—had it been?—a scream; she shot out of bed; Lydia was placidly snoring; Deborah was tightly curled, choking for breath—

'Darling— *Debby* ...' It was some while before Deborah surfaced, and then it was half-heartedly; she blinked at the light Judy had switched on and said without evident relief:

'... Oh ... Was it only a dream?'

'Yes, darling ... It's all right now ...'

'Not after *that*,' said Deborah curling up again, rejecting comfort.

Dring had not stirred. Judy told him: 'Debby had a nightmare,' and he said 'Oh,' uninquiringly.

In the morning they were still silent with each other, and during the day occupied themselves separately. Deborah stayed in bed, saying coldly that she was perfectly all right, thank you. The family did not gather till Lydia came home from school and began practising her skipping. This, shaking the house, seemed to shake both Dring and Deborah into signs of activity; both wandered down to the kitchen where Judy made tea and set out yesterday's rock buns.

Lydia came through, panting and trailing her rope. 'You don't need to kill yourself over that skipping, surely?' Judy encouraged her.

'First you say I'm too *fat*—' protested Lydia grabbing a bun. 'And you needn't think you're going to stop me and throw me out because I've *got* to do a hundred without stopping—'

'All right ... Only, it's a bit noisy for everybody else—'

'Well everybody else in this house might as well be *dead*.'

At that, Deborah visibly flinched, sloshing tea out of her beaker. Dring said: 'That'll *do*, Lydia,' with a severity that was even harsh; Judy sighed, audibly admitting helplessness. Lydia, noting this effect on everybody, felt she had gone too far, without, as ever, quite knowing why; she reacted by muttering with her mouth full: 'Bloody awful rock buns. Not enough currants.' No one took any notice. Finding a hard-baked currant from the top of her bun, she spat it vigorously in the direction of the sink.

Each of the other three had, as it happened, the feeling of having somehow gone too far in their various directions, and the more so because it was no use looking to any of the others for help or sympathy. Judy, the habit of materfamilias persisting, made an effort to start general conversation:

'I heard today, when I met Gwen Martin: Miss Mitchell's going to live in Eskdale House, or somewhere, if they can find a place for her.'

'Poor old beast,' said Dring glumly.

'Oh, but it'll be much the best thing for her. She wasn't really looking after herself properly—was she, Lyddie?'

'She'll loathe being in a home all the same,' said Dring.

'She'd rather die,' stated Lyddie, taking another bun.

'Oh, Lyddie, don't exaggerate. Nobody wants to die. As

soon as she's warm and decently fed, she'll cheer up and adapt herself—'

'I *hate* it here!' exclaimed Deborah, so loudly that everyone jumped. She slapped down her beaker on the table, spilling the rest of the tea over the plate of buns. 'I've got to go away. It's too *dead*—'

Judy, after a glance at Dring, who was watching Deborah darkly, went round the table to her. 'Where do you want to go?' she asked in a humouring tone, putting her arms round the stiff shoulders. Debby shrugged her off and said, more calmly—practically:

'London. Isn't that where I'm supposed to be? What the hell am I wasting time here for anyhow?'

Dring and Lydia still watched her, Dring warily, Lydia's mouth gaping half full of bun. Judy hesitated, decided to evade the issue of Deborah's semi-official detention, and murmured instead:

'Well, darling, for one thing, you know how much the train fare is—'

'Oh, why do we have to be so poor, just because somebody wants to try and write crummy *poetry*?'

On that Deborah flung herself out of the room. Dring's eyes widened for a moment—why pick on the poetry?—but he did not meet Judy's consulting glance. Lydia said: 'Coo. She *is* potty.' Judy said: 'You're making crumbs all *over* the floor. For heaven's sake try to behave yourself sometimes.'

Just now Deborah's dreams were so much more valid than her waking hours. Last night, Mellbreak had split as she clung to him and revealed a black abyss just out of her reach. She couldn't even fall into it. This morning when she looked out of her window he had closed the rift again and pretended to be solid. But she could never trust him again. And just now in the kitchen, what Lyddie had said had thrown up a picture of Miss Mitchell lying face down on the scree of Mellbreak with her poor little white head and twisted hands on the lonely sharp greyness. Deborah liked Miss Mitchell, who had a lot more wit about her than most of the bumpkins round here. She went up to her window and saw that mist had come down low; who knew what Mellbreak was up to, behind it ... Death was everywhere here, seeping through the mist. But what was it she'd just thought of, to get away from it ... Oh yes: London.

All this *forgetting*. She was sick of it. But of course she forgot, stuck away here in the mist with ineffective people who didn't know anyway. What Deborah now knew—gaining a resigned desperation from admitting that everybody here was useless, and *glad* to be on her own—was that the thing was: London. Once she got there and saw it, she'd begin to remember everything else. If she got to Euston, she'd know where next— She'd find Bill—Tom? What was his name? Anyway she'd go to ... where was it ... anyway, wherever the house was. She'd know. She'd find somebody to tell her.

The thing was, not to linger here but to start off before she began to dither and try to remember. The impulse she had lost was in London, so she would have to get there and join up again with herself, and then, she'd be able to live again. She thought, because Judy had mentioned them, of trains. A train was the quickest way. And if you hadn't got any money, there were methods of getting round that, which probably wouldn't occur to anyone as mistbound as Ma, but which Deborah could easily employ ... once she got started. She shivered in her silent room as Mellbreak watched her invisible, offering no farewell.

8

ALEC MCBRIDE WAS TICKET INSPECTOR on that particular train. He was no sort of fool. He caught up with the girl in the yellow jacket not far south of Warrington. She came flitting out of the toilet and found Alec had backtracked and was waiting for her.

'Your ticket please,' he said and looked at her lugubriously. He knew how it would be. And she looked back at him. She didn't run. She was young and her fair hair was clean. Thin in the face.

'I've got a platform ticket,' she said, and said it virtuously. She held it out to him. 'I hadn't got enough money for a real ticket.'

'You'll be aware you need a real ticket to ride the train,' Alec said as he assessed her. Well-spoken. 'And how far were you wanting to travel?'

'I've got to get to London. It's important, you see.'

'It is; aye.' Alec leaned a little closer. Drugs? His lugubrious brown eyes inspected her candid grey ones ... Likely, not. He was not a fool about human nature either.

'And when I get there, somebody will pay for my ticket.'

'They will, h'm? You're being met at Euston?'

'Yes, my friend ... One of my friends ...' She went blank for a moment and said: 'I've forgotten his name ...'

'You have? M'hm.' Alec nodded. 'And where did you come from?'

'That doesn't matter. I can't go back, you see. I simply must get to London.' But she dropped her eyes before Alec's. She tore up her platform ticket into small pieces. It didn't seem to surprise her, when he said she'd be put off at Crewe and the people there could sort it out. He said it quite gently. He could see she was upset, a wee bit touched maybe. Not a regular ticket-cheat.

He handed her over at Crewe and watched her being led away.

She was taken into an office. Its lights were bright after the train's. A faceless man asked her questions across a desk.

'I've only got to get to London,' she explained, patiently.

'You understand,' he said in an unnecessarily loud voice, 'that you can be prosecuted for this offence?'

When she was asked for her address in London she said: 'I don't know.' She wished they'd all shut up. On the other hand, to be prosecuted would be a nuisance.

'... Of course, if your fare were to be paid ...'

That was an idea. When they asked for her parents' address she gave it. It would do them good, those misty people, to have to fork out. They'd have to admit the harsh realities of the world into their refuge. So she gave the telephone number. Somebody rang Broom Cottage. She wondered what time of night it was there. Or, for that matter, here, wherever it was ... Crewe.

After the telephone conversation, which was a long one—and which she hoped Dad would have to pay for—they told her she was to be put on the northbound train and: 'They will meet you at Carlisle. And if they settle with us on the spot, there need be no charges.'

'Who?' she asked, curious.

The two men now in the office looked at each other and then at her.

'Who's going to meet me?' It made a difference. She didn't want the whole family piled into the car. But they could hardly just send Lyddie, this time. No, don't be stupid, Lyddie couldn't even drive a car.

No one bothered to explain to her that her mother on the telephone had made out a good case for her daughter's state of nervous near-breakdown. It was evident to Deborah, though, that the people here suddenly turned kinder. Someone brought her a cup of tea.

'Your parents are coming to meet you. Now, till it's time for the train, you may as well rest ...'

So she was led away again to a waiting room. Dim figures with suitcases peered at her without interest. Perhaps they wondered why she was given VIP treatment, told to lie down on the bench, and covered with a striped blanket. She wondered why herself, but was as dim as the other figures; not really interested.

'We won't let you miss the train,' somebody assured her.

'What time is it?' She was remembering the kitchen at home, trying to guess whether Dad would this time have put his boots on and set out to look for her.

'Never mind; we won't let you miss it.'

When she woke up it felt like no time at all. The small hours were so small they had petered out. The blanket was hotly prickling her chin and the world smelt of ancient soot. 'Come along, my dear,' a tubby man was urging her. He had ginger hair and a uniform like a railway porter's. 'We've got to get over the bridge. Ups-a-daisy. Shall I give you a 'and?'

He helped her up. She looked, Jim Adams thought, like a ghost. He put his hand under her elbow as they started up the steps. 'That's the way, love. Plenty of time. Train's not due for six minutes yet.'

Her legs ached. Cold dead-time air blew along the platforms. It reminded her ... It woke her up. And woke her up twice.

So far the journey had gone like a dream. It had been easy. She'd got good hitches, and there had been a train surprisingly soon. But in the heavy sleep just now, that dream had dissolved. With it, another dream enclosing it had vanished.

What the *hell* was going on? All she remembered now was a journey on a night like this, northbound, on a horrible train, with Ma. They're stopped at Crewe *then*, for God's sake.

[103]

For *God's* sake, she couldn't start that all over again.

More than waking up, she came to. She stopped, clutching at the hand-rail with both hands.

'Come on, love,' said Jim Adams.

'I *can't* ...'

'Just a few more steps. We'll get you on that train some'ow.'

But that was just what they wouldn't. Not this time. Nothing had ever been such hell as those days—weeks—at home. At the moment they were a blur because she couldn't even remember why they had been hell, or what she'd been thinking of, to let them happen.

She wasn't like *that* at all. She was a positive and original person and now remembered it. A violent shiver loosened her grip on the hand-rail but cleared her vision. As the ginger-haired man shoved her on, she was lucidly 'here', in the wide tiled passageway with posters and signs to other platforms and to her right, the way out. She took it, so suddenly that she seemed to herself airborne, a bird shooting out of a cage.

So she almost seemed to Jim Adams and to the ticket collector, so unexpectedly did she dart away and past. She was outside the station before their shouts followed her. She ran on, so fast that only shouts could follow, and those not for long.

She could run for ever; the night was hers and she was free in it. She was wearing her baseball boots and they scudded along without sound on the dry pavements.

It didn't seem to matter where she went, as long as it was away. But after a while, feeling sick rather than breathless, she slowed and considered. Better keep away from trains. Hitch, then. Why hadn't she done that in the first place? God knew. —Where? Oh yes—London. Back to Mortimer Gardens— There; she remembered the address of the squat, all the time.

The thing was, find someone driving towards the motor-way, which couldn't be far from—where was she: Crewe.

Funny, she'd never imagined there was a *town* called Crewe, with shops and things. Pretty grotty it looked too, at this time of night. Maybe, at this time of night, nobody did drive through a place like this? She couldn't imagine who on earth would. But she walked briskly on, hoping she was facing in roughly the appropriate direction.

Jakes was making for the motorway. Must make up time. They'd expect him to do this. But, even chance. He watched, behind for headlights, ahead for fog. Knew the map well; he'd not wasted time, meeting Gibbon off the Irish Mail at Chester, delivering him at the farm. Mission accomplished.

Jakes was at war. His intelligence was wired direct to his nerves. Thoughts didn't stray and emotion was short-circuited. When he noticed the girl thumbing at the town's end he doubletook without a blink. He stopped.

They didn't know this car but they knew Jakes. A passenger, a woman specially, might fox them.

'Oh, thanks. You aren't going as far as London, by any chance?'

'Get in.'

'Thank God ... I've got to get to London and I was beginning to think everybody was *dead* in this part of the world ... Not a single *car*'s passed ...'

Not listening to her, Jakes noted that. Once on the motorway he'd improve his chance. Fog might be to the good. Except for time. Make the Finchley house by ... eight. Alternative: Could contact McConnell later through the Three Feathers—

More or less open country. A car passed; dipped its headlights. The girl was chattering. Pause in the chatter; he felt her staring at him. But the lousy tweed cap was well down over his eyes.

'Where are you going?'

(*... He knows where he's going, at any rate. He handles the car damn well. How nice to be with a man who's hard*

[105]

and purposeful—it shows me I'm back in the real world again ...)

Jakes did not answer. Another car passed. Its headlights blazed and it slowed. Jakes did not alter his speed. In his mirror he saw its rear light receding. Yes; that would be them. Most likely the Anderson man. Act on the assumption he'd double back soon and follow.

'... I just wondered, why you should be driving at this time of night ...'

The motorway. Clear of traffic and fog. Jakes accelerated. They'd no chance now of finding where he'd stashed Gibbon. They were more likely to try to trail Jakes to Finchley. He watched behind; no headlights.

'... Look, *are* you going as far as London? You didn't exactly—'

They ran into fog. After the first impact, not too thick. Jakes wound down his window, leaned out and kept going.

'... You're going *far* too fast ...'

Revised plan: get off the motorway at the next chance and lose them. Delay in contacting McConnell but couldn't risk Finchley till the stuff was shifted out of there.

Better lose his passenger too. Fog was thinning. Jakes cut across to the hard shoulder, leaned over her and opened the door.

'Out.'

'What? I can't get out *here*. You oughtn't to stop here either—'

He silenced her with one neat clip, ran round the car and dragged her out. Dumping her on the grass he was on his way again in seconds. Next turn-off about six miles ahead. Might make good enough time by the old A41. Fog permitting. He prepared his report for McConnell as he drove. Gibbon at the farm and the girl on the motorway verge were ahead of him as items in the report. Like a good soldier Jakes never looked behind him.

*　　　*　　　*

They were all singing their heads off when they came out of the show and they went on singing as they piled into Joe's car, Ted and Tracey again plus various odds and sods, but a couple of them got lost somewhere and then this chick Ted had collected, she wanted to get out at Rusholme, said she lived there. Well Ted had the idea he was taking her back to town with him or something only she started creating, and there was a set-to in the back, and she managed to get the door open and it hit a lamp post. Well, that did it for Joe. He was trading this car in soon. He told Ted to let the chick go and Ted hung on to her and there was a bit of a rough-house and Tracey sat there in the car singing, that thing from the show:

'What's wrong with the world is
It's GOT NO LOVE in it ...'

You'd have thought they were all tight or something, only music always got them a bit like that. In the end the chick got away and Joe shoved Ted back in and Ted began singing too. It was all right for him only Joe wanted to get to work tomorrow. He didn't want to lose another day's pay what with the down payment on the new car to raise. Tracey wanted to stop for a drink but Joe said they'd be shut by now. He kept his foot down and thought, thank God they'd get on the motorway soon and she'd have to stop arguing. He could have done with a drink himself really to keep him awake. Maybe if he kept singing that'd do.

'—If it's GOT NO LOVE in it
It can't go right ...'

The motorway was jampacked with bloody great lorries. At this rate they wouldn't hit Hendon before midday.

'What's wrong with you is
You've GOT NO LOVE in you ...'

'Smashing group, the Mandarins,' Tracey said and yawned.

Ted must have started on her because she began yelling at him and so did Joe; she wasn't his girl, only he didn't want a set-to in the back while he was getting past these damn lorries.

Then, Ker-ist, they ran into fog. Ted said, let's stop some place, but Joe told him not to talk daft, there wasn't anywhere, and Ted said anyway he wanted a leak and Joe said Ted could bust for all he cared, he wanted to get on out of this lot and home. Tracey piped on:

'What's wrong with me is
I've GOT NO LOVE in me ...'

And then she said, 'Hey listen:

'What's wrong with Ted is
He's TOO MUCH PEE in him ...'

After that they all began making up verses about what was wrong with people and the fog thinned a bit and things got a bit more cheerful. Still they were all getting rather bloody-minded with the music wearing off and a hell of a way to go yet.

'What's right with the world is
It's GOT YOU AND ME in it ...'

Ted said: 'Hey, look—'

It was a girl standing right there on the hard shoulder waving at them.

'Bloody 'ell,' said Joe astonished.

'She can't hitch on the motorway,' said Tracey. 'Silly bitch.'

'The cops'll pick her up,' Joe agreed.

'Why'n't *we* pick her up?' said Ted.

Yeah, that was an idea. As long as nothing was coming. It wasn't. Joe stood on the brakes, and backed towards her.

She came tumbling up, Ted and Tracey shouting at her.

'Get in quick!' he shouted, opening the near front door.

[108]

too, and got in. After she'd stuck her head in to have a look at them.

(*They're all right. They're young. My age, human* . . .)

'Thanks awfully—'

'Thenks *evah* so,' said Tracey talking posh, and she began singing: *'What's wrong with the world is—'*

'Bloody lucky to get anybody to stop for you,' Joe told the girl.

'I know. You're about the first car. There were lorries—'

'Bloody silly place to be too.'

'What's right with the world is
It's got OUR LOVE in it . . .'

'It wasn't *my* fault. A man threw me out of his car.'

'Did he rape you too, duckie?' asked Tracey and screamed laughing.

'He hit me. He knocked me out.'

'Cor, listen to her. She's had a fate worse than death. *What's wrong with the world is, It's got TOO MUCH RAPE in it* . . .'

'Could've had my leak while you stopped,' Ted remembered.

'Would've had to be a bloody fast one,' Tracey said.

'Yeah, well I'm a fast worker. What's your name, chick?'

'. . . Deborah. I want to get to London—'

'Who doesn't,' said Joe. 'We been to Manchester for a show, specially. The Mandarins.'

'They're smashing,' said Tracey. *'What's wrong with the world is . . .'*

'Come over in the back with us, chick,' said Ted grabbing hold of the girl's hair.

'Turn it up,' Joe told him. Ted's elbow had rammed his and made him swerve.

'That *hurts*,' said the girl in a whiney voice. She wasn't much of a looker but then Ted hadn't been getting far with Tracey and he'd lost his chick in Rusholme. Tracey by the sound of it was pulling the girl's hair too. The party had perked up now they'd got company. Still you couldn't have them sillybuggering about in a car and Ker-ist, some more fog was looming up too.

—Made his eyes go funny . . .

*'What's right with the world is
It's got DEB-OR-AAAAH in it . . .'*

'Here, I only gave you a feel— You frigid or something—?'
'My neck hurts, where that man—'
'Yeah, you forgot, Ted, she's just been raped—'
The car juddered along a kerb and that hadn't been the goddam fog, it was Joe damn near falling asleep. For all the racket this lot was making. 'Watch what you're doing,' Ted bawled at him.
'Look, I could do with a break. What about—'
'Who couldn't. Give Ted a break, Deb-*or*-ah—'
'—stopping at the services it said about, back there?'
'What d'you want to bloody stop for? *You* were in such a rush to get home—'
'*You* were in such a rush to pee—'
'Yeah; there's that. Okay then.'
*'What's wrong with the world is,
It's GOT NO LOVE*— Oops, Ted, that was *my* bloody foot—'
'—If we can find the bloody place in the fog,' muttered Joe, slowing. Not a clue where they were. Motorways, they're like a different country. If they'd never been invented he wouldn't have got let in for taking these erks all the way to Manchester, and why couldn't Ted do some of the driving for godsake even if he'd got his licence taken away, nobody was going to worry, this time of night . . . Here: lights, signs, all a bit dim in the tail end of the fog. Well if it was clearing they might as well push on— No, he'd go to ruddy sleep if he didn't have a coffee . . . He turned into the parking space and ran up alongside the one or two cars there.

'Not much doing,' said Ted. 'Think they're open?' But they all piled out. Except their pick-up. She said: 'I'll wait for you.'

'And pinch the car,' said Tracey. 'No thanks.'

'Well, are we going to stop for *long*—'

'Come on,' Ted said, and got hold of her and heaved her out. Being Ted he made the most of that. The bint started kicking at him and whining again. So Joe went round and said: 'Break it up. I want a coffee.' Tracey put her arms round his neck and said she'd lost her shoes and where was the Ladies, it looked like the fresh air was making them all a bit turned-on, only Tracey was a silly cow anyway and Joe didn't bother. He shoved her off and began pulling Ted off the other girl he'd got flattened against the side of the car. '*Break* it up—' What with all this he'd never get in to work tomorrow. Looked as if Ted had bust this chick's neck or something, she was all flopped against the car and flopped on to Joe when he shoved Ted off her. She felt kind of soft and clingy and for a minute Joe went for her himself, but then Ted came back in, using his feet. 'Gerroff, you sod, she's mine, isn't she—'

Joe wasn't having that. He used his feet back on Ted, not letting go of the girl, so she was jammed between them and Tracey was yelling at them to go on, rape the bitch, she was used to it, and *What was wrong with the world was*— That bloody song again, Joe had enough of that for tonight, so he yelled at Tracey to belt up.

A man came towards one of the other parked cars and took a look at this bunch and started getting into his car fast, and Joe didn't blame him, they must have looked like a gang of maniacs. Still he wasn't letting Ted grab the chick off him as easy as that, Ted and his bloody get-all-I-want big-headedness, Joe'd never been able to stomach Ted now he thought of it. It was high time Ted got his. He gave Ted a real good one right in the nuts with his foot and Ted bellowed like a bull and Tracey began screaming at Joe to lay off him, as if Ted'd be grateful for *her* championing him, but as Ted took a breath and came at Joe again, the girl who'd been whining away all this time got out from between them and screamed at the bloke in the other car:

'He-e-elp!'

Bloody dramatics. Anyhow the bloke took no notice, he was starting his car, he'd got the sense to keep out of trouble, specially anybody else's. The girl began running and Tracey grabbed her by the arm and told her to shut up, but the girl got free and Tracey tottered and sat down on the asphalt and *she* began whining, and Ted seemingly hadn't quite decided whether to go after his chick or come at Joe again, and by this time the girl had chucked herself right across the bonnet of the car as it moved off and yelled:

'Oh *please*— Take me away from them!'

Well seeing the bloke couldn't bloody well drive off down the M6 with a bint draped over his bonnet he had to slow up, and when he did she was round to the far door in no time and he did let her in. Good luck to him. Maybe she was in for her second rape of the evening but once she was away, Joe didn't bother.

Once she was away Ted calmed down a bit too. 'Sod you, Wilkinson,' he said to Joe, but as if he was saving it for another time. And Joe said: 'Sod it all. Come on, we've wasted enough bloody time, let's see if we can get a coffee.' So they went off towards the caff, Tracey in one shoe, holding on to both Joe and Ted and starting that effing song again about what was wrong with the world.

Reg Emmett hadn't the least intention of getting mixed up with a crowd of scrapping hippies. Driving overnight you came across all the riffraff. God knew he wouldn't have *been* driving by night if it hadn't been for the pile-up of work waiting for him at home, and nor would he have been so late if he hadn't stayed on for a noggin with those two chaps from Newcastle. Point was, you went on these courses partly to meet up with other types in the organization and exchange

[112]

ideas that weren't strictly what the firm sent you on the course for, but nevertheless came in useful. You had to think in every direction at once if you wanted to keep afloat in this rat-race of a life. No wonder he had an ulcer, or what ruddy well felt like one; he'd have to try and fix up a visit to the quack as soon as he'd caught up on his paperwork— No, hell, he'd got all that Bromsgrove nonsense to sort out this week, he'd never have time. And so it went on. No wonder his guts were playing up, ulcer or not, after that splendiferous nosh he'd been putting away all week. One thing about the firm, they did you well on these courses, that hotel in Blackpool had been good. But God they made you work for it, and if they ever found out you were keen enough on your work to drive back overnight to catch up on it, would they be grateful? Big laugh. And nothing much else to laugh at in this squalid world, except the same old dirty stories those chaps came out with after a few whiskies, and then Reg's laugh was only polite, Ha Ha Ha, keeping up the all-pals-together myth while his guts griped (and *now* he remembered the one good story he himself knew, about the girl with the cucumber) and it was all right for those others who rolled off into their hotel beds to sleep it off while Reg, keen energetic type, took to the dreary motorway and stopped every time he came to a gents. And if he had to stop, he hadn't the least intention of picking up a hitch. However, rather than mix it with the rest of her gang, he took this girl on board and drove off fast.

'Oh *thank* you . . .' she said, collapsing into the passenger's seat. 'They were so *awful* . . . Where are you going?'

'Birmingham,' said Reg tersely.

'Oh—I want to get to London, but that'll help. I'm sorry really to chuck myself at you like that but I've been having such a night . . .'

Reg didn't want to know. Luckily the fog was a lot thinner and the traffic less. At this rate he might make it home while his guts were quiescent. He lit another cigarette and un-

buttoned his coat and settled behind the wheel. The girl said:
'Have you come far?'

'Blackpool,' he conceded. 'Breezy Blackpool.'

'... On holiday?'

'Big laugh.' He overtook a crawling tanker and added:
'Been on a course for my firm.' They whooshed under a wide
bridge; the outer lane was empty in a greyish glimmer that
could have been dawn. 'Monitex.'

'... Textiles?' she said, vaguely.

'Christ, no. You must have heard of Monitex. Steel press-
ings, allied materials for the building trade. Bloody powerful
concern. Except that it's going down the nick fast like the
building trade. Depends on it, of course. For that matter
every trade in this benighted country's going down the nick
nowadays. It's a shambles. Reorganize, economize, bugger
about, you never know whether you're coming or going and
personally I'm just about past caring. Chap in one of the big
oil firms was telling me the same thing. And it's us reps, the
men in the field, who get the rough end of it every time.'
He came up behind a Jag doddering along at fifty, as if the
outer lane was a bloody country tootle, but when the Jag saw
his lights it sailed off ahead doing at least ninety—bloody
idiots you saw on the roads nowadays, talk about speed limits—
Big laugh.

'For instance,' he went on, seeing no point in chasing the
Jag, cramming his half-smoked fag into the ashtray where
it dislodged several others from its pile, 'this year they suddenly
increased my area to include Leicester. I'd already had Rugby
stuck on me—bloody fantastic. How'm I supposed to cover
that lot?' He lit a cigarette and mused: 'I'd jack it in but I
don't know how the hell else I'd earn the money and besides,
they make sure there are half a dozen eager young types
snapping at your heels just to keep you awake—'

His guts seemed to have calmed down at last. Maybe
having someone to talk to kept his mind off his troubles.
'And they send you enough paperwork to make a full-time

[114]

job on top of everything else. The table in my flat's absolutely stacked with bumf I haven't had time to read—as for laying it to have a meal on, big laugh. Can't get near it. Anyway I usually eat out, no time for mucking about cooking. Comes expensive, but they say that's the kind of thing they pay you a high salary for. See how they get you; you spend all their salary trying to get their work done. Honestly it's bloody tyranny, I'd rather we went communist and had done with it. It'd be more honest. And it might do something for the economy. Couldn't be worse than the cockup all *our* governments make of that. D'you know what I had to pay in income tax last year, to keep all those layabouts and hooligans living in comfort? Blokes who could quite well find jobs if they tried but do better on the dole. They tax you out of bloody existence. That, and the sweat of keeping up with old Papa Monitex, and the *price* of every damn thing— Look at cigarettes; it's fantastic— If I lose this job it won't be my fault, they'll have bloody well persecuted me out of it, and how'm I to find anything else at my age—over thirty—and with no training for anything but slogging around in a car. D'you know how many *thousand* miles I logged in the last quarter?—and chatting up moronic clients ...'

He stuffed his cigarette on the ashtray and flicked at the stubs that cascaded down his trouser leg. Experimentally he switched off his headlights. 'Thought it was getting light,' he said gloomily. 'Should be, I suppose. Spring nearly here, if I had time to take any notice. That's another thing they're bloodyminded about: holidays. Changed me round when I'd signed for a fortnight last month and had it okayed—some bugger got 'flu, was their tale—so I only got a week's skiing ... Snow was lousy at St Moritz then too, and I damn nearly tore a tendon. I can still feel it. I was in agony for the last few days. Damn waste of money, nothing to do but sit around tippling and waste some more money ... Honestly, you can't win ...'

And now, all he had to face was his flat with its piled ash-

trays, unemptied garbage and scattered heaps of bumf. He
looked at his watch; appointment in Bromsgrove at fourteen
hours, it was no joke. No time for a kip, and God knew if
he had anything in the place for breakfast. Which reminded
him that he quite fancied the idea of bacon and egg. Might
call in at the Beacon Dining Rooms ... Get a shave at
Monty's, maybe. Buy a paper. Slide into the new day without
having to cope with the flat. Get around to it this evening,
except he'd be too buggered by then ...

Musing on the evening, the warm pub or cosy solitude
with television, he recollected his passenger. She hadn't been
any trouble. Hardly nattered at him at all, unlike most women.
He said:

'Where did you say you wanted to go?'

'London.'

'I ought to have put you off at another services. Otherwise
I don't know how you catch a ride ... I turn off any minute,
to get home.' He hoped she wasn't going to be a nuisance
to dispose of. 'You know the form though, do you? Hitch
about a lot?'

'Sometimes. Last night I started off by train, but they
threw me off at Crewe and tried to put me on a train back
north, so I decided to hitch.'

Reg positioned himself in the nearside lane, then asked:
'Why should they send you north if you're going to London?'

'Oh ... I hadn't paid for my ticket. I haven't got any money.
They rang my father to meet me at Carlisle.'

'And meanwhile you beezered off in the other direction,
did you. That sounds a crazy idea.'

Since she did not elaborate on her idea, he summed up:
'Best thing would be, to get back, if your father's meeting
you. There'll be a train from Birmingham.'

'But I don't want—'

'Or a bus,' he interrupted, firmly. 'More buses than trains.
Tell you what, I'll run you round to the bus station. How'll
that be?'

(I might as well be there as anywhere ... He just wants to be rid of me. He hasn't once looked at me yet ...)

'All right.'

It was out of his way, but Reg believed in giving a helping hand to people when you could. When he called 'Good luck' to her as he drove away, he felt he'd done his good deed for the day and that it was pretty generous of him too, considering all he had on his mind. The strains of life with Papa Monitex hadn't stopped him yet from being a human being, after all.

9

IN A COLD DAYBREAK, in Birmingham, in a bus station, Deborah reviewed her situation with understandable melancholy. She sat on a bench tenderly feeling her neck and head. She wasn't sure quite where that heavy man in the tweed cap had hit her, but she ached in her throat, both ears, and behind her eyes. She was bitterly cold, empty, and had—when she counted it —one and a half pence in her anorak pocket.

Her encounter with the 'real world' had bruised her more than physically. The various people she had fallen in with during the night had been 'real' enough—in the sense of, substantial and undeniable—but not one of them, since the doggy-eyed ticket man on the train, had looked her in the face. Nobody, simply, cared at all.

And, here, it was obvious nobody would. People were setting out early to work by now. Grey and grim they strode by, hunched against the bleak prospect of another day. No one so much as glanced at her.

All the same, she *was* in the real world, ever since she'd rushed out of Crewe station, and this livid dawn threw a new light on things. For instance: London. What had been the panic about getting there? Now she realized that the squat had been bust up and everybody was scattered—two of them at least, into prison—and, furthermore, nobody in London cared a damn about her either. Not really.

Which was, in a way, a relief. It meant that she need not depend on them. She had 'come to' without assistance. 'To' from what, she only vaguely wondered— God, I must have been barmy.

Quite what she had been expecting to result from her return to London she wondered even more vaguely. The thing was, immediately, that she was stranded in this dismal city; and aching and miserable. So, what to do about that?

Because there was no perceptible point to doing anything very positive, she thought rather wistfully of going home. It would give her time to reconsider, and at any rate there would be something to eat. And the pure air of the fells ... God, Birmingham *stank*.

Well then: Home. By bus, as the badly-used man who'd dumped her here had suggested? Not very brightly, considering she'd told him she hadn't got any money. Trains, she didn't feel equal to risking again. Fleetingly she thought of Dad having to fork out for even more fare ... Then thinking of family, she remembered Uncle Michael. He didn't live terribly far from Birmingham. He was rich. Or anyway he might *lend* her the money for a ticket so that she need not land Dad with a socking great bill as soon as she got home.

She got up from the bench with some effort. Her injuries, or sheer fatigue, had made her rather limp. It occurred to her that if she could get a bus—to Kenilworth, might it be? That was the nearest town to Uncle Michael's house—she could tell the conductor she'd post him the money if he'd let her have a chit for it. It was the only expedient that came to her. She hadn't even enough money to telephone Uncle Michael.

The conductor on the bus, which Deborah eventually found and boarded, didn't think her idea a good one at all. She was summarily thrown off the bus when he came to ask for her fare. So she was stranded again, in outer Birmingham, and feeling even colder, and bereft of ideas. She could just have sat down and died, till she saw a distant policeman. Police were supposed to do something about the destitute, weren't they? Even if they booked her for vagrancy they might lend her enough to telephone Kenilworth ... She ran weakly after the striding figure, gasping: 'Help—'

So it was that Michael Dring was telephoned at twenty

minutes to eight that morning by the police, who informed him they had a Deborah Dring here who said she was a relative of his and might he please come and fetch her?

Fiona had telephoned Judy once since the visit to Broom Cottage just to 'ask how they all were'. This was how intercourse between the households was usually initiated and carried on. It would never have occurred to Alan or Judy, elusive as they were finding Deborah at present, to notify or consult Knott Leigh, which was the name of the Michael Drings' pleasantly situated house verging on the Forest of Arden.

'That', announced Michael ringing off, 'is Deb. The police have got her.'

'What's she done *now*?'

The Michael Drings had been awake when the telephone rang, but not yet dayborne. Michael had been shaving and listening to a radio account of earthquake damage in Turkey; Fiona had been still in bed deciding what to wear for her Heart Foundation coffee morning. She looked up at Michael in faint alarm.

'Nothing. Well, it seems, she's run away. I'll have to go and get her. Damned inconvenient ...' He went through to the bathroom and switched on the shaver again. Fiona sat up and called after him:

'Get her— Where? Where is she?'

'... I've got an area meeting at eleven. Nothing much before that, though ...' Above the buzz of the shaver he said more loudly: 'If I bring her here I can ring the office if I'm going to be delayed. God knows what's going on. I told the police she was a nervous breakdown case and they seemed prepared to believe it ...'

So was Michael, especially when he had Deb in the car and began to question her. She looked like nothing on earth to start with, in a grubby anorak and baseball boots and her hair all over the place, and a mumpy bluish swelling on one side of her jaw. Her face was pinched and pale. When he greeted

[120]

her, kindly if quizzically, with: 'Hullo; what are *you* up to?'
she said in a collected enough tone:

'I'm sorry to bother you like this, Uncle Michael. All I
wanted was to borrow my fare home if you could lend it to
me.'

'Home, eh? How come you've wandered so far from it?—
Come on, let's get going. Hop in ... Well—'

'Where are we going now?'

'Home. Knott Leigh. Right?'

'All I really want is to be taken to the station—'

'Well, I haven't had my breakfast yet,' he said, diplo-
matically, 'and I bet you could do with some too?' Nor was he
dressed; he'd shot out in slacks and sweater, in case this were
some sort of rescue operation; about which, he wasn't yet too
sure. '... Then we'll see about putting you on a train if you
like. I'd like to hear, though, how you came to fetch up in
Small Heath at this hour of the morning.'

'It's just that Dad was meeting me in Carlisle hours ago—'

'He was? Does he know where you are?'

'No, you see, after they rang him I ran off— Maybe, they'd
ring and tell him I wasn't on the train?— No, why should
they bother.'

' "They?" '

'The people at Crewe. It was after that I decided to hitch.
Then a man slugged me—but I don't think I can have been
out for long. Then those ghastly other people picked me
up—'

'Where was this?'

'On the motorway somewhere, I don't know.'

'Nobody would stop and pick you up on the motorway.'

'Well, they did. But the next man picked me up—at least
I threw myself at him—at a services somewhere. He took me
to the bus station, and after that I thought of you, so I was
trying to get to you when I got chucked off the bus. So I asked
a policeman what to do next.'

That sounded like the first sensible idea she'd had. What

to make of the rest of her story, Michael didn't know. Probably a tissue of nonsense, but in the event, here she was on his hands, and he'd have to decide whether she was fit to travel, and whether she seriously intended to go home or, given money, would go gallivanting off somewhere else again. 'Look here: did your father know where you were going?'

'... Oh no. I just went—'

'Just ran away?'

'I suppose so ... More or less.'

'I see. We'd better ring them right away then.'

Deb persisted: 'As soon as I know what train I'm arriving back on.'

The fact remained, to Michael, who was something of a psychologist, that whatever Deb's protested intentions, *here* she was; flying to him—and Fiona—for refuge. He thought for a while and then said in a gentle, reasonable tone:

'I'm glad you've decided to go home. It shows you've got some sense of responsibility to them. In the end, you can never duck out of life by running away from it. Can you? ... Fiona and I are always ready to help. You know that. But it's a case of where your roots lie ... Old Alan may be a bit head-in-the-clouds at times. But his heart's in the right place, when it comes to ... essentials.'

If his recommendation of his brother appeared a little tepid, it was because Michael was trying to be delicate, not to intrude upon another family's situation. In any case this was a difficult sort of speech to have to make when you'd had to drive twice round the county without breakfast, but Michael was never reluctant to face up to his responsibilities. Deborah, listening with a flash of interest— Was Uncle Michael going to be any *help*?—then felt only a disappointment, a blank in his picture. Head-in-the-clouds, yes, but what was *in* those clouds didn't matter at all to Uncle Michael. She said:

'He's writing poetry nowadays.'

'Yes, well ...' shrugged Michael, as if that were something a sensible daughter would make allowances for.

But to Deborah's way of looking at things, had she been able nowadays to look clearly, the writing of poetry was heroic. Unliterary, she placed some vague but tremendous value on the praeter-human that may have been obscure to her but was evidently a blank to Uncle Michael. So *he* was useless too. So she sighed, and looked out of the car at the 'real' world, to which she was still glad to have been restored, but seeing it cold and mechanical.

It was cold; the daylight had slid in under a leaden sky. And there was something mechanical—essentially, she felt, practical; everything *worked*—about Knott Leigh, which they soon approached. The garage door lifted itself for the car to enter. In the kitchen, Auntie Fiona preparing breakfast manipulated switches like someone manning a power station. Machinery for beating, grilling, washing, drying, and who knew what else, was lined up round the walls.

However the house was gorgeously warm and bright. Deborah sat in the dining recess gratefully shivering, between a rubber plant and the purple-flowered curtains. Uncle Michael, beaming, sat opposite her. 'Well—hungry, old lady?' She loved him.

'What would you like, darling?' urged Auntie Fiona, hovering in a very posh velvety housecoat. Fiona never did dress before Michael had left for the office; this morning a sense of crisis suspended had paralysed her. 'Michael, what would *you* like...?'

'My breakfast, of course, woman,' he said slapping his hand on the table. 'Haven't you got it ready?'

'Oh, yes, just about ... But I wasn't sure what ... when ...' She flicked some more switches. 'But Debby— Would you like ... Some warm milk, or Bovril...?'

'Anything,' said Deborah fervently. 'Whatever Uncle Michael's having.'

'Oh. Yes, if you ...' She had been expecting some sort of invalid. What Michael was having, as usual, was orange juice, muesli, crisp bacon and ryebread. Fiona hurried to it. Let

Michael talk to Deborah, he'd do it better ... They seemed to be talking about the garden.

'... We cut back those conifers and made that rose bed ... How long is it since you were here anyway?'

'I don't remember.' Turning from the window, Deborah watched the food coming. There seemed to be a good many gaily coloured packets and the bacon, with half a tomato, made a poor showing in the middle of a large bluebell-patterned plate. Uncle Michael, whose grasp of the practical she much admired, said:

'What about an egg for Debby, too?'

'Yes *please*.' Also, without much pressing, she accepted four slices of toast, popped-up by the machine in a corner. 'We don't eat it ourselves,' mentioned Fiona. 'It's lucky I had some bread in ...'

Meanwhile Uncle Michael and Auntie Fiona were planning their day, which sounded incredibly complicated, even allowing for the complication Deborah had brought into it. Auntie Fiona *must* go to this coffee morning because she was staffing the cake stall ... After that, could she call at Worthings about the glasses ... Yes, if he gave her a cheque, and what about a wedding present for the Schein girl ... Oh, a small thing would do—a table lamp. He'd ring Bruce from the office, by the way, about the seventeenth ... Oh, and did he remember the Stephens tonight, what time...? They needn't get there till seven and they'd be home by soon after nine ... Then, salad for supper? She'd write to John today, and the man was supposed to be coming about the boiler ... He'd confirm the bookings for Tuesday week but would she see about her car ... Yes, she'd take it in on her way back from tea with Barbara, and did he remember they'd probably ask us to dinner on Friday ...

Uncle Michael went up to change. Auntie Fiona removed the dishes and stacked them in a machine. 'I've got the bed made up in the pink guest room, if you're tired—'

'Oh, I'm not *staying*.'

'No?' This surprised Fiona; she couldn't help sounding pleased. Which Deborah could understand; it would have been tiresome, fitting a visitor into the Knott Leigh schedule. It would have been managed, of course, and willingly, but one would somehow feel rather like a plate, slotted into the appropriate slot, to revolve smoothly.

When Uncle Michael came down dressed for the office he was impressively white-collared; a figure of authority. 'Now,' he began, 'what shall we do with you, Deb?'

She'd been thinking. 'Well, if you could lend me some money, I might get into Birmingham and pick up the express bus there for Whitehaven. It goes through Cockermouth and that'd make it easier for them to meet me. Besides, it's cheaper.'

That struck Michael as highly rational, also responsible. He sat down again across the table smiling thoughtfully at her. 'You really want to do that? Feeling fit enough to travel? ... Right, then.'

So the mechanism was switched on. Michael would forthwith ring Broom Cottage and Deb might have a word with them herself, to explain her movements. Then Michael would ring the bus station to establish the times of the Whitehaven bus. Then Fiona would drive Deb into the bus station at some juncture dependent on the coffee morning and the advent of the man-about-the-boiler. Money would be supplied, with no question of 'lending', for journey expenses. As soon as Fiona had seen Deb off, she would ring Broom Cottage again to fix the time whereat Deb was to be met. In case of anything unforeseen, Deb must carry with her Michael's office telephone number. Okay?

'... You know,' he said, confidentially, 'I wish there was more I could do for you. I know you've been having a sticky time lately in one way and another. We all do when we're young. But specially nowadays young people have problems, with so much so-called freedom. And with the world in the state it's in. We've tried to let our two think for themselves but we've given them a certain amount of discipline too. We think it gives the character a bit of stiffening and that's all to the good in the long run. Cathy for instance doesn't have everything her own way. She wanted to go to Italy at Easter with some gang of pals she's made at the Art Society here, but I told her there's time enough for all that when she's got her A-levels ... You see, it's just a question of putting first things first and sticking to your own job, and you achieve far more in the end. I don't expect you agree, coming from a family like yours, but I'm just putting my own point of view. Now, if Cathy for instance were to go off the rails as you have lately— And I'm not saying it's impossible; nobody's perfect—I know what I'd do about her. I wouldn't preach at her. I'd take a sympathetic line and try to get at what her problem basically was. And supposing I couldn't—though she's always been able to talk to me; we haven't had any rows in this family— I'd say: Right. Let's call in the experts. This girl needs help. And—I was telling your parents this when I was up there— I know an excellent man in that field. A Dr Foster, who has a place not far from you. He's had enormous success in sorting out young people's problems. If I were you, I'd think about that.'

But Deborah was for the moment incapable of thinking about anything. The food and warmth were taking effect. Her elbow that was on the table slid forward, her head zunked down on to it, and she was immediately sound asleep.

On the night of Deborah's return home, the leaden sky dropped its load of snow. It was March snow, soft and heavy, sliding down the roofs in blankets as soon as the strengthening morning sun touched it. The fells looked like meringues. The lakes were dark blue, and lichen and catkins acid-gold. Lydia, making snowballs on her way to school, felt them disappear between her hands whispering.

Deborah slept till midday and woke into silence spangled with the brisk dripping from gutters. The day was polished white and blank; nothing had been said; her mother had been delighted to see her.

'. . . And luckily, Stan Martin happened to have seen you walking down the road, so we knew at any rate you hadn't gone on the fells . . .' So, you might think, everything was all right. If they had suffered any alarms at Deborah's disappearance, they didn't describe them. So Deborah was not impelled to give any account of the alarms of her own journeys. The return home had blanketed them over, as if with snow.

She went downstairs. The snow-glare stuffed the house with glossy silence. 'Where's Pa?'

'Working.' Ma stopped doing whatever she'd been doing, put the kettle on, made toast simply by holding a piece of bread on a fork over the stove fire. Days here were elastic; nothing needed to be planned. Deborah yawned and said: 'I must wash my hair.'

In any case, she wasn't interested in remembering the unlikely adventures of the last couple of days. Far worse memories were beginning to bother her. Life was crazy—time went round in cycles; now, this time round, she was remembering all that had happened in London before the *last* time she came home. How she'd come to forget it, she couldn't imagine. Freud would say, she'd wanted to. Well, thought Deborah uneasily, Freud was probably right.

Even in the turmoil stirred up, she desolately said to herself: It's all very well to keep saying: I must have been crazy. That doesn't let you out of anything.

For the first time she couldn't help wondering: *Am* I crazy?

This question, one can't answer alone.

Dring and Judy were still, in spite of Deborah's escapade, in their state of tense, and artificial, separation; as if both had started to speak at once, both said: No— You. . .? and then both hesitated for too long, so that contact was lost.

[127]

All Dring did say, abruptly, late at night after Deborah's return, was: 'Why on earth did she go to *Michael's*?'

Judy said: 'I've no idea.'

The implications of the question were more than Dring could go into, even with himself. As it happened, the peculiar isolation he had been forced into just now had an unexpected effect: his poetry stirred. He sat for lapsing hours at his table, hardly lifting his head to look at the pillowy fellside and its black crack of gill.

There was another sudden snowfall on Thursday morning, but no wind, and so no drifting. Judy, coming back from shopping in the car, ran confidently at the virgin rise of the lane. The wheels whirled, but she was sure she felt solid ground underneath. She reversed to try again, nearer to the wall. Gwen Martin, on her way round from her coalhouse, called from the yard:

'Are you stuck? Come in and wait a minute. It's thawing as fast as it comes down.'

Judy left the car where it was and went into Gwen's kitchen, glad of a change of scene. Dinner, at twelve o'clock here, was over. The long table was scrubbed and an afternoon stupor, of curled-up cats and ticking clock, had descended. The teapot was still on the hob and Gwen poured Judy a cup. Judy wondered how Gwen would take it if she said she loved this house because it was so *farmhousy*.

But Gwen raised the topic on her own mind: 'Did you hear, Miss Mitchell isn't at all good?'

'Yes; Mrs Granger said Mrs Mossop had been to see her—'

'She should have been out of hospital by now. At first we heard there wasn't much wrong with her. Even now, they don't seem to know what is.'

'Well— She's getting on. Eightyish? And she never looked after herself very well—'

'That's just it.' Gwen's cheeks flushed. 'There was many a little thing I could have done for her and gladly, but you

[128]

know, she wasn't—isn't—an easy woman to get on with. I mean you never felt you could just pop in and ask how she was. And often enough I could have taken things down, when I'd been baking, but she did put you off ... I know Lydia used to go every day, and she put up with *her*, but you can't expect somebody her age to notice little things that might be wrong, and I told her nephew, I'd have gone more often myself only she did make you feel you were thrusting yourself in—'

Judy took the point. 'You couldn't have been a better neighbour, honestly. She just didn't welcome help at all—*and* let you see it. I ought to have gone oftener myself instead of just letting Lyddie, but I'd only have felt I was butting in, as you say ...'

They persuaded each other unadmittedly that neither was to blame for Miss Mitchell's plight. Gwen began to feel better; Judy too was restored by this farmhousy feminine chat. She thought: Why don't I come and see Gwen more often, or get her to come and see me? The snowflakes had melted off the windowpane and sunlight dazzled again on the fields. The car took the lane at a slithering rush. She was late, but there was cheese in the pantry if Alan or Deb had got hungry—

It seemed they hadn't. Her kitchen was as silent as Gwen's, but with activity withdrawn, rather than completed. She looked into the sitting-room; Deborah was lying on the couch; asleep?

If she had been, she jerked herself up with remarkable speed. She stared wildly, propped on stiff arms, and said:

'Mummy— Am I mad?'

Judy's greeting smile and words died. Automatically she said: 'No, of course not.' And then, weakening the effect, but shaken herself by Deborah's distraughtness: 'Whatever makes you think that?'

'Because I think such ridiculous things, and then I forget what I *have* thought. And I forget what's happened—'

'Yes, everybody does.'

[129]

'—And I don't know why I've been doing things or what I've been doing, even—'

This was a genuine crack in the defences and Judy, taken so much by surprise, wanted only to run for Alan. Not that Debby was mad—or if she were, that it wasn't a situation to be coped with like any other—except that it was bigger than any other— Or, that Debby was within reach, trying to catch hold, but, for how long? With the back of her head Judy seemed conscious of the silence upstairs that was Alan—why so silent, she couldn't at the moment remember. Feeling brave and useless she knew she had to cope on her own, and as she went to sit by Debby on the couch, putting her arms round her, she still remembered: *This* doesn't work, I've tried it before—

Today, to baffle her, it seemed to work. At least Debby burst into tears and clung to her mother in sheer fright, crying like a small child and then stopping at last and remarking in a cool, adult voice: 'However, *that* does no good.'

Still, if it had calmed her for the moment, it had done a little. When Judy suggested something to eat Deborah nodded, came with her to the kitchen and efficiently helped to make cheese sandwiches. When they sat at the table Deborah seemed tired and detached. She said:

'I never did tell you about the things I got up to in town.'

'When? ... Before you ...'

'Yes, before I was run in, and ever since I met Matt and Sophie when I first got there ... Did you mind, that I didn't come home for Christmas?'

'It seems a long time ago now ... Yes, it was rather dull without you.'

Deborah began to talk about the university, her various friends, the meetings, the parties, the fleeting copulations, the schemes for apolitical sabotage ... Interested Judy was, horrified, but it was at a remove; because that was how Deborah saw it. She wanted to say: But that's all over now, darling;

yet she sensed, Deborah thought so too; that was, now, the trouble—

'It just doesn't', said Deborah finally, 'feel as if it was *me*.' She took her plate to the sink and filled the kettle. 'Coffee?'

'Please ... Then what's still worrying you?'

But Deborah's face was cold and closed. 'I don't know.'

Well, Judy certainly didn't. Letting the subject drop, she tried to be normally cheerful, and Deborah, in a polite and dejected fashion, seemed to try to respond. Lydia coming in, Alan coming downstairs, apparently noticed no change in the atmosphere. Judy felt as if she and Deborah were two women with a secret they dared admit to no one. Later, at night, she told Alan:

'Debby's afraid she's mad.'

Not to her surprise he said: 'I don't wonder.'

She left it.

She didn't sleep much; this new worry was sharpened, subtangible. Next day she and Deborah seemed to resume their mute alliance. There must be *something*, Judy insisted, I could say or do. She's expecting me to, but doesn't know what either, and she's being so quiet about it because she's frightened ... So was Judy. Menace hovered as if—as in fact, rather—some terrible illness threatened one's child. That this was Friday, evening-class day, did not cheer her up as much as usual. If anything, it depressed her to remember that in a week or two classes would be over for the year, heralding Easter, the visitors, summer, a year rushing by while Broom Cottage was pinned down to its point of non-reality.

The classroom, when she got there, was real enough; only Judy was inclined to come and go like a defective bulb. She made an effort to pull herself together, and it helped that Miss Dunn was back; she'd been missing last week. Miss Dunn was always good value. She was a retired headmistress (looking, actually, not unlike Judy's old headmistress at school) and undoubtedly knew far more French than Judy did, but was an angel in the class. She admitted that she *read* a good

deal of French but liked to practise her conversation ...
Which she did at no one else's expense. This evening, the
sight of her wise, toadlike face gave Judy heart. During the
coffee break she fled to Miss Dunn as if for comfort.

'... I was afraid you'd got 'flu or something...?'

'Oh no; I've been away, staying with my sister in Kent.
I came back on Wednesday, on the same bus as your daughter.
I saw you meeting her.'

'My daughter—' said Judy, astonished. 'I didn't see *you*?'

'No; quite a number of us got off. I noticed her when she
got on, in Birmingham, but didn't speak to her. I had a feeling she might be the kind of young woman who would find
it a bore to have to talk to an old trout she'd scarcely met, all
the way home—'

'She'd have been— *Has* she met you? Oh yes, at the Rose-
hill thing, that time—I wish you *had*—I mean, did she seem
all right on the bus? I'm sure she did, but it was before—
You see, she'd just run off and wound up at her uncle's,
though we'd been told to meet her off a train—' And un-
stoppably, out it all came. Judy was telling Miss Dunn all
about Deborah.

Angelic Miss Dunn listened, nodding.

'... I'm sorry to bore you with all this. It's just that it was
such a coincidence, you being on the same bus— It's not as if
there were anything anybody else could *do* about it—'

'No; I don't expect I can,' said Miss Dunn. 'The only thing
that comes to my mind is: Do you know, or know of, Dougal
Foster?'

'Dougal...?'

'He specializes in what he privately calls "adolescent birth-
trauma". I've had dealings with him over a pupil—this must be
seven years ago—and he was very helpful. I know him personally, too, through some friends in Langholm. He's a very
sensible man, in my opinion.'

Miss Dunn's opinion counted for a good deal, but Judy
felt a slight chill at the idea of handing Debby over to a

[132]

psycho. Still, one had to face it, that might be the best thing. One had to face more immediately, however, the emptiness of the coffee room and the waiting class. Apologizing to Miss Dunn Judy rushed them both back to the classroom and made another effort to concentrate on French. After the lesson Miss Dunn, hurrying because she was being given a lift home by someone from Madrigal Singing, said only:

'I do hope Deborah's soon better, and let me know if you have any thoughts about Dougal Foster; I might perhaps have a word with him.'

Thanking her, Judy drove home over roads washed snow-less; only small gobbets in the hedges skimmed crystalline through the headlights. Her thought-pattern was disrupted; tomorrow's shopping, Lyddie's education, were trivial in the dark confusion of the near future. She dashed damply into the house— Was it actually raining?—and found the kitchen lit, smelling of toast. *Alan*—

But it was Deborah, in her kaftan, hair demurely plaited, taking a plate from the bottom oven. 'I remembered, some-times you feel like a little something, when you come back from the class ...'

'Oh, darling, how nice of you.' But Deborah's face was still as taut, as if she would never smile again. Judy tried to, sitting down with her plate. She tried to chat, describing the class. The surface broke and she said:

'You know Miss Dunn? I was telling her about you— Just in outline, you know— She's very experienced with people and I always think, so sensible ... What she said was, and it's only an idea— If you felt you'd like help— There's a man she knows, Donald somebody— No, Desmond ... Anyway, I think, called Foster—'

'Near Dumfries?' said Deborah looking up.

'Maybe. That rings a bell ...'

'Yes. Uncle Michael said he told you about him.'

'... Did he? Yes—I believe he did. What a coincidence.'

'Uncle Michael was telling *me* about him too.'

[133]

'Was he ... How funny. That we should be told twice—'

Deborah's eyes woke up and glowed. 'I wish I could go to him,' she said, urgently. 'I'm *sure* he'd help.'

That was enough to snap Judy back into focus. No more panicking. She had a purpose. Finishing her toast and licking her fingers she went purposefully upstairs, along the passage without glancing into Lyddie's room, and opened her own bedroom door to the familiar sight of the bed in shadow, white paintwork dully gleaming, and Alan's back humped intently in the far light of his table lamp.

'Listen darling. You remember that man in Dumfries Michael was telling us about? Debby wants to go to him.'

'M'm?' said Dring, not turning. She crossed the room and perched on a corner of the table, half-facing him.

'But Michael did say his fees were high. How much money have we got?'

The very baldness of the question prevented Dring from putting up any guard, had he wished to. He was surprised into answering it as it came, merely moving aside, with deliberation, an open notebook Judy was almost sitting on. 'It'll all be in the green folder. I think the current account stands at about a hundred.'

'Lord. And when's the next coming in?'

'... Money? I shall get my half-yearly statement at the end of the month, but can't be sure what it'll come to—'

'Yes, I know about that, we did reckon it up after Christmas. We decided it was just about what we'd need till— In fact, it's all pledged. I meant, *new* money?'

Dring pondered, then conceded: 'The next sum I'll receive will be the advance on acceptance of *Nothing to Lose*. If it's accepted.'

'Yes, it will be. Fordman said so when you started it. Could you ask for an advance of the advance—get the money *now*?'

'I hardly think so. If I did, it would inhibit my writing of the novel—'

'When,' she asked him, inexorable, 'at this rate, *will* you get it finished?'

He sat back, irritably raking his hair. 'God knows. It's pretty well stuck.'

'Well, couldn't you please unstick it?'

For the first time he appeared to notice something unusual. He was slow to revive from what had been a bout of deep inspiration. '... Couldn't I *what?*'

'This is important. If Debby believes that doctor can help her, we've got to give her the chance.'

'*What* man? Some quack Michael's heard of at second hand—'

'Miss Dunn actually *knows* him. But that isn't the point. Even if he's a quack—which isn't likely—Debbie *wants* to go to him. I'd better find out what it does cost. Maybe he's in the phone book— Miss Dunn would know his address though—'

'We can't afford pricy fees as a speculation.'

'We can't afford them anyway. So we've got to *get* the money. How quickly can you finish this novel?'

That flabbergasted him. With his hands behind his head he gazed at her, expressionless. She persisted:

'It might mean dropping your poetry but you could carry on with that afterwards. Look, darling, just for Deb, couldn't you push on and finish *Nothing to Lose* in a hurry?'

Dring's jaw sagged; then he recovered. Sitting upright, fists clenched on the table, he said quickly and coldly: 'Oh yes. I could finish it off in a hurry. I could just leave *out* the whole 1848 episode, for instance. No one would miss it. And I could kill off a couple of characters who don't quite fit into the plot. And make the hero and heroine fall into each other's arms regardless, just to make a quick happy ending.'

Judy hadn't at the beginning of this speech recognized the sarcasm. When she did, her mouth shut grimly. 'All right,' she said. '*Do* that.'

They measured each other, strangers.

[135]

Again the lack-of-contact silence caught them. Judy, feeling it, made an effort: 'It's for Deb,' she said, more gently.

'I see. She's worth my ... career? I must botch my work to send her on some dubious cure—'

'It isn't like that. She's worth *anything*, anyway. You know that.'

'It is, unfortunately,' said Dring with his head on his hands, 'very much like that.' He would have given his life for Deborah. Judy knew *that*. '... But this, in a way,' he said almost apologetically, 'isn't mine to give—'

'Well it isn't anybody else's,' said Judy. 'Don't be so *stuffy*.' Her lack of sympathy was like a calculated slap in the face. Looking up at her, Dring seemed to wait for her to relent. When she did not he murmured:

'You're exaggerating, you know. You've been too worked up about Deb all the time—'

'What you don't seem to grasp is, that *she's* dangerously worked up. She's *ill*, for God's sake. And frightened. And you won't put yourself out to help—'

'I'd do anything to help, except the impossible ... I'd expect *you* to see that. Surely you put some value on my writing, as such?'

'Yes,' she admitted. 'But, just now—'

'I've depended on that. And you. You want me to scramble off some piece of fiction instead of ...' He hesitated and added rather uncertainly: '... doing my own thing ...'

'Your own thing can *keep*.'

'I doubt it. Once I discard my standards for expediency—'

'Oh—"I, I, I—" ' she interrupted losing patience. 'We aren't talking about *you* and your precious writing. It's Deb.'

'It's me, or Deb?' he asked simply.

'Just now— Yes.'

'You're trying to put me in a thoroughly false position, instead of letting yourself perceive that it's Deb who's in one.'

'Of course she is; that's what's the matter with her—'

'Not quite as I mean it. Your own standards are rather

wobbly ... Don't you see,' he said, reasonably, 'that in any case, if you carry on like this, it's the last way to get me to write anything? All this time, it's been your faith in my writing that's made it possible for me.'

'What? To write?— Yes, but I keep telling you, I *have* got faith in your writing. Obviously. Or why should I have put up with all this for so long?'

'But you haven't much faith in *me*.'

As she frowned down at her twined hands, either not knowing how to answer that, or not wanting to, Dring suddenly recollected: 'You've put up with all *what*?'

'... Oh, I don't know— This life, I meant,' she said, shrugging.

'This *life*? Here?' He was astounded. 'I thought—I was sure—you were happy?'

'I suppose so,' she said, absently. 'Yes, it's been lovely in some ways. Only, it's gone on, rather.'

'We hoped it would?'

'Nothing lasts for ever,' she said, still absently, her mind on Deb and finances and failing alternatives.

'But look— You never said a word of this— You weren't, I'm sure, fooling me— You *wanted* to come here and live as we did— For me to write—'

His agitation began to come through to her. Sighing, she yielded: 'Oh yes, yes. But I didn't see us just doddering on on our beam-ends till we faded away from poverty like poor old Miss Mitchell. Did *you*?'

'What did you see, then?'

'I don't know. Yes, of course, I expected you to write and be famous. And then we'd— Oh, live here, most of the time, but have enough money for maybe a flat in London too— And travel, and have a villa in Italy, and meet famous people, and— Oh, whatever famous authors *do*— I've never met one but surely they do lead interesting lives, even nowadays?'

Dring was silent. When, noticing that, she glanced at him, he said quietly: 'I see.'

[137]

'You see what?' asked Judy, distracted.

Instead of answering that he remarked: 'I never imagined you capable of such vulgarity.'

Her mind taken off Deborah now, she reacted the more vigorously because *she*, let alone Debby, seemed to be deprived of his sympathy. '*You* can call it vulgarity but to anybody else it would look like a quite normal human wish. Yes, and I'd like to have some decent clothes too, and maybe even jewellery— Is that the *depth* of depravity? You go on about *your* life-work and doing your own thing, but to hell, *I've* got a life too and I'm supposed to be a person and maybe I've even got a *thing*, though you probably wouldn't recognize it . . .' He had accused her of exaggerating; now, she certainly was, in the perverse relief of saying what she'd not let herself think. Justifying her outburst, she added: 'The trouble is, I've overdone the wifely subservience for too long. And been too cut off from the world. God, I was in Gwen Martin's for half an hour today and I felt as if I'd been to the Buckingham Palace garden party . . . Even if I do get a job,' she threw in, her preoccupation cutting in like a crossed telephone line, 'I couldn't get a regular one till September now, even if there were one within reach, and they say supply teaching's overstaffed in this area and it's *now* we need the money.'

'It all seems to centre round this question of money,' said Dring neutrally.

'Well, life does, in practice, doesn't it.'

He said, to himself: 'I never imagined you were capable of saying that, either.'

This interview left Dring unnerved. That word he would have found exact; his nerves, as well as his nerve, had sunk into the greyish passivity that swamped him.

He knew, naturally, that Judy was wrong, just as his brother Michael was wrong. Conceivably the whole world except Dring could be, and was, wrong, but that did not make Dring 'right'—or if he were, he assuredly did not feel it. He felt

[138]

nothing—except a petulant resentment at being 'put' in the wrong.

'Unfair.' But this he knew to be childish and could suppress. What he was more objectively aware of, as he went through the motions of domestic life, was his exclusion by the women of the household. Judy and he had barely been 'speaking' for days already, and Deb had taken virtually no notice of him before or since her absence; but in these days, grey as his mood as the rain washed away the snow, he sensed the tacit accord of Judy and Deb. He fancied that it was against him, and in part he was right. He did not, negative himself, assess its negativeness; he thought they might be plotting something; he knew they were at any rate waiting for him to make a positive gesture.

He was, newly—perhaps for the first time—sorry for Deb now. There was no 'dramatic' element in her jumpy dejection. She did not seem to disappear, or hover, as she had; she was always here, quiet but edgy. Without her hysterics she seemed older, curiously dignified by some remote disaster, like a widow.

He couldn't consult Judy about her, much less ask her direct how she was feeling. Thrown back on himself, his anxiety became self-reproach; all they would say, he imagined, if he made any offering, would be: If you want to do something to help, get on with that novel.

Which he couldn't. Guilt about this may have been false but it weighed on him. It made him wonder seriously: How *could* I earn money? Leaving aside my writing ... which obviously I'd have to ... Or, what about hack writing—articles or reviewing or magazine stories?

No; he hadn't the facility. It would be half a loaf. Neither his heart nor his will would be in it. What about, for instance, giving lectures? He doubted that there would be much money in that, and, though not so long ago he'd taken school assembly and orated to speech-day audiences without giving it a thought, nowadays the thought he'd have to give it would be enough to put him off. He just didn't feel equal to putting himself on public show.

But as a matter of fact there seemed to be just about nothing he did feel equal to. Brooding on this led to a downward spiral. He was apparently reduced to the 'appearance' of himself that he'd so far avoided: self-indulgent, scruffy, idle and spineless.

Even if he climbed down altogether and applied for a teaching job, he couldn't suppose either that he'd be equal to that nowadays, or that any education authority would take him seriously.

Judy and Deb were apparently spring-cleaning cupboards. Lyddie was playing marbles, making a noise as irritating as her skipping as the things rattled and bonked against skirting boards or across her bedroom floor. Dring, self-punishing, dared not go out and walk even when the rain slackened, lest it be thought he was enjoying himself. He sat at his table and watched the swollen gill wasting from the upland bog. Forbidding himself to look forward to meals, he was agonizingly hungry.

What Judy was plotting emerged after three or four days of this. She said, casually, in bed, out of her silence:

'I rang Miss Dunn, and she's got in touch with Dr Foster. She says he's rather full, but it might be a good thing for him to interview Debby. It would, I suppose. It would settle it in one way, if he said Debby wasn't suitable. Or if she didn't take to him.'

'Or what,' said Dring with foreboding, 'if she did?'

'I can easily take her, there and back inside a day,' went on Judy ignoring him. 'So I fixed an appointment for the day after tomorrow.'

'I see.'

'So I hope,' she ended courteously, 'you won't be needing the car that day?'

He said suddenly: 'We might mortgage the cottage?'

Judy seemed to reflect, then said: 'And have *that* to pay off?'

Her contempt checked him. All right; he himself was merely a liability.

She and Debby went off to the interview without saying goodbye to him, leaving a covered bowl of risotto in the bottom oven for his lunch. They treat me, he thought, as if I were the dog ... He allowed nothing for their own apprehensions. Judy, as she drove off on the long route in and out round the Solway, was thinking: He didn't even see us off. When I'd bothered to leave lunch ready cooked for him, too.

Both were, at this stage, given to thinking of various wounding or spiteful remarks they might have made to each other had they been on speaking terms. But, had they been, the remarks might not have been necessary; they had had no practice in quarrelling.

When he heard the women coming home Dring did not at once go downstairs, from a diffidence that was probably misinterpreted. Deciding that he ought to show interest and that, besides, he *was* interested, he went down to the kitchen just as Judy had made some tea, which was open to another misinterpretation.

Judy was wearing her go-to-town suit and looked—Dring's instant word for it—schoolmarmy. She did not meet his eye. So he had to ask Deborah:

'How did it go?'

Deborah met his eye, for the first time in recent weeks. In her eye, he saw what Judy had seen on Friday night: a glow of hope; a flash of the old Deb. He realized then how quenched she had been lately. It touched him. She said, rather flatly: 'Dr Foster was all right.' Dring waited, but she turned away and sat down at the table, hands folded, waiting for her tea.

Deborah herself knew she was 'quenched'; she could not have enthused about Dr Foster, or anything, because she had to be so careful nowadays, to behave well, not to give away how mad she was. What she had felt about The Hollies, which Dr Foster's place was uninspiringly named, was that it might be all right to be mad there. Dr Foster, a drab little man who said nothing much, yet somehow gave that impression. She'd been disappointed when she first saw him, and he'd asked only dull factual questions about her health and things, but when she'd come out of his office she'd acquired this feeling— She wanted to go back, because if she did say what she really wanted to say, he'd listen. Or, he'd make her listen to herself ... Deborah, concentrating on good behaviour, hadn't understood the financial issue; only that they hadn't got enough money for her to go there. But if she asked about this or complained, she might start crying and fussing and give herself away. So she sipped her tea, sitting upright, being correct.

Dring, turning away too, trudged upstairs. He forgot about tea but, remembering, decided he didn't deserve any. Presently he took out the manuscript of *Nothing to Lose* and laid it in its sections across his table. The first chapter looked faded, battered at the corners, old as cold toast. He spread out his notes.

Lydia's marble-racket began. Rain began, veiling the view. At six o'clock Dring went down and shut himself in the sitting-room, banging the door to indicate he wanted no interruptions. ... Michael had just finished an afternoon's gardening. Dring might have delayed this call till Michael had had time for a drink, but he was so sure of a rebuff that he was in no mood to be diplomatic.

Nor was Michael. He said so exactly what Dring had known he would that Dring felt gloomily vindicated.

'... But for heaven's sake I told you ages ago, it was idiotic to realize all your capital at once ... What d'you want a loan for?'

'We want to send Deb to that doctor you recommended.'

'Oh. Good idea. You'll find he's a splendid chap. But look, surely you've got something stashed away—nobody with any wit lets himself get reduced to rock bottom. What about those National Savings Father left, surely to God you didn't cash those...?'

'We needn't go into all this in detail. I only wanted to ask—'

Well, it didn't happen to be convenient for Michael to part up with any money just now, glad as he'd be to help. He didn't organize his affairs so that he had loose sums idle ... Why wasn't the writing bringing in anything? Had Alan dried up or what? In that case, it would be sensible to make a break and get a decent job—

Dring, failing to see why he should foot the telephone bill for all this, thanked Michael tersely and hung up. He had swallowed a massive dose of I Told You So, abased himself, to no effect. Cutting off Michael, he was humiliated. Then he began to be angry with Michael, which roused him a little. By the time he had flung himself out of the sitting-room, treading on a marble and lurching across the passage to clout his shoulder on the kitchen doorpost, and stamped upstairs, he was furious enough to slam down a clean sheet of paper on the table and, glaring at it, say aloud: 'All *right* then.'

This was a task. Look on it as that. Right, then: scrap the 1848 episode. Its point had been, in essence, to show the childhood of Weinberg's son in the blissful dawn of Marxism. Skip Weinberg, cut—in the terminology of the cinema—to Victorian London. This was, God knew, straightforward enough. Any sixth-former could do it, like an examination essay: 'Show in not more than 5,000 words how Weinberg's son starts a clothing factory, exploits his employees and gets rich.'

It would mean scamping Weinberg's son, 'making' him do this and that, pushing him about like a chessman, but that was all part of the task. Dring had been looking forward to meeting him, this appealing rogue who loses out in his first round with Mammon. Come to think of it, he hadn't got a name yet ... Dring pondered, waiting for the name, and then realized that he was slipping already— That wasn't the idea

[143]

at all. *Give* the bloke a name and get on with the job. Hans, Johannes, anything ...

He unscrewed his pen, pulled the lamp nearer and started work. He needed to keep busy, to protect himself against what he had suddenly become conscious of: loneliness. With the departure of Weinberg's son, he had lost a friend. Nor would he come back. After this sort of betrayal, a character like Weinberg's son, too, was capable of tipping off the rest of the character-world to keep clear of that hack Dring ... For God's sake; *'Chapter XXV'* wrote Dring heavily at the top of his paper. He was getting whimsical, let alone morbid.

Loneliness persisted, as if the rainy dusk seeped into the room and encircled him. He didn't suppose he'd caused any rift between himself and Michael—Michael in fact would be feeling more 'in the picture' and would quite likely telephone again later with some more admonitions—and be answered, quite likely, by Judy; to whom Dring had chosen not to confess that he was approaching Michael. Had he been able to consult her beforehand he probably wouldn't have done it; that he couldn't talk to Judy about all this, was the loneliest part of it all.

Recognizing only now how lonely he was, Dring looked up; surely in the wide world there was somebody he could talk to? For the last six years he'd had Judy, the people in his books, that interesting girl Deb and that appealing child Lyddie, and life had seemed crowded with company. It was appalling enough to be bereft of all those at a stroke, without beginning to wonder why there was nobody else. He thought back; Bateson, he'd talked politics with all night; John Marshall, he'd climbed with as a student; Peter, of course, he'd known since they were at school ... He began to track them down mentally, trying to remember when they or he had last written—

God. Apart from anything else, had his concentration gone all to pot nowadays? *Chapter XXV* ... Let's get a few outline headings down. For instance, dates. If Weinberg's son—

[144]

dammit, Hans—were born in ... say ... 1830, then by 1877 he'd be ... Arithmetic kept Dring gratefully occupied for some minutes. He began to feel he was getting somewhere.

... For all he knew, this was how real authors worked. He'd never met one (as Judy pointed out). He'd read, though, about authors who set themselves so many words a day and he'd heard, even been asked, the question that everybody is believed to ask on meeting an author: 'Do you write for set hours, or just as the spirit moves you?' It implied that the spirit need not. But something must. What, Dring hoped he would presently discover. He might be glad of all this, as he got used to it. It might be just the discipline he needed.

Completing the calculation that Weinberg's son—*Hans*—must have been born in 1835 to fit in with the rest of the date-scheme, Dring screwed up his pen exhausted, wondering how long it was till supper-time. Just a mouthful of hot coffee might buck him up. No; there was to be no slacking. No self-indulgence. He was undertaking this task for Deb and he'd do better to keep reminding himself of that.

So, what was the next thing. Yes, W—Hans's factory. Whereabouts in London ... And it was no use sitting here imaginatively conjuring up a cobbled yard with gas lamps in the fog; Dring went bustling downstairs into the sitting-room, pawing along the bookcase. He shouted:

'Who's got that London Street Maps book?'

Judy from the kitchen had the effrontery to ask: 'What d'you want that for?'

He came to the doorway. 'In connection with a clothing factory founded in 1857 by a certain Hans Weinberg,' he said forbiddingly, 'probably in Stepney. It appears in a novel called *Nothing to Lose* which will soon be approaching completion.' Having announced that, he'd be committed; he felt relief and a sinking alarm. Judy looked at him, her mouth pinched.

'I'm glad to hear it,' she said without a trace of gladness. She sounded as if she didn't for a moment believe him.

She was writing at the table; there was no sign of supper. Deb was at the far end of the table—knitting, of all things; making heavy weather of casting on stitches in pink wool. As after a pause she looked up too, Dring smiled encouragement at her.

'—So with any luck,' he said, 'the family will be in funds again before too long.'

Deb didn't smile back. Her glance, not quite meeting his, was vaguely sad. Well, he hadn't exactly expected gratitude, but— But. Never mind. This was his own task and he could manage it without anyone's support.

'Cheer up,' he said to Deb, but she had bent her head over her knitting again and didn't seem to hear him.

Judy, like many neurotics, was ready to admit how neurotic she 'used to be', but couldn't see that her reactions to any immediate circumstance were anything but objective. Particularly as the last several years hadn't been troublesome, she felt she had taken all this about Debby very calmly, considering, and that she was wholly in command. In command, anyhow, she had to be, in view of the uselessness of Alan. About this, she agreed entirely with Debby, or with the judgement Debby had expressed not so long ago, when she was still expressing anything. She couldn't have said so to Debby, had she wanted to, because Debby at present was so uncommunicative again.

Isolation gave Judy what she took to be courage. She was 'facing up to' the problem. In effect, finding it insoluble, she was staring it out of countenance. This produced in her a curious mental block which prevented her mentioning the matter of fees to Dr Foster while she and Deborah were at The Hollies. She merely told him she'd let him know soon whether they wished to ask him to take Deborah on. She would have been surprised to hear that Dougal Foster found her uncommunicative. Judy thought she'd displayed great poise, considering.

Later that evening she did, as Dring had anticipated, answer the telephone to Michael.

Michael, after his drink and a little soothing television, thought over Alan's call, and remembered that it was Deb who mattered. The loan was asked on her account. He remembered that Deb had so lately been here, a refugee. He remembered incidentally that nothing had been said about paying him back for her bus fare ... This borrowing lark simply wasn't on; it wasn't in the ethics of the thing at all. He knew Alan thought so too. What the hell, Michael wondered, could have got into him— He remembered that it had been *his* idea that they send Deb to Foster, and hoped to God they didn't imagine that because it was Michael's idea he was somehow liable. You never knew what muddle-headed constructions those vague types might put on things ... Still and all, as he ate his dinner, a very delectable moussaka, he began to feel an interest in the Broom Cottage set-up. Blood was thicker than water, et cetera. He said to Fiona:

'... I might ring Alan back and see just how he *is* fixed.'

With a fraternal curiosity that he took for fraternal intimacy, he exposed himself again to Alan's awkwardness. When Judy answered the telephone he was rather relieved.

'... Old Alan pretty well hung up on me, earlier this evening—'

'I didn't know you'd rung?'

'I didn't. *He* did. Didn't he say? Telling me about Deb—'

'*What* about Deb?'

Lord, she sounded in a twitch. 'Just, about your sending her to Foster. Damn good idea.' He thought fast: Did Judy know Alan had tried to touch him? If not, better not let on.

'Why on earth should he ring and tell you that?'

Cornered, Michael said in a friendly tone: 'Oh— You know. Just about lolly. How it could be managed. I've been thinking about it. Haven't come up with any bright suggestions yet I'm afraid, about how it could be raised. Just wondered—'

'Nothing's been decided yet,' said Judy quickly. She had

[147]

thought as fast as Michael. If Alan had been trying to borrow money from Michael, he must have hit bottom— She couldn't have believed it of him. 'We saw Dr Foster, but we're thinking it over.' Especially with Michael, her mind blocked off the money question totally.

'Well— Don't think too long, that's all. Poor Deb needs help. And maybe Foster has a waiting list—'

'Seeing he let her come home again, he can't have thought she was as bad as all that. And I know a personal friend of his who'll be able to get her in, any time.' She quailed at the notion that Miss Dunn might ever get to hear of that statement. She rushed on: 'So thank you for ringing, Michael, but really I'm sure there's nothing *you* can do to help.'

He murmured affabilities and accepted dismissal. Back in his armchair he observed to Fiona:

'I think I see why old Alan was like that: Judy's been bitching at him.'

'I don't blame her,' said Fiona, loyal to Judy, whom she had liked on their recent visit more than she used to. Happily getting in her shot at Alan, to whom she thought Michael was far too loyal, she added: 'He'd drive me bitchy in one *week*, that man.'

Michael gave her a tight smile. 'You can be bitchy as it is, my dear, without Alan to set you off.' After further cogitation he added: 'But I don't see why I had to get a brush-off like that. I mean, one does like to share in one's family's troubles. That's what families are *for*, I've always thought.'

10

TWO DAYS AFTER THAT Prunella Mitchell died. The event seemed foregone rather than expected, and was hardly an event, so narrow was the line between death and whatever she had been continuing for the last several days in her hospital bed. Charles Mitchell had been assiduous in visiting her although the nurses had warned him: 'She won't know you, I'm afraid.' What troubled Charles, more, was that he hardly knew *her*; she was bleached-out like a fossilized monkey. Nothing could be deader than that. When they told him she had 'gone' he involuntarily glanced about him; they could only mean that she had revived?

He felt sadder than he'd expected, because he hadn't anticipated the quality of his sadness; what he felt was, disconsolate—cheated, almost. There was nobody, now, to be kind to ... She had left him with all he'd had to offer her—solicitude that, practised, warms into affection—on his hands.

Also on his hands he had all her affairs, such as they were. He drove out to see Mrs Martin, who had been keeping the cottage aired and redirecting the scanty mail to him. He knew he wouldn't be the first with the news of his aunt's death. It had occurred during last night, and the tidings would have sped to anyone who knew or cared. Or, who felt they ought to have cared; Charles sensed that he wasn't alone in such a sentiment; Aunt Pruey had had a remarkable gift, and in death still exercised it, for making people feel they ought to have been different, without ostensibly expecting anything of them.

Expected of, Charles would have known how to deal with

things. He stood at the Martins' yard gate and looked along the puddly side track to the cluster of branches concealing his aunt's cottage. There were buds on the sprawling lilac and towering sycamore.

'... It was very peaceful,' he told Mrs Martin perfunctorily.

'Well, you'd expect it to be,' she said, disconcerting him. 'You can't see her suffering much, can you? Not unless she wanted to.' Then as if she had surprised herself too, she added formally: 'It was all for the best really. A release.'

'I suppose so ...' He refused a cup of tea. He didn't want to hang about here. Soon, he'd have to come up and sort out that cottage. He wondered for the first time whether it might be his? There would be a will, presumably to be read after the cremation, but quite likely Aunt Pruey would have left the place to the National Trust. He hoped she had. Charles loathed the place. If it came to a cremation, he'd rather put a match to that, than bother to dispose of the desiccated little remains from the hospital— So much less, he uneasily felt, the true 'body' of his aunt.

'... No, thank you, I really must get back.' He'd been neglecting work lately, far more than he would have, had there been anything he could *do* for Aunt Pruey. Doing something, he could thereafter have turned his attention to his job. Still lingering, he stared towards the cottage, unhappy in the yard gate in his city suit, his face red with the shrill wind, his thin hair lifting. He looked, Gwen Martin noticed, older, lately ... Following his gaze, she said: 'It's soon to speak of it, but d'you think we might have you moving in there now? It'd make a nice little holiday cottage, if you cut a few of the trees down and let the light in. Maybe, you could retire there...?'

'I'm not retiring for another five years or so ...' protested Charles, knowing and resenting that he must look seventy today. But what Mrs Martin said had cheered him up just a little. Painted up, with a porch to keep out the wind, the foliage hacked away, the cottage could be given a fresh life and should, in this area, and nowadays, sell very well, and make a very nice little holiday place for somebody or other. And Charles need never see it again.

It struck Gwen that she might slip up and make sure the Drings knew. Except for Lyddie on her way to school she hadn't seen any of them today. She fetched her coat and headscarf and walked up the lane, to see Deborah leaning over the front wall of Broom Cottage, picking idly at lichen, her hair adrift on the wind. She looked at Gwen as if she had never seen her before. Nor had Gwen seen Deborah since her return home. My word, thought Gwen, she does look a bit rough. 'Hullo, Deb. Have you heard about poor Miss Mitchell?'

Hearing the news, Deborah went on staring for a moment. The bruise she had sustained had spread oddly before it faded, leaving a greenish stain at the side of her chin and under one eye. It surprised Gwen the more when tears began to run down this marbly face.

'Don't let it upset you, love— She was in a way glad to go. She'd have hated it in that home—'

But Deborah, not waiting for consolation, had turned and run to the house. Gwen watched, then, supposing Deb's mother was in and would comfort her, set off home. She'd never cared much for Deb—a cheeky girl in her smooth way— but today felt really sorry for her.

So did Deborah's mother, although when she heard the explanation of these unexpected tears she reacted with a defensive annoyance. 'Miss *Mitchell* ...' — As if: Is *that* all! '... Well, darling, we more or less expected it. She was old. And it was peaceful ...' Putting a pair of scissors away, Judy shut the drawer with firm finality. She was sorry about Miss Mitchell, but in the circumstances death was probably the best thing for her, and Judy wasn't going to let such an event upset either Deb, or the calm routine Broom Cottage had now settled into. 'We'll have tea soon,' she said.

[151]

Lydia was heard singing in the yard, and immediately, Dring's footsteps creaked overhead. Already, according to the routine, he came down for his cup of tea as soon as Lydia came back from school. The household was geared to the production of *Nothing to Lose*, and tea-breaks were allowed for.

Judy was able to tell them both at once about Miss Mitchell, and was glad to get it over. She told them as soon as she had poured out the tea. Deborah was still silently weeping but no one had asked why. Lydia glanced once, wide-eyed, at her mother but said nothing. Dring said: 'Poor Miss Mitchell. But I suppose it could be called a release. You'll miss her, Lyddie.'

'Me? She's been away ages already.'

Judy said to Dring: 'Children soon forget.'

'Evidently,' he agreed, sipping tea.

'Nobody *cares*,' Deborah exclaimed, to nobody.

'Well, darling, she *was*—'

'Don't say she was *old* again. It isn't what anybody means. *You* might at least be sorry,' she accused Lydia.

Lydia was beginning to eat a slice of Swiss roll, unwinding it with her teeth. Through it she said: 'She died on purpose.'

'Lyddie, don't be silly,' Judy reproved her. 'Nobody does that.'

'Jesus did.'

There was a silence; both parents recognized from Lyddie's authoritative tone that this topic had recently been dealt with at school, in preparation no doubt for Easter; but it was not a topic that any of the other three was equipped to discuss, or even felt it necessary to.

Judy said vaguely: 'But that was quite different ...' and left it at that, with Lydia left, if her purse-lipped expression were anything to judge by, victorious.

Only later, Dring, back at work, wondered if that had not been an extraordinary thing for Lyddie to say. Relating it to Miss Mitchell he wondered if it might be true. At which he felt all at once drained and deserted, as if Miss Mitchell

[152]

had run out on him. Tiresome old creature— The more as he suspected her quite capable of dying for a principle without being able to imagine what, in her case, the principle could possibly have been.

He found himself envying her. What; her escape? Perhaps, her silence; her unshared crisis. The dignity, of taking a decision alone and acting on it without self-justification. There was a cool finality about it that was of a piece with Miss Mitchell whom *now* he would never be able to ask, or query; she had a completeness.

Which meant, he reminded himself, taking up his pen, nothing except that he was using the poor old lady as a tool for self-pity. 'There's nobody on my side now ...' Extraordinary notion.

However, the thought intruded: She—and for that matter Jesus, from what I remember—died for something they believed in; and I've got to live for something I don't believe in; which is a damn sight harder.

He re-read his last sentence and resumed work, which at present was becoming a refuge. He was surprised, and pleased, to find that the task was fairly absorbing. The necessity of speed and conciseness gave it added interest, and he appreciated his position in the household, which had fallen into place round him as it never had when he was labouring towards pure creativeness. Even, Lydia had been forbidden to play marbles, and had been told to go out and dig her garden instead, ready for seedtime. He enjoyed his meals and brief vigorous walks, feeling he had earned them. He liked being able to report to Judy how many words or pages he had completed during his 'set hours'. It was a relief not to spend dull wastes of time brooding at his table. After a good spell he would think: Is this what it's like, being a 'real' author? And almost, he thought he might telephone Fordman and raise the question of the advance-on-the-advance, now that he could calculate pretty well within a day or two the time of the work's completion.

Or so he'd thought, till he heard about Miss Mitchell. He'd never really been aware of her, in or out of hospital—not sufficiently to account for this sense of her dereliction. Only now that she, as it were, yawned behind one shrivelled little hand and turned and walked away, did he notice a new gap in his circle, through which the cold wind of loneliness was let in.

At supper he was listless; not hungry. Judy asked: 'Work not going well?'

'I'm in a dull patch, I think. I'll pick up later ...'

Determined to fulfil his stint for the day he wrote on, into the spring twilight with a blackbird chipchipping in the sycamore. When Judy put a cup of coffee beside him he didn't notice it. He tore up two pages because he suspected he was forcing things; his style was both formed enough, and resilient enough, he'd been pleased to find, to put up with a little bullying along; but, tonight, he was conscious of over-doing it; caution, or taste, raised its weary head under his assaults. Re-assaulting from a different angle he still found he'd used the same adjective twice; he did not hear the infuri-ated sigh this drew from him but heard Judy say:

'Darling, isn't that enough for today?'

He was surprised, turning, to see that she was in bed, not even reading. 'Is it late? I'm still not to the end of the ware-house scene—'

'No, but I'm sure you're tired. There's no sense,' she told him kindly, 'in overdoing things.'

'As a matter of fact— I *am* tired,' he admitted. Perhaps that was all it was.

'No wonder. You've been working so hard for three whole days. Come to bed now. You can always make an earlier start in the morning.'

He came to bed, not bothering with his late-night snack. Sleep would be the best thing ... But Judy was inclined for conversation in the dark.

Judy was a good deal more at ease with herself, and with

[154]

Alan, now that he'd pulled himself together and taken his responsibilities upon himself. At least life was *moving* again; in the tense interlude of their non-communication she had felt something inside herself might freeze up. Thawing, she communicated with an ease that left her no time to weigh Alan's response. Curled comfortably round, watching the star-lit window, she asked:

'*Did* hearing about Miss Mitchell depress you?'

'Depress me?'

'I thought you went rather quiet, somehow. I never thought you were specially fond of her. Or Debby; wasn't it funny, how *she* cried? I know, you used to talk about books and things to her—Miss Mitchell—once, before she got so anti-social, and didn't come up the field for her little walks any more ... But that was ages ago.'

'Lyddie said, she's been away for "ages". She gives that impression.'

'Who does—Miss Mitchell? —Did? She didn't honestly make much impression on me. She wasn't an awfully positive person, really.'

'No?'

'Well, look at the way she kind of faded out. She didn't put up much of a fight. She was supposed to be so cultured and brainy but as soon as life got difficult, she ... Well, I suppose, she just lost the will to live.'

'Or found the will to die,' muttered Dring into the pillow.

'What?' And as he did not repeat himself: '... The will to *die*, you said? Well, surely it comes to the same thing, and, either way, it's wrong. Isn't it?'

'M'm.'

'The *will*'s terribly important. You've got to hold on to it. You see, that's what worries me about Debby just now. She seems to be losing that *will*.'

More wakefully, Dring said: 'Yes. I do wonder— Will she ever be *gay* again?'

'If she just gets back some of her ... energy, that's all I

care about. For a start anyhow. She was so miserable about Miss Mitchell but not—you know—as if she really *minded* ...' Judy thought about that, and added: '—It was as if it meant something inside *her* but not ... It wasn't a thing she could share with us ...'

Had there been anything to share. Dring suggested: 'She's rather out of touch—'

'Yes, that's exactly it, and when I think about it now, I think that's where we made a mistake.' Judy bounced over to face Dring, raising herself on an elbow. 'You see, what we did, when we brought her home, was to lift her right out of her own world. No wonder she seems cut off. No wonder either she doesn't seem quite alive. It's too quiet here and she *is* cut off from what matters to her. I can imagine, she feels quite unreal.'

'M'm?'

'It's made me think. That's been the trouble with us, too. We did cut ourselves off. So no wonder we haven't been quite alive, either.' She could dimly see that Alan's eyes were open; she assumed, as one does in eloquence, his fascinated acquiescence. '—It all hangs together. What we used to call our principles—you know, non-violence, and all that stuff—was a reaction against what had happened in the world before. Just because we were so sincere, we rather overdid it. Our way of passive resistance was really a way of opting out—not of *dealing* with things. So the world moved on without us and look at the way it's going. Violence increasing, everywhere. Nothing to control it. You can't duck out of violence— You've got to *meet* it.'

'With violence?' suggested Dring, as she paused on that challenging note.

'Well,' she admitted, 'no ... No, obviously not. What I mean is that you can't just damp it down. It pushes it underground. And you can't just ignore it. That leaves it rampaging about ... The point is, you've got to find a *positive* way to meet it. *We* haven't. We haven't dealt with Debby positively and that's why she hasn't any faith in us. We've just—'

'I daresay you're right about that,' said Dring, dejectedly.

'About what?'

'Deb's faith in us. In me, anyway.'

'Oh well, you haven't been a frightfully *alive* person at all, have you, since we lived here, apart from dealing with her ... *That* was why she smashed Fiona's present. You see, in spite of everything, true feeling does somehow break out—'

Horrid sounds from outside the bedroom door checked Judy and brought Dring's head up. He said: 'Good God— What ...' but Judy was already in action. 'Lyddie,' she said curtly, throwing aside the quilt. 'I thought she'd grown out of ...' She was gone.

When she was little, Lydia had been the sort of greedy child who gorges at parties and is quite unexpectedly indisposed in the middle of the night. Years had been improving both her digestion and her powers of anticipation; usually, now, she got herself to the bathroom in time. Tonight she had not. Judy, filling the house with brisk bustle and the smell of disinfectant, could be heard speaking words of reproof rather than sympathy. Dring hid his face in the pillow. When Judy came back he asked queasily:

'She all right now?'

'I hope so. Anyhow I've left her a pottie. I don't know what it is—a chill or something. She doesn't seem to have *eaten* anything queer. But really, she's too old to be so uncontrolled—' She settled herself, tucking the covers round her neck, gaining authority from having dealt with a distasteful duty. Sensing which, Dring meekly said:

'Sorry to leave jobs like that to you ...'

'Oh well; you never did like facing up to unpleasant things, did you. It's just not in your nature.' She sighed, relaxing. '—What were we talking about?'

'I forget ... But if I want to start work early tomorrow, what about getting some sleep?'

'All right,' she conceded, after considering. 'You go to sleep, darling.'

Dring closed his eyes and obeyed.

Deborah was frightened, and precariously annoyed, by the way she couldn't help minding about Miss Mitchell. She told herself that she didn't, *really*; which made it worse ... Unreal feeling—normal sentimentality—had no place in her present scheme. To keep crying like this was a giveaway; luckily, nobody seemed to notice. Trying to keep her mind off the death of that pathetic little gallant person, Deborah involuntarily forced up a vision of herself going to the funeral, leaping on to the coffin and throwing aside all the flowers and wrenching up the lid and shrieking: 'I say unto thee, arise!' Whereupon Miss Mitchell's cool little blue eyes would smile gratefully up at her ... This vision, over-detachedly appraised by Deborah, took on the strength of a hallucination.

But in any case, no one from Broom Cottage did go to the funeral. Nothing more at all was said about Miss Mitchell. Deborah fancied the subject was being avoided on her account; but she certainly wasn't going to mention it either. So another barrier appeared between her and the others. She liked this nowadays; it made her safer. What she didn't like was the sheer monotony of her own good behaviour and the recent routine of the house. Okay, so Dad was working hard to make money for *her*, but she thought the less of him for it. She had, not long ago, scorned him for being 'useless', but, now that he was useful, she hadn't even scorn left. She would have admitted that she was bored if boredom, admitted, wouldn't have led to compensating activity. She went on with her knitting. She was making a scarf from some hideous pink wool Mum had left over from something; why a scarf, Deborah had no idea.

Judy, noticing that Deborah had stopped crying, hoped that that was the end of it and that we'd heard the last of Miss

[158]

Mitchell; at any rate, Alan seemed to be settled to work again. Lyddie's term ended tomorrow, so she would be around the place to be quietly employed, but otherwise there should be a clear run now, to the novel's end. Then, one could think about new beginnings.

On a clear and peaceful morning Lydia, setting off for school, met the postman at the gate and, for once obliging, clumped back into the house to throw a letter in front of her father. She was halfway out of the door again when he called: 'Whoa— This is for you.'

'*Me?*' She hardly ever had letters, and certainly not letters in long white envelopes with typewritten addresses. She examined it, scowling. 'Miss Lydia Dring'. 'Shall I open it?'

'Why not?'

She thumbed open the envelope, dropping it to the floor. 'Coo. It's from these people ... solicitors.' She read, biting her lip. 'Oh. Miss Mitchell has left me that picture in her will.'

'Let me see, darling.' Judy read the letter and confirmed to Alan: 'Yes. An oil painting, "Glebe Woods" by Hugh Mostyn. —Well, wasn't that nice of her, Lyddie. You see, she must have been fond of you after all.'

Lydia said, loftily: 'She was my friend.' Adding, reflectively: 'I wish it'd been the kaleidoscope.'

'You'll be able to hang it in your room to remember her by. —But you'd better run now, or you'll be late—'

It wasn't till midday that Judy, reading the letter again, said: 'I suppose a picture like this couldn't be valuable?'

'I've no idea what Hugh Mostyn's rating is nowadays. But an early picture—of the kind he'd give away—or that Miss Mitchell would hang on to ... Probably, not worth much.'

'Still, there'd be no harm in ringing these solicitors, just to thank them for the letter— They might have some idea ...' Feeling that she was grabbing at any straw, Judy went to the telephone. She came back breathless.

'Much you know about paintings— The solicitor says Miss Mitchell had this one insured for *five hundred pounds*—'

'That may prove nothing.'

'Oh, Alan, she wasn't *that* batty. Nor is any insurance company. You realize what this means: We're *saved*!'

Dring was at first more cautious. He said that at any rate they must have an expert opinion on the picture, but a secret optimism must have echoed Judy's, because he agreed to telephone—in the middle of the day, too—an art dealer in London who might give them a rough idea. 'You remember, that man Felix worked for— What was his name? Not that we've got a London directory—'

'Oh, *remember* his name, for heaven's sake, and ask Inquiries—'

So Dring worked his way through to the art gallery off Conduit Street and held on while a senior member of the staff was found, who explained at prosy length that, from the description, as far as he could tell, though naturally the picture would have to be examined and authenticated, in so far as he could risk an opinion, if this were a Hugh Mostyn of what was nowadays referred to as the 'dark phase', the picture might not have outstanding artistic merit but would be classed as a collector's item, since Mostyn himself had, subsequently, destroyed all his paintings of that period. It was interesting to hear that there might be one still in existence. In Cumbria? In a private collection? . . . Yes, of course, about its value: compared with the Mostyns of the mature period, of course, it wouldn't fetch a high price, but . . . At a guess, two thousand pounds, though the gallery had a client who would quite possibly go to two-five-hundred, and if there were counter-bids, if the picture were to go to auction and other collectors were interested, then, possibly, three thousand . . . It was hard to say . . .

'I *told* you,' said Judy when Dring recounted this.

She and Deborah were still at the kitchen table. She jumped

up, went round to Deborah and hugged her. 'So, darling, it's all going to be all right. I'll get in touch with Dr Foster right away and you can go there after all.' And, to Dring: '—And you can finish your book as slowly as you like and just *how* you like. Isn't it marvellous. Dear old Miss Mitchell— I wish she could *know* what she's done for us all ...' She stretched both arms above her head, turning to the window; she might have been greeting a new world. '... I didn't ask Dr Foster, you know, how much his fees actually were or how long he thought he'd want to keep Debby there. It didn't seem worth it. But now we'll be able to plan properly— And we might be able to pay off that awful Richards man at last, for instance. And, come to that, you needn't finish this book at all, darling, if you'd rather do something else for a while ...'

'That', said Dring in a curiously flat tone, 'might be quite a relief.'

Relieved he indeed felt, but also flattened. He wasn't yet sure he wanted his toil of the last ten days or so to become redundant. Judy glanced at him, concerned.

'I don't mean you *needn't* finish it, heaven knows—I'm sure it's going to be just as good as the others. Only you needn't rush, now. You've been so *good* about it but I know it's been a sweat, even if it was all for Debby—'

'*I* didn't want him to sweat,' put in Deborah.

'Well, darling, he *had* to. A bit. But now—'

'He didn't *have* to.'

'I don't suppose I *had* to,' allowed Dring, an impulse outgoing towards Deborah, who seemed as dazed as he under Judy's exhilaration. 'I wanted to, you know.'

'Yes, *well* ...' said Deborah wearily, denying him; he thought: One can't do a thing right, for that girl.

'It seemed a good cause,' he murmured, shrugging.

'There couldn't be a cause worth mucking up your work for.'

'But he wasn't mucking it up, don't be silly,' Judy resumed. 'And anyhow, all that's by the way. The point is, that *now*—'

'*Now,*' announced Dring standing up, 'I think I'll go out for a break.'

'Yes, do. Take a breather ...'

His cheerfulness over the financial deliverance was half-quenched in what he unwillingly recognized as Deb's disapproval of him. Because it in part coincided with his own, he couldn't see it as mere immature censoriousness. He *had* been wrong to force his writing, in whatever cause. Perversely, too, he felt at a loose end this afternoon without his 'stint' to tackle. He went, not on to the fell, but down towards the lake and woods, where elder was in leaf, and bread-and-cheese starred the hedges. Equally perversely, as he stood with Loweswater lapping at his boots, watching the waterfowl and thinking about the amount they owed the Richards man, the real name of the Weinberg boy came to him: Wenzel. Of course; that was it. Wenzel Weinberg, whose face, clearly sub-visual, grinned wickedly at him across the lake wavelets. He was quite a different person from the stuffed puppet in the manuscript on Dring's table. Oh, what the hell. Dring turned his back on him and trudged home.

He hadn't walked far, and was home before Lydia, who had yet to be told the news of her valuable inheritance. Dring was still unlacing his boots when she came puffing in, laden with all the clobber she seemed to amass at school during the term. 'Broken up,' she proclaimed, kicking the door shut behind her and dropping the pile at her feet.

'*Darling,*' Judy cried, hurrying to her, 'do listen— What d'you think, such wonderful news: That picture Miss Mitchell left you is worth about three thousand *pounds*. Daddy rang up an expert in London. Isn't it fantastic.'

'Crikey,' remarked Lydia hitching up a sock.

'—So now, Debby can go to that doctor to be made better, and Daddy can get on with his proper work, and we can pay off some bills so that we can get this place organized, and I needn't go and get a job, and it's all going to be *much* easier for us all—'

'D'you mean you want to *sell* the picture?'

'Yes, of course we must—'

'No,' said Lydia, planted square-faced in the middle of the kitchen. 'You can't. Miss Mitchell wanted *me* to have it.'

'Oh, don't be silly, darling,' said Judy who naturally couldn't take that at all seriously. 'Of course she did, but when we need the money so badly, other things are more important than a picture.'

'Not this one.'

'It isn't even a very good picture. The artist himself didn't think so. —Anyway, we'll *have* to sell it, I'm sorry.'

'You can't. It's mine.'

'You don't understand,' said Judy, slowing down. 'Just now, we're absolutely broke. Daddy was trying to finish a book in a hurry but it's being such an effort for him and might put him off his real work. You know how important that is to him. And you know how Debby isn't at all herself. She really needs to go to this doctor. It might mean her whole *life*. You can't hold on to a picture and do so much harm to other people.'

'Yes I can.'

'Don't you realize— Three thousand *pounds*. I don't expect you can imagine so much. We're talking about real *money*.'

'So what.'

'I'm trying to explain to you *what* ... Oh, all right, we should have *asked* you first. It's your picture, after all. *Please*, Lyddie, let us sell it? —Is *that* better?'

'No. You can't.'

'Oh, bloody hell—' exclaimed Judy spinning round. 'You'll see sense in a minute. You're just being obstinate. —Let's have tea.'

Lydia, still planted with her heap of clobber at her feet, stated her position. 'Miss Mitchell wanted *me* to have it. So I'm going to keep it. Because it's that picture. And she was my friend.'

[163]

That, to Lydia, summed it all up most lucidly. She had been thinking on and off, all day at school, and had begun to discern why she had been entrusted with the picture instead of the kaleidoscope: Miss Mitchell knew that Lyddie had been growing up with the picture and would pretty soon, in any case, grow out of the kaleidoscope. Miss Mitchell wanted her own life, the important part of it, to be continued in somebody else who valued it as she had, or would come to. Lydia couldn't have expressed this; what she had expressed, she expected Mummy to find adequate.

'—You didn't even like her much,' pointed out Judy, banging the kettle about. 'You were always saying so. You were always moaning when I told you to go down and see her.'

Lydia thrust out her lower lip and said nothing.

'—Besides, I don't expect you like the picture much, either. I remember the one. She had it hanging opposite the door in her kitchen. A nasty smeary little dark thing.'

'She knew the man when he was alive,' said Lydia sulkily.

'But that's pure *sentiment*. Really, one can't be bound by other people's sentimentality. —Tidy up all that rubbish, and wash your hands. You're just being utterly childish but one forgets how young you *are*. You'll feel better when you've had your tea. —Go on, pick it up and take it *upstairs* . . .'

As Lydia sullenly went, Judy turned to Dring, who had been listening boot in hand to the exchange: 'She can't mean it. Can't *stop* us—'

'Unfortunately, it *is* her picture.'

'Oh, don't be maddening . . .'

'But she can't really mean it,' he soothed, not too certainly.

'No, she can't,' agreed Judy accepting the reassurance and calming down. It was inconceivable that such a small thing as Lyddie's selfishness should blot out the family's brightened future. —You might have known, though, that Lyddie would make herself as awkward as possible—she'd *been* awkward enough lately, God knew. With her hands on the handle of the kettle, Judy clenched them, irritated anew by the memory

[164]

of Lyddie's obstinate blob of a face— Great cussed hulk she was; but, only a child, one had to remember ... Towards Lydia at this moment Judy felt the kind of murderous hatred one feels towards a harmless old lady who gets in the way when one is frantically running for a bus. This alternated with prudence— One would have to manage it tactfully ... Staring at the wall above the Rayburn she noticed the cracked tile and remembered:

'It's only like Shaun and the pebble. Remember? She only wanted it because *he* wanted it. She's just trying to make an issue ...'

'She will, too, if you go on like that—'

'Well for heaven's sake somebody will have to go on like *something* to get her to part up with the thing ...'

'We'll think of something,' he said, putting on his slippers.

'Why should we have to *think* when it's so obvious she *must*— Oh well.' Checking her exasperation again, Judy took the teapot to the dispenser. '—I was thinking, we could ring Michael this evening, too ... You know, it might seem we're taking her picture away and using the money for ourselves. Surely there ought to be something in it for her?'

'That's an idea.' Fully aware of Judy's frustration, he added: 'I'll talk to her when she comes down, shall I?'

'If you'll be *firm*—'

Deborah came in. Having been told she needed fresh air she had spent an hour leaning on a gatepost in the back track, to avoid any sight of Miss Mitchell's cottage. She looked cold. When she heard that Lydia refused to part with her picture, she said: 'Oh. I never thought of that ...' in a resigned lack of protest that Dring found saddening. Perhaps she had done well not to let herself be cheered by the good news this morning; but that the bad news didn't cast her down either, gave him a fresh concern for her. She came to the tea-table with her knitting in her hand. Lydia, at the second time of being called by Judy in a studiedly sweet tone, presently came too. Her face was blank and stiff; justifiably, she expected discus-

[165]

sion. Dring decided to let her fortify herself with her usual mounds of carbohydrate, but Judy began:

'Daddy wants to talk to you about this, Lyddie. So please listen.'

Lydia raised her eyebrows and put her elbows on the table. 'We told Deb we can't afford to send her to Dr Foster's after all,' Dring said casually. 'And she didn't blame you for it.'

Lydia shot a startled glance at her sister and then buttoned up her face again.

'... In fact, nor do we blame you, Mummy and I, for wanting to keep something Miss Mitchell intended you to have. It's quite an honour, to be remembered by someone like that. And the picture is something she valued—apart from its money value, I mean.' He drew a breath; now for the approach: '... But you do know, one can attach too much value altogether to *things*. Possessions. I daresay they tell you that at school when you do your Bible readings. What they call, the things of this world—'

'Miss Mitchell said one shouldn't lay up treasures on earth,' said Lydia implacably.

'... Yes, well, that's just what I mean ...' But Dring somehow felt he had been circumvented. 'The picture's only a *thing*, isn't it? A treasure, if you like. But other values do come first— What we call the imponderables. Such as health, and generosity—'

'You're being too vague,' broke in Judy. 'Talking right over her head. What would Lyddie want an *imponderable* for? Look, darling, I've been thinking. If we sell the picture we surely won't need *all* the money. Even if we have to use it just now, there'll be enough left over for something you'd like. For instance, if you'd like a trek-pony over next winter— We had to say no last year, but if you'd like one *this* year ...'

A pony. Of her own. Even a borrowed one for six months ... Dring saw Lydia's face turn scarlet. When she said in a stifled voice: 'I'm going to keep that picture,' he was in spite of himself impressed.

'Did Miss Mitchell mean as much as that to you?' he asked mildly.

'She was my friend.'

'But she wasn't a *close* friend. Not a person a little girl of your age could get to know well,' insisted Judy, failing to see, as Dring failed to see, that that was rather the point; how narrowly they had missed each other, Prunella and Lydia, passing in opposite directions through a doorway. '—Anyhow, Lyddie, if you're so anxious to do what Miss Mitchell wanted, how do you know *she* wouldn't have wanted to sell the picture if she needed the money?'

'No she wouldn't.'

'You can't know that. You're just being pig-headed. *I'm* quite sure if Miss Mitchell knew how badly Debby needed help, she'd agree to selling it. Anybody sensible would.'

'Well she *didn't* know. So.'

At that, Judy reached across and snatched from Lydia's plate the chunk of apple cake Lydia had not been eating, but picking at with her fingernails. '—And we won't have you stuffing sweet things, *if* you don't mind. *Or* being sick in the night again. You can just stick to dry toast for a few days.'

Lydia, who as a matter of fact had been in robust health since her one midnight calamity, bore this deprivation without comment. It was Dring who looked at Judy askance; the gesture had seemed, in its suddenness, almost vindictive. Dry toast had not been prescribed till this moment. He cleared his throat:

'What Mummy means, Lyddie, is that we're not taking anything away from you. We might borrow this money, because we need it just now, but when we can pay it back, it'll be all yours. It'll be quite a lot. You'll be able to do more with it than you could with a picture. It might even pay for some training you want when you're older. We can invest it for you till then—'

'I don't want any money,' said Lydia.

Judy snorted. 'So you say *now*. But you'll see.'

[167]

'No I won't.'

'Oh, stop being so *silly*. What you won't see is that you're being cruel and wicked as well as childish. What have *we* done to *you*, that you've got to plague us like this?'

'Nothing,' said Lydia indifferently. The question had anyhow, Dring assumed, been rhetorical. Nevertheless it hadn't been a bad question—

'Yes, Lyddie, *do* you feel you've got a grievance against us so we deserve not to be helped?'

She shrugged heavily, silent; possibly not wishing to surrender even a negative advantage. The other three all looked at her, the awkward plain lump of disagreeableness in their midst. Judy said:

'It'd have to be a damn big grievance to excuse *this*. You'll *have* to see sense, sooner or later. Are you just enjoying this —having us all at your mercy? —Listen. Daddy promised we're only *borrowing* the money— We're not stealing anything from you—'

'Yes, you want to. My picture.'

'For God's sake, what's a *picture* worth ... Besides, what are you going to do with it?'

'Hang it on my wall,' Lydia muttered.

'But how can you possibly live with it, looking at it and being reminded you've spoilt so many people's lives to get it—'

'That's rather a gruesome thought,' Dring agreed.

'Oh, I don't expect it'll bother Lyddie. She doesn't care how many other people she makes miserable as long as she gets her own little way. Honestly I never realized what a *monster* we'd produced.'

'That's a bit strong—' intervened Dring.

'It's not a bit too strong. I wouldn't have believed anybody could be so bloody-minded. —Anyway we probably shan't have a wall for you to hang it on for long, because we'll have to sell the house and move, God knows where, at this rate— And *that* might please you, of course, to break up the home—

[168]

If you know what you're doing at all, or are you as crazy as your precious Miss Mitchell— Because that's what she was, a dotty self-obsessed old *spinster*—'

'No she wasn't. *Shut up*,' roared Lydia, and Judy did shut up, shocked herself by the echo of her shrill, rising voice round the low-ceilinged kitchen. A silence closed in, heavy and motionless as if their sinking boat had hit bottom and rested. Indeed, family life had never descended to this before. Dring was pale and furrow browed, Deborah was fiddling shakily with her knitting, Judy was running her fingers wildly through her hair. Lydia alone appeared unshaken. She muttered:

'Talk about *dotty* . . .'

'That'll do,' Dring reprimanded her sharply. Whatever else, Lydia was in no position to get away with impertinence. She stood up, as if he had dismissed her, and went upstairs, thumping her feet. When her bedroom door had slammed, Judy said:

'Oh, I'm sorry— But I got so *furious* . . .'

'I know. Never mind. —She may have a point, though, you know: *Have* we been paying her too little attention?'

'Lyddie? Good Lord, we've paid her nothing else. How could we fail to, when she's always in the way, bumping into things, making some impossible noise or other—'

'Yes, that's what I meant. Was it all attention-catching?'

'Fine time to think of that,' complained Judy, who couldn't at the moment be bothered to.

'Well, now I do think of it, we've been paying far more attention to Deb lately than to her. And she may not have understood why.'

'There was a very good reason why.'

'I know. But how can Lyddie see, at her age . . . Or that', he modified it, 'is what I've tended to think. In some ways, she's not a child any longer. But we've treated her as one.'

'She behaves like one.'

'Yes, that's what I meant—'

'Oh, shut up about what you meant. What do you *mean*, now, present tense? What are we going to *do*? You've simply made her worse with all the guff you talked. —Listen. Surely, since she's a minor, she can't hold property except under our guardianship, legally? Why didn't we think of that? We don't have to have her consent, in law, to dispose of her possessions as we think best?'

'I don't quite know', said Dring doubtfully, 'what the legal position is. But anyway I'd hesitate to make off with anything so irreplaceable as a picture … That she *is* only a child would make it seem worse—'

'For heaven's *sake*, you're as bad as she is. And you'd *hesitate* whatever you did—' Her voice was rising again. Dring interrupted:

'I'd hesitate to upset Lyddie, who does count, after all. It may be too late to say it, but hasn't she always taken a bad second place to Deb? For instance last Christmas when Deb wasn't here, didn't we more or less say Christmas was going to be a washout and not lay on anything special—seeing it was only Lyddie—'

'Last *Christmas*— How far off the point can you *get*? What are we going to *do* about all this?'

'From what you say,' Dring reminded her coolly, 'I've made a mess of reasoning with her, but I can't see that you've done any better. —Deb, what about you? D'you feel like persuading Lyddie? It's in your interest, as much as anyone's.'

As he and Judy waited, Deborah noticed their silence and looked up. '… What?'

'Were you listening?' Dring asked her, not unsympathetically. 'We were trying to think of a way to get Lyddie to part with her precious picture.'

'Debby can't do anything with Lyddie. Lyddie's been beastly to her ever since she came home. Don't *bother* her,' said Judy.

Deborah was considerably bothered. Something about this whole acrimonious teatime had been bringing her to the verge of the unthinkable. She had hoped nobody would notice her. 'I'm all right,' she said mechanically.

The inconsequence of this distracted Judy for the moment. 'Yes, of course you are, darling. Somehow or other we'll get you to Dr Foster's— Might we', she asked Dring, 'borrow money on that picture, is that an idea? —And for heaven's sake, if Lyddie does keep it, shall *we* have to pay insurance on it?'

'I don't want to go to Dr Foster's,' said Deborah quietly.

'You don't ... But why not?' asked Judy, turning back.

'He'll say I'm mad.'

The other two both watched her, not even contradicting, because they seemed fascinated by what she was doing: she was unravelling her pink knitting, pulling and pulling at the wool with feverish fingers till it fell in its crenellated strands into a heap on the floor.

The paradox struck Dring: if she didn't want to go to Dr Foster's, that meant she must. And as an insurance against anyone's failure to persuade Lydia, he ought to press on with his own contribution to the situation. Wenzel—he meant Hans—Weinberg waited upstairs.

Leaving Deb to her mother, he went up to his table. This morning, going down to lunch, before his release and re-imprisonment, he had been about to start a new paragraph. His notes were beside the page. Now, the whole thing looked to him like Deborah's knitting.

It had been in a way a mistake, Judy saw, to admit Dr Foster to their circle; it was an admission that she and Alan were not sufficient to cope with Debby. On both sides. Or had Debby been making that plain all along ... However it was, she simply didn't know what to make of Debby now or what to do about her. Once you invoke the experts, your own knowledge is automatically cancelled ... But, thought Judy on her weary way upstairs, we always did understand her so well—

'We'. That was the factor that, as much as any knowledge, had lost value. As a solid parent-front, she and Alan conspicuously failed at the moment. One thing Debby's troubles had achieved was to divide *them*.

Judy wasn't yet ready to accept re-captivity. When she went into the bedroom, everything about it was stale and repellent. She shoved the sweater she had brought up into a drawer, kicking it when it, as usual, stuck. All the white paintwork was disgustingly tatty. The Indian rug had a hole, and that useless curtain half-separating the sleeping area from Alan's table was faded, and looked anyway like the market-stall remnant it was. And Alan, humped over his table in a grimy cardigan, looked as if he'd grown, fungussy, out of the wall.

'Supper-time?' he said, without turning.

'It's only six o'clock.'

Sitting back and jabbing his pen through his hair, he sighed. 'This damn thing's fallen to bits in the course of the day—'

'Oh God, *God*, I knew you'd say something like that!'

That made him turn round. He looked nothing but surprised.

'—Well,' rushed on Judy, throwing herself flat on the bed, 'as if there weren't enough *nuisances* without you moaning—'

'I merely said—'

'Oh shut up.'

After a pause he remarked, staring out of the window: 'Lyddie will come round, you know. The position she's taken up just isn't tenable if she wants to remain a member of the family.'

'Oh, I suppose so ... She can't expect to get away with this dog-in-the-manger act.'

'It's interesting that, if she wants power over us, she doesn't exert it by giving us the money but by denying—'

'I don't see anything interesting about that. —It'd hardly be *giving*. She's no more moral right to the money, as things are, than anybody else—'

'But it would involve taking what is legally hers. I don't

[172]

care for that. Of course we'd pay it back—'

'With what?'

Dring turned again. 'With whatever I subsequently earn, I imagine.'

'And what's *that* going to be? It's all very well taking this high moral tone—'

'I'm not,' he broke in indignantly. 'It was you who started talking about moral rights—'

'—But you'll be let off the hook too, I might point out. You'll be able to sink back into your trance— '

'That's hardly fair—'

'—and spend some more time writing unsaleable wiffle-waffle, and *then* what, when we run out of money again? We're not getting anywhere by all this. I tell you, I can't face beginning all over again.'

'Beginning what?' he asked apprehensively.

'*This*. Stewing away in this place, propping you up—'

'I'm sorry if that's been such an *effort*—'

'You know bloody well it has. —And every time there's a crisis you let me down. You always have.'

He was silent, thinking back. They *were* back, as if the last ten or so years had been only a truce; Judy desperate to provoke him, Dring desperate to keep the relationship calm. Dring shuffled a few papers on his table and said, calmly:

'I really did think, you know, you were happy when we came here—'

'I doubt you gave it a serious thought. *You* were happy and you assumed that would be enough for me ...' In an equally calm tone, her hands behind her head, she went on: 'The trouble is with you, you've never had to *work* to get what you wanted. First of all your father died and you got that money on a plate, and then all you had to do was sit around waiting for inspiration, and now, Miss Mitchell dies and some more money falls into your lap. No wonder you're still basically ... half-baked.'

Yes; she'd said that kind of thing fairly often, recently, and still it gave Dring the vague feeling that something was unfair ... He said at random:

'Miss Mitchell's money isn't exactly falling into my lap, if Lyddie has anything to do with it.'

'That's right; dodge the issue ...' Bored with him, she rolled over. 'Friday ... I wish I were going to my class to-night ...'

Cordially, Dring said: 'So do I.'

ON THE FOLLOWING MORNING Dring received the half-yearly statement from his agent. Judy took charge of it. She spread out the contents of the green folder—significantly—on Dring's writing table and put her glasses on to reckon up the situation, while he hung unhappily about behind her.

'. . . It's a bit more than we expected,' she announced at last, 'but we can use it all and more. There's simply no margin.'

Dring could only think of: 'Oh well . . .'

Outside the window, sleet plastered itself greyly against the pink sycamore buds. The weather was preparing for holiday. Other schools than Lydia's had broken up, tomorrow was Palm Sunday, and the 'season' was beginning. In any case, this threat to winter's solitude would have made Dring restless. Broom Cottage's remoteness didn't protect it nowadays from increasingly numerous and venturesome visitors. Cars edged up and down the lane, usually disgorging an occupant to knock at the Drings's door and ask: 'Does this go any further?' Often, people knocked to ask whether they did teas or bed-and-breakfast. Walkers searching for a way on to the fell sometimes clambered over the garden wall, looking abashed or indignant to find themselves knee-deep in rhubarb. Late on summer evenings, arrivals with tents or even caravans wanted to know if they might camp here.

This, if the weather did not relent, was probably going to be an Easter of sodden, exhausted, lost souls wanting to know where the bus stop was. Dring, watching Judy snap shut the green folder, thought: Oh well . . .

They were being 'nice' to Lydia, who was apparently un-impressed. She had not yet uttered a word today, but gobbled down the scrambled egg Judy gave her for breakfast in surly silence, then put on her gumboots and departed. To Judy's pursuing question: 'What are you going to do, darling—dig your garden?' Lydia had merely said: *'That—?'* before she banged the back door.

Deborah was red-eyed and inactive. Asked whether she'd like to go shopping with Judy she merely said: 'I don't want to go out *ever.*'

Dring merely pummelled at the puppet Hans Weinberg.

Between sleet showers Judy hung out a little washing. If she and Alan were both now resuming distasteful tasks, she had no pity for him; rather any amount of paperwork than Lyddie's patched and faded pyjamas. She prepared lunch in numb amazement that she should still be *here*, not indeed quite believing it. Not believing that *something* wouldn't happen even now— All this was a mistake.

In the early afternoon a car growled up the lane: the Allisons, the first of the seasonal callers. Pippa Allison had been one of Judy's earliest pupils. She had married young and now had two boisterous sons, who racketed about knocking stones off the wall while Judy made tea for Pippa and her tame husband. 'Hadn't Stephen and Jeremy better come in-doors?' suggested Judy when a gluey squall splattered the window. 'Oh, this'll do them good,' asserted their mother. 'It'll toughen them, and besides, they won't want to miss a minute of being in the Lakes. You've no *idea* how I envy you, being here all the year round ...'

Judy might normally have called Alan down, in the ab-sence of her own children especially, to help entertain she Allisons; today, afraid that might make them stay longer, she did not.

'... and even in bad weather it's still lovely here—so peace-ful, all on your own with nothing to worry about ...'

Naturally Pippa did not expect contradiction; she wanted

only to tell Judy what *she* had to worry about; which she did, till her husband managed to interrupt and point out that the boys had vanished some while ago and might have fallen in the lake by now. Pippa sent him to look for them, meanwhile tying on her fur bonnet and asking: 'How are your two— all right, I hope? You're lucky having girls. The worst thing about boys of Stephen's age, I find, is . . .'

Lydia, coming in late for supper, borne up the lane on Fred Martin's tractor, had evidently not been tactfully or cravenly keeping out of the family's way; she had simply had a busy day. Lambing, she said, had started at Susan's cousin Dick's. She was full enough of this perhaps to have forgotten all about Miss Mitchell's picture and its disposition. Though nothing was said about that, even Lydia must have become aware of the tension at the supper table; after a few un-answered observations about lamb-birth, she lapsed into the general silence.

Missing her, some time later, Judy wondered whether she had actually gone to bed without being told. A sense of her own defection was mixed in Judy with remorse, and pity for any child neglected; she ran upstairs to Lydia's room, and was reassured to find Lydia there. (If I forgot you, darling, it wasn't really because I *wanted* to . . .) It was reassuring too to find the room so much as usual, with that indefinable but inevitable smell of childhood, and its ungovernable scruffiness; scraps of torn paper, a jam-jar of greenish water, the banished marbles in the lid of a shoebox, clothes scattered broadcast, and the crooked picture of Mrs Tiggy-Winkle on the wall, all had the permanence of normality. Lydia, sitting up in bed with unbrushed hair and a heap of pebbles on her lap, fell back into place; Judy automatically said:

'Have you done your teeth?'

'M'm,' Lydia compromised.

'Did you have a nice day? Your hands look cold. Why don't you snuggle down now?'

[177]

Lydia raised her eyebrows and moved three pebbles deliberately into a separate heap, ignoring the suggestion in an undefiant manner that faintly alarmed, as well as annoyed, Judy. This was no child, but a stubborn strange adult; a changeling. Sitting down on the bed, Judy said pleadingly:

'Look, Lyddie darling, you mustn't feel we're all against you. Or that we don't understand.'

The eyebrows stayed up; two more pebbles were shifted across.

'... But I do wish *you'd* understand, too. You're getting so grown up nowadays. Surely you can see other people's points of view ...'

'What about?' inquired Lydia without interest.

'Well, about anything at all. You're old enough—and bright enough—to see what's going on around you without always having to be told—'

'Why should anything be going on?' asked Lydia with a nerveless placidity that made Judy feel baffled—resentful—rebuffed. She could say only:

'Well— Things do, you see; that's all ...'

'Oh,' conceded Lydia, quite unconcerned.

'It doesn't matter to *you*, then?'

Lydia returned the obvious: 'What doesn't?' Leaning out of bed, she dropped half a dozen pebbles into a paint tin on the floor. Flinching slightly at the noise, Judy said:

'So you're still only a little girl, then, are you, after all.' From the straining of another pair of patched pyjamas across Lydia's plump bottom she could hear only irony in her own tone. The room *was* cold; mechanically, Judy tried to tuck the pyjama jacket into the waist of the trousers, a gesture that Lydia denied by heaving herself back into bed and then lying flat. She closed her eyes.

'Never mind, then,' Judy said resignedly. 'Go to sleep, darling.' But as she pulled up the covers the back of her hand touched a warm pink cheek and suddenly she knelt by the bed and put her arms tightly round the solid, solitary figure—

'Oh, darling, you do love us really, don't you— Don't *harden* ...'

'I'm not,' protested Lydia, embarrassed, affronted, and sounding genuinely surprised. '—Goodnight.' She rolled over, bundling herself off. Judy, not to admit defeat, folded up a few of the scattered clothes before withdrawing. She saw herself definitely *needed* here. The idea that she might, after all, have to go and get a full-time teaching job was now quite intolerable.

Judy, and Dring, both had great affection for Lydia and every sympathy with her at every stage of her development. Unfortunately, the ulterior motive behind their desire to understand her at this juncture inhibited their expression of it. In short: Sunday morning was still tense with 'nothing said'. Lydia came to breakfast with tousled hair and dull, grumpy face. She took no notice of anyone, and ate several pieces of toast with dogged greed, as if to indicate that her parents would have denied her food hadn't she grabbed it for herself. Whatever her offence against the family, she was incapable of mitigating it by any grace of manner.

Dring went out, the day being dry, to replace the stones knocked off the wall by the young Allison hooligans. One had squashed a patch of snowdrops. The garden, such as it ever was, looked tattier even than it usually did at this time of year. Lydia had left the fork to rust beside her scratty little bed of dead weeds. He stood for some time morosely regarding the places—three of them now—where the wall had collapsed and been temporarily repaired by himself with posts and wire. Only there was nothing temporary about his repairs except the style of their execution; the barbed wire in the first gap was by now rusty and all the posts looked wobbly. I always, he brooded, botch up jobs ... Drystone wall building may have been a craft Dring did not aspire to, but that didn't really excuse this mess. It looked as if he took no pride at all in his property. Which might, he sadly reflected, be true. He couldn't live up to the place.

When he went indoors, Judy was cooking, while Deb sat on the stool by the Rayburn with her hands knotted round her knees. She seemed, as she always did nowadays, like someone all packed-up and waiting to be collected, all interest lost. Dring, like Judy, deplored the negative power Dr Foster exerted over her situation. He said, throwing his gumboots aside:

'Why should there be smoke coming out of Miss Mitchell's chimney?'

At that, Deb jumped so suddenly that she overbalanced, clutched at the edge of the stove, missed, and fell on all fours to the floor. She scrambled up with a half-glance, both furtive and horrified, towards Dring, and ran out of the room with tears starting.

'That was tactless of you,' Judy complained.

'Why the hell—'

'Haven't you noticed, she *minded* about Miss Mitchell. Much more than Lyddie—'

'I've noticed so much that Deb *minds* lately that it confuses me—'

'I've noticed *that* ...'

He and Judy apparently couldn't begin to converse now without bickering; to avoid which, Dring went upstairs without pursuing the topic of smoking chimneys. The explanation did not come till late in the afternoon, when the Drings were gathered for tea, and Charles Mitchell knocked at the back door.

Lyddie went, from habit and curiosity, to open it, and he stepped inside, a paper carrier in his hand. 'Good afternoon. I hope I'm not disturbing you—'

'Not at all— Won't you have a cup of tea?' said Judy rising, also to the occasion. Charles Mitchell, even casually dressed for Sunday, was inescapably a businessman. He impressed Judy the more, when rarely they met, because he was so old to be a nephew; his unexpected years rendered him venerable. Today his face was purplish and tired, for which he obliquely accounted:

'No, thank you— Mary's waiting in the car; we're just off home. We've spent all day clearing out that cottage—'

'Oh yes. We saw the smoke.'

'I'm afraid,' he said grimly smiling, 'we did cause a fair amount of atmospheric pollution. There was so much rubbish in the place. —What I came to say, though, was: I see no reason why *this* shouldn't be here, as well as anywhere else?' He held up the carrier, and as the four faces turned to it with no conspicuous expression, he added: 'It's that picture.'

This, they had all guessed. In the silence as no one immediately reacted, Charles Mitchell went on: 'I suppose it would be all right by the solicitor-wallahs for me to hand it over. I'd rather, than leave it unattended in the cottage, or bother to take it away with me and bring it back later—'

'Oh yes— Thank you. We'll take charge of it,' Judy said.

'As a matter of fact,' recollected Charles, 'it's yours, isn't it?' He held out the carrier towards Lydia, benignly.

'Well, *take* it, Lyddie,' said Judy sharply.

Lydia, scraping back her chair, went to receive the carrier. She tucked it under her arm.

'—And *thank* Mr Mitchell.'

'Thanks,' said Lydia, mumbling.

Dring thought it suitable to say: 'We'd no idea the painting was as valuable as the experts we've consulted say— Of course, they haven't seen it yet. We rather hope your aunt realized what a splendid legacy she was giving Lydia. We all appreciate it.'

'Oh, not at all— She probably knew what she was doing. She usually did,' said Charles Mitchell with a return to grimness. 'And she was fond of Linda, I'm sure. Didn't she help her a bit around the house?'

'Lydia. —Oh yes, now and then,' took up Judy. 'But not to *that* extent. The thing is, too,' she thought it suitable in turn to offer, 'I hope it won't make a big hole in the ... estate ... That it isn't—well, depriving *you* ...'

'Oh, think nothing of that,' he urged her. 'In any case I'm sure you can use the money.' He managed to say this not at all offensively; his glance round the kitchen was sympathetic, rather than critical; and he added: '—Who can't, nowadays. I shall be jolly glad of what I get from the sale of the cottage, I can tell you. It ought to be something respectable, wouldn't you say? —And for all I know, there might be some more valuables among all that junk. I'm going to take some of the books to a dealer, on spec. Mary thinks we ought to have those oddments of silver valued too. We might strike lucky again, you never know.'

'I hope so. —You're selling the cottage, then?' asked Dring.

'Well, yes, I can't see myself using it. —Not that I've anything against this area. It's all right for people who want to get away from it all, you know. In fact it's just the spot for a holiday cottage for somebody who could afford to do the neccessary improvements.'

Dring reassured himself: But we can't see the place from here ... He was surprised by the depression that filled him as he pictured that cottage all tarted up with a local slate patio, and carriage lamps by the pastel-painted door. And they'd hew down the old sycamore and sweep away the ancient moss with some efficient modern chemical ... What was depressing was that the depression surged up and sank again like a blind underwater beast, knowing itself in the wrong—knowing Dring, that is, to be in an underwhelming minority; nowadays, *everyone* liked fresh paint and patios; the Lake District, like everywhere else, was changing; it was 'progress'. A man who liked mossy walls without mortar, but couldn't even build one, had no place at all; it was as if his time were up. He sighed loudly, drawing upon himself a puzzled look from Charles Mitchell.

'Yes,' put in Judy, wifely tact persisting, 'you ought to sell it well. Specially if you put it on the market now, in spring—'

'Yes; there's that. It was helpful of Aunt Pruey to depart at this time of year. —Well; I must depart too. Mary's waiting. See you again, I hope ...' And he nodded himself out.

As soon as the door had closed, Deborah said: '*Bloody* man.'

'Why?' inquired Judy indulgently.

Deborah looked amazed. 'What? —Nothing. I mean—I don't know what I was thinking ...'

'I think he's a rather nice man,' remarked Judy as if to smooth over Deborah's confusion. 'Anybody want more tea?'

'Oh so do I,' said Deborah, clumsily beginning to gather up plates.

'Lyddie,' said Dring, 'aren't we going to see this picture?'

'Why?'

'For God's sake, why not?'

His petulance bounced off her. She left the table and went to rummage in the deep cupboard.

'What *are* you going to do with it?' Judy asked her. This had the sound of a final challenge; now that the picture was in the house, a decision could reasonably be forced. Dring appended: 'Yes. Let's talk about it, Lyddie.'

Backing out of the cupboard dragging the toolbox, Lydia said: 'I'm going to hang it on my wall how you *said*.'

'... But that,' Judy reminded her, 'was *before* ...'

As far as Lydia was concerned, 'before' was irrelevant. She went out, carrier under one arm and toolbox under the other, her out-thrust behind a monument of insolence. They heard her clambering upstairs with her burdens, panting and clonking the toolbox against the banister.

'She seems to mean it,' observed Dring. Judy, also gathering plates, did not answer. From above came a rumbling crash as the toolbox was dumped on Lydia's bedroom floor. The ensuing silence began to strike Dring as ominous.

'Apart from anything else, is Lyddie safe with a hammer?'

'If she hits her thumb I shall be pleased,' said Judy tautly. Deborah turned to give her a hollow stare.

'And apart from her thumb, what if she punches the hammer through the canvas? We didn't ask Mitchell about who's paying the insurance meanwhile—'

'You think of everything.'

'No, seriously; I wish you'd nip up and keep an eye on the operation—'

'You wish *I* would?'

'—Because heaven knows how she's setting about it, but one can hardly bang nails into these walls ...' He paused, catching up on Judy's tone. 'Yes; why? Won't you?'

It irritated Judy, that he should be surprised that she hated the idea of coping with Lydia at the moment. 'Why should you always assume it's *my* job to run after the children— Won't I "just nip upstairs" like a housemaid—'

'It seems natural to me,' he said coldly, 'that a mother should take action if a child's wielding a dangerous weapon—'

'It seems to me far more natural that a *man* should deal with a job like putting up a picture ...'

What each, not admitting it within, was equally unwilling to see in the other, was a reluctance to have anything to do with Lydia—practically, a disgust with the girl. They understood each other well enough to avoid each other's eyes. Judy began hunting for the soap powder, to wash up; Dring rose and straightened his chair, neatly. Dring might have excused himself the more simply (Lyddie had been damned obstreperous for long enough, and now all this on top of it, and besides, he was tired today) but Judy—anyway of fierier temper, and possessing the maternal nerve-conscience that warns against the obverse of maternal affection, against the baby-battering demon—felt profoundly guilty and took it out on Alan:

'... You haven't done a *thing* to make Lyddie climb down. You just make her worse, for instance asking to see the picture—'

'So I did want to see the picture; why not?'

'All right, go up and look at it *now*.'

He felt hardly in the mood. But, reminded by distant

[184]

sounds of stony battering, he still felt someone should go—
'Deb', he said, 'won't you go up and see what Lyddie's doing
and tell her to stop it, as the old joke says?'

This had come to him as an inspiration. Before, they'd sent
Lyddie to reclaim Deb in a crisis. It committed neither parent;
it showed some solicitude; it mightn't be a bad thing for Deb to
take an active part in the family for once.

Deborah gave her habitual start and gazed at him blindly,
but turned to the door. 'Good lass,' he encouraged.

'I don't know what *that* will achieve,' said Judy, adding:
'I'd have gone myself as soon as I'd washed these—'

'I'd better go and finish that wall-mending,' said Dring,
going for his gumboots.

Deborah made her way slowly upstairs, hauling herself by
the banister. Several chunks of the ivoried white paint had
come off, revealing old grained wood beneath. She wondered
what it was Dad had told her to do. Whatever people said to
her, she quickly shut off, just as she shut off her own thoughts
as soon as they had come to her. Even her inward impulses
she contradicted, so much was she on her guard against mad-
ness. It was no wonder she was in confusion.

Round and round her prison she seemed to go, finding one
door after another and then remembering not only that she'd
tried it before, but that it was a trick; 'they' wanted her to
emerge, so that they could tell her she was crazy. She had to
deny everything so that 'they' couldn't trap her; she had
to say she didn't want to go to Dr Foster's, otherwise they'd
know she was mad; only mad people would want to go to
him.

Yet things had, if not reality, continuity. Secretly from herself she was quite *au fait* with the story of Lyddie and Miss
Mitchell's picture. —And *that* had been awful, how she nearly
gave herself away when that ghastly man came and talked as
if he'd been cleaning out a pigsty— He'd obviously been pawing over Miss Mitchell's private belongings like a looter after

[185]

a battle, seeing nothing but what he could *sell* ... Nobody remembered Miss Mitchell now. Nobody mourned her.

Nor dared Deborah, any more. Suppressed grief—if for the Miss-Mitchell-part of her own self—churned up a hidden hope that Miss Mitchell wasn't dead at all. Anyhow, nothing like so dead as these vultures who picked over her poor dead cottage ... Whose chimneys, you see, suddenly of their own accord yielded smoke; but if you showed surprise at that, they'd think you were hallucinated.

She opened the door of Lydia's room and stood blankly watching. Lydia was having a difficult time. As her father had pointed out, one can't just hammer a nail into a stone wall. Plaster had descended in quantities; the mat at the foot of the bed looked as if a dog had been eating puff pastry on it. Lydia, crimson in the face, turned and glared.

'Go away.'

The picture lay face up on the bed, the carrier pulled off. Deborah advanced to look at it.

'You heard— *Go away!*'

'That's the picture,' Deborah observed, tentatively. Her compulsion to study it had for the moment betrayed her; and Lydia, since Deb took no notice at all of her wall-pulverizing efforts, and was anyway so dim, couldn't really much resent her presence—

'Don't you touch it, that's all!' she warned, and scrabbled in the toolbox for another nail. She'd made a fair-sized hole, in the middle of the dust cloud; a thinner nail might fit into it ... She hadn't looked at the picture yet herself. Till she'd got it firmly on her wall, she'd no time to waste. But, envious of Deb's scrutiny of it, she came across with nail in hand. 'I used to think it was bears,' she confided.

Deb, lifting back her hair with both hands from her lowered face, still said nothing. 'You know what,' went on Lydia, 'Miss Mitchell knew the man. *I* think they were lovers.'

She had no one with whom to share any of her sense of the painting's significance; which, naturally, reinforced her ob-

[186]

stinate clinging to it. Having bestowed this information on Deb, she felt revived and fell upon her work again with vigour. Fitting the thinner nail to the hole she smacked it powerfully; with a musical *twoing* the nail flew out and disappeared, possibly on to the bed: it was not heard to fall. Lydia scowled about looking for it, and then looked at the wall again to see that a new crack had scribbled itself on the plaster. From very rage she swung the hammer at the crack; a chunk of plaster the size of a cod fillet dropped out, hit the floor with a hollow bonk and scattered into fragments that rattled across the boards clear of the mat.

'Bloody *hell*,' said Lydia with finality. 'Well, I'll just have to leave it down, just for tonight. Tomorrow I'll get Mr Martin to bring his power drill and make a better hole. Only anybody who touches it had better look out,' she threatened, tenderly gathering up the picture and setting it on a chair, propped up so that she could see it as she lay in bed. 'You heard what I said—' she added; but Deb had gone.

Deborah in her own room was looking out at the picture of Mellbreak on a spring afternoon. On the old larches in the foreground, rosy-pink pompons swung in the wind. Hugh Mostyn's dusky Glebe Woods were the actual landscape to her. Between his tortured bear-trees she had seen a glint of purpose. She lay down and closed her eyes. Be careful. They're trying to lure you out. —But it wouldn't go away. Perhaps this was sanity. Perhaps, something she hadn't tried before.

She let it begin to jigsaw together. She let herself remember that somebody had said Miss Mitchell had been cremated. Horrible idea. She should have been buried full-fathom under the yews. The bloody man had done that to her. The smoke from the cottage chimneys was his signal to the world: I'm polluting the atmosphere. I'm a sordid, brutal little man pulling Aunt Pruey's private nest to pieces now she's helped me, departing in the spring. —But she hadn't gone far. She was lying on the scree of Mellbreak ... Hiding in those shadowy woods? At any rate she was somewhere. This was what tugged at Deborah. Miss Mitchell wasn't dead enough. Not yet. And the point was: Did she *want* to be?

On consideration, Deborah decided: Yes. The interval of consideration, of waiting for the conclusion to present itself, had made her mind calmer, and receptive to a consequent purpose that slipped in before she could distrust it. So she began to see the overall picture of the jigsaw. Miss Mitchell's splendid gesture of dying was in danger of being ruined by these vultures who hung on to her personal possessions to turn them into cash, but bundled off her body and got rid of it— Altogether squalid; quite the wrong way round.

What Deborah was required to do about this took shape slowly. She tested it, remembering quite clearly that she *had* tried this before, and it hadn't worked—when she smashed the porcelain figurine in the presence of the assembled families— but that had been different. She'd been doing it to liberate herself. This time, it would be to liberate Miss Mitchell, which laid an obligation from the outside. The picture had got to be smashed because it was the last important thing tethering Miss Mitchell to earth. Important to Miss Mitchell, as the rest of the things weren't; the rag-pickers could have those.

When Deborah opened her eyes again it was dark. She might have been asleep. No one had woken her for supper; nowadays it was understood that if she missed a meal she'd feed herself; her carefully 'sane' behaviour included looking sensibly after herself. So, sensibly, she went downstairs, put on the kettle, and brought the biscuit tin from the pantry.

Purpose had survived. Now, though, she was more aware of the drawbacks. She didn't in the least want to damage the painting; it was rather terrifying to think of it rending and cracking under her hands— And, anyhow, would it? It was a tough old canvas, even if she could get it out of the frame. —Was the toolbox still in Lyddie's room, incidentally? It'd make a row, when Deb lifted it and brought it down, just as it had when Lyddie lugged it up.

But then, she hadn't *wanted* to smash the figurine. That had

[188]

been the point: it was a compulsion—or, a 'dare'. She'd just have to force the courage. What she also wanted to force, naturally, though she didn't realize this, was something or someone to prevent her. She ate a couple of biscuits, waiting for the kettle, which was slow to boil because the stove had been dampered down for the night. Recollecting this, Deborah mechanically opened the spinwheel and then, because it wasn't too warm in the room, opened the fire door too and drew the stool closer. Soon, blueish flames crept and licked through the black fuel. —That was a better idea; she'd burn the painting— Cremate it, as a tribute to Miss Mitchell.

As she ate another biscuit she reflected dolefully that the loss of the picture would mean the loss of her own chance of going to Dr Foster's, maybe of getting out of all this muddle at all. —But that was fine; it made it a sacrifice; worthy of Miss Mitchell; there was a touch of the superb, a flash of Deborah's own genius, in the unexpressed decision: better a crazy heroine than a sane traitor. On it, she became practical.

She needn't lumber herself with the toolbox or waste time sawing and nail-yanking. If she took the picture out to the byre and put it on the chopping-block, two or three good swipes with the big axe would reduce it, frame and all, into sections small enough to fit into the stove. It'd be quite easy. Right, then.

She went upstairs shivering, reluctant. Lyddie had, unusually, closed her bedroom door. The latch snapped, the door creaked— Good, thought Deborah in defiant cowardice, that'll wake her up ... But it didn't. Lyddie's heavy breathing rumbled on, filling the room. There was enough light to show the outline of the picture, propped on its chair at the foot of her bed. Ghostly, Deborah glided across to it. It was smaller than she'd remembered. This was all going to be too easy ... As she went out of the room she closed the door too firmly. The latch this time cracked like a pistol. Oh *hell*, thought Deborah, standing transfixed outside; *that'll* do it ...

She hadn't long to wait. Lydia woke, sat up, looked down

[189]

the bed and saw the picture missing, and burst out into the passage tumbling over her feet and bellowing:

'Come back with that— Give me that picture you bloody bloody *beast*—' She hurled herself at Deborah.

The uproar instantly woke Dring and Judy. Dring muttered: 'Whatever's that...?' but as usual left the answer, since it audibly concerned the children, to Judy, who, startled out of a nightmarish sleep, was out of bed before her eyes opened. She reeled out of the room and switched on the passage light.

At the top of the stairs Lydia was yelling and pounding with her fists and feet at Debby, who, two steps lower, stood cowering, her head bent under the assault and her arms folded round a flat object—a shield she would not use. Something about her meekness, to Judy's bewildered glance, made Lydia's aggression ugly. Deborah's head jerked under a savage punch, her hair swung, her slender neck might well have snapped— '*Stop* that!' commanded Judy, rushing forward.

'She's got my *picture* the *bitch*—' roared Lydia, not desisting.

'Leave her *alone*—' God, as if Lyddie hadn't made enough trouble, without hurting Debby like this— Not quite thinking: You've got to *meet* violence ... Judy under an impulse strange to herself seized Lydia roughly by that immediate handle, her hair, as when highly exasperated she had occasionally in the past. This time, the weight of Lydia's body, resisting, called for more than exasperation. In white rage, Judy tugged Lydia round with all her strength, gave her a hard slap across one cheek and then the other, and grasping her plump shoulders shook her till her head rolled like a marionette's and Judy herself was breathless. 'Stop that or I'll kill you, d'you hear, I'll *kill* you ...'

When she let go of Lydia, Lydia staggered for a moment, then turned away, descended a stair and snatched the picture out of Deborah's arms, landing a vicious kick in Deborah's stomach as she did so. To feel that she had made no impression, that Lydia was in every way impervious to her, brought

[190]

Judy to murder-point. She pounced on Lydia again, thrashing at her as uncontrollably as Lydia had been thrashing at Debby. '*You ... damned ... little ... pest ...*' she screamed. Deborah cowered again as Lydia lost her balance and, with a piercing shriek of alarm, tottered and went slithering and bumping to the foot of the stairs, the picture still clutched to her chest.

She hit the stone flags of the lower floor with a sickening dull flat thud. For a few seconds there was silence. Then Deborah roused herself and went down the stairs nearly falling herself, landing on hands and knees, peering into Lydia's face. Before she could speak, Lydia drew in a gasping breath and began to bawl in loud boo-hoos, a child hurt:

'—*Ow ... Ahoo, ahoo ... I've broken my back ...*'

Judy said from the top of the stairs: 'I wish you had. Get up.'

Still bawling, Lydia rather surprisingly did. She rubbed at her back, then bent to pick up the picture, turning it in the light from above to inspect it for damage. Apparently satisfied there was none, she all at once stopped bawling. She climbed stiffly up the stairs again, softly sniffing, ignoring her mother. Deborah knelt, watching her go. No one said anything. With a strange bruised dignity, her picture in her arms as if it consoled her, Lydia hobbled into her room and quietly closed the door behind her.

After a moment Deborah stood up and came up the stairs. She looked at Judy with a kind of cold curiosity and remarked:

'You're absolutely *mad*.'

Waiting for no reply, she too went into her room and quietly closed its door.

12

DRING, incredulous that his family should be fighting on the stairs in the middle of the night, was still wondering whether he ought to intervene when Judy came back to bed. She explained nothing, but lay with her face in her pillow, crying, allowing no comfort. He'd have to leave it till morning, when perhaps she'd feel better. Presently falling asleep himself he was still half-listening for sounds in the house. Waking before Judy, he was glad to get up and be first to start the day's chores. A vague sense of something out of order was in part explained when he went down to the kitchen to find that the Rayburn had been left at full blast all night and had burnt out not only itself, but the bottom of the kettle which had been left on the plate. This was a substantial gloomy-Monday predicament. Kettles were expensive items nowadays, without worrying about the fire-grid of the stove ... That, however, seemed more or less intact. He put on a pan of water for coffee and opened the back door to moist sunshine.

The others came down late, singly and silently. Dring was inclined to suppose that there had been some crisis during the night from whose nature he was excluded. Now he became aware that not only he was excluded; each of the others, excluding everyone, was as alone as he. Deb was, as usual, in some introvert-world of her own; Lyddie was stuck in her dog-in-the-manger isolation; Judy was haggard and withdrawn.

However, they *had* assembled. They sat round the table on which Dring, dumbly helpful, had laid plates and food. Judy cut slices of bread; Lydia helped herself hugely. No one had said as much as 'Good morning'. This brooding quiet, suggesting to Dring some aftermath of calamity, began to suggest too a calamity menacing; as if rather than the family's having suffered fire or death during the night, it was today to face eviction; they hung together for a last meal in mute apprehension.

Judy had not even noticed the burnt-out kettle.

Hearing a car in the lane, Dring in his semi-fantasy supposed doom was now approaching. Whether the others heard it, or shared his apprehensions, they all started extravagantly at a violent knocking on the front door.

This in itself was irregular. Everybody who knew them came to the back, which faced the yard gate. 'Who...?' said Judy, gripping the edge of the table. 'Lyddie—open it ...'

Lydia hauled herself off her chair as if she had sciatica, but went obediently enough into the front passage; the key of the door could be heard squeaking in the lock. The three waiting in the kitchen, heads turned, saw daylight fall on to the flags and heard a clear and emphatic female voice declare:

'This's got to be Broom Cottage.'

It sounded rather transatlantic; certainly determined. Lydia said: 'M'm ...'

'And a Miss *Dring* lives here. She in?'

There were sounds as if the visitor had stepped indoors. She had; she thrust Lydia back before her and appeared in the kitchen doorway. 'Miss Dring?' she inquired.

'What's she done?' asked Judy faintly.

Not attending to that, the arrival looked them over, rapidly critical. She was not a prepossessing figure. Young middle-aged, solid, with short strawy hair, a slit of a mouth, florid face, stained suède coat, check trousers and grubby white boots, she stood with a smoking cheroot in her hand surveying Judy and Deborah as if they exceeded some worst expectations. 'Which of you is this Lydia Dring?'

'Oh,' said Judy, relieved, 'that's Lydia. Behind you.'

The woman turned and glanced at Lydia and said: 'Mph.'

[193]

It was a brief sound of indifferent scorn. *'Her?'* she asked, turning back to fix her eye on Dring. *'She's* got this picture?'

'What picture?' He knew perfectly well what picture it must be, but saw no reason to resist his instant dislike of this truculent female.

'The dark period Mostyn,' said the female succinctly. 'He wants it.'

'Who does?'

'Oh Christ,' said the woman. 'Here he comes.'

There was a fumbling movement at the front door, a patch of shadow on the flags, and another figure came shambling into the doorway of the kitchen. The woman shouted with a rancorous edge to her already unpleasant voice: 'I told you to stay in the bloody *car.'*

All the Drings were staring astonished. Dring thought: *Can* it be? Who told me he was dead? ... But I went to an exhibition of his when I was a student, for God's sake, and he was a veteran *then* ... It was Judy who said, only half aloud: 'Is this ... Hugh Mostyn...?'

Nobody introduced him. The still unintroduced woman was shouting: '... If not in the bloody *hotel* ...' and Mostyn himself was intent only on getting into the room. Letting go of the doorpost he reached for Lydia's empty chair, using it as a crutch to propel himself a little further to the Rayburn, beside which he sat, turning the chair and dropping on to it from a reckless height. He must once have been a tall man. Now his thick tweed coat didn't hide his skinniness. His wrists, as he laid his hands to warm on the stove, stuck out of his cuffs like leathery twigs. He had a black beret askew over wispy white hair, and a face carved, battered and weathered by eighty-seven years of strenuous living. A cigarette was crumpled between two fingers; a dirty rattle in his chest choked out of him as he tried to regain his breath; he looked peevish and bitter and cruel and oblivious. And he smelt, rather. But his eyes were, in their red rheumy pouches, small and crystal-sharp. He coughed, spluttering, let his cigarette fall, poking

[194]

automatically into his coat pocket for another, and said in the lightly hollow voice of the deaf:

'Well, have you got the picture?'

'Where is it?' his companion (Wife? The how-many-th?) demanded at large.

It was Dring who said quietly: 'Get it, Lyddie.'

She shot him one imploring glance, which Dring blocked with one of warning. Lydia probably understood that if this pair wanted her picture she didn't stand much of a chance; but Dring understood that if Mostyn had come so far he must at very least see it. Apropos of which he asked, as Lydia not too hurriedly went upstairs:

'Where have you come from? This is a long way from anywhere—'

'Bloody right it is,' agreed the podgy woman, moving round to lean against the sink, but making no move to sit down; she didn't intend, evidently, to stay. 'We had a hell of a time finding it.' This accusation the Drings were used to; specially to this lady, Dring wasn't going to apologize for his house's remoteness. 'We drove up yesterday and spent the night in a hotel some place. *He*—' with a jerk of the head at Mostyn, 'couldn't wait till the thing was brought to *him*. Cussed old bastard.'

She said this with no undertone of affection; but then, it did seem Mostyn was deaf. Glancing at him to check the assumption, Dring saw the old man struggling to strike a match for his new cigarette. The box lurched in his cold hand. Dring leaned over and took it from him, extracting a match and offering the flame. Mostyn drew on his cigarette and then emitted a snarl that sounded like: '... 'mbloody dotage ...'

'He loathes being helped,' remarked the query-wife, as ungrateful as Mostyn.

'I imagine you have to drive the car for him, though?'

She ignored that, possibly as over-obvious. 'Where's that kid?'

'She'll bring the picture. She's rather attached to it, you see ... How, by the way, did you know about it? That it was here?'

She shrugged, stared towards the stairs, and then admitted, as one might as well talk as not to fill in the time: 'Tim Pettinger rang him. Said you'd rung *him*. Told him you'd got a dark-phase picture. Hugh didn't believe it. Made such a bloody fuss ...'

Oh, of course: the gallery. Still, it had been only—what—three days ago that Dring had telephoned them. The news must indeed have electrified Mostyn— Might, the art world in general? And, still, this bullying female *had* brought Mostyn at his wish, all the way from wherever it was—somewhere in the south, most likely, it didn't matter. And anyway, Lydia could be heard now, stumping downstairs.

She came into the kitchen with the canvas hugged to her stomach, back-side-out. Dring was about to tell her to turn it round and bring it to Mr Mostyn when Mostyn himself moved. With amazing agility he heaved himself off the chair, lurched forward and took the picture from Lydia, swaying round to place it on top of the kitchen cabinet where it would receive the fullest light from the window. He set the picture down delicately but then jammed himself clumsily against the cabinet, supporting himself on extended arms, and gazed at the picture, immediately absorbed. Everyone was, involuntarily, as if respectfully, quiet; waiting.

Mostyn's movement had brought him so closely past Dring that the tweed coat had brushed across Dring's face and the old-man-smell for a moment enclosed him. But it wasn't this that made Dring swing round to follow his passage and gaze at Mostyn, absorbed in him as Mostyn in the picture. During the passage, looking up into the old man's face from so close and strange an angle, Dring had seen it as alert as a twenty-year-old's. The mouth might slobber in eagerness but the little crystal eyes sparked intelligence. And the old scarecrow's hands had touched the picture with expert gentleness.

It wasn't, even, that; it was a sharp pang of—loneliness?—that disturbed Dring. He witnessed a meeting—reunion—between Mostyn and the long-lost work of his creation. It had been rather like the meeting of lovers— When you're waiting for a train, for instance, and so are various strangers, and off the train gets someone that one of the strangers is in love with— How those two leap to each other and their own world exalts them and everyone else is forgotten, left cold on the drab platform ... So, Mostyn had flown to his love—his child—excluding everything else ... Shaken, Dring could only think: Would I, after another forty years, feel like that if I saw one of my books again?

Two answers came, not of his own uttering:

The first, simply: *No.*

The second: *My poems, I would.*

The truth about oneself is often over-simple and usually inconvenient. If one comes suddenly face to face with it round a corner, as Dring had, it is not readily recognizable; it needs, anyway, a little explaining, adapting, to render it palatable and fit it into the scheme of things. For which, Dring had in any case just now no leisure. Telling himself: H'm, yes, I must think about that ... he shelved the question as Mostyn was speaking:

'This is it. This is it. Where's it *been?*'

'It's one of yours, all right?' shouted his companion.

'Yes. Yes. Remember this one. Good God. Burnt them all, y'know—all this lot. Always wondered why. After I'd been in that stinking hospital. Depressed, they called it. —Daresay I was. See it, here— This sloping perspective. And here— *Overtone* shadow. What the devil colour did I use—'

'Never mind all that.' The woman levered herself off the sink and threw the stub of her cheroot behind her. 'If that's the one you wanted, let's get going.'

She reached past him as if to pick up the picture, but was checked by a snarl more vicious than Mostyn had emitted

when Dring lit his cigarette. Not wholly deterred, she said:
'Well—*what?*'

He shook his head impatiently and went on studying the
painting, now more critically, narrowing his eyes. Absurdly
egotistical old bastard, noted Dring— He doesn't give a damn
about anything but his picture; I bet he's no idea where he is
or what's going on. It was impossible not to admire him.

'Old fool,' said the woman, not admiringly. She seemed
prepared to wait for a moment, however, and Judy seized the
chance at last to enter into the occasion.

'Do I understand,' she began in a high-pitched voice, rising
from the table, 'that Mr Mostyn wants to buy the picture from
us?'

'*Mph.*' The snort was charged with most offensive derision.
'Buy his own picture?'

'It's not his. He painted it, yes, but now it belongs to our
daughter. It was left to her by its owner.'

'Yeah. Well, that still makes it his. Sorry.'

'Have you any idea what it's been valued at?' persisted
Judy. Two red spots burned in her cheeks.

'Quite a bit, I guess. But you hadn't to buy it. So it's no
loss to you.'

'It would be a *great* loss to us. A good deal depends on our
having that money. You can't just walk in here and carry it
off—'

'Stop me,' said the woman indifferently.

It was apparent to everyone attending that Judy would
gladly have done just that; she tensed, moving her hands as if
they groped for a weapon. At that moment Deborah, still
sitting at the table, raised her head and looked at Judy with
keen inquiry; Judy half-glanced at her, drew a long breath,
and resumed, dropping her hands to the table:

'Besides, the will hasn't been proved yet. The picture's only
in our possession by courtesy of the family—'

'Never mind the courtesies.'

'I can see *you* never do,' retorted Judy. The woman, merely as if bored by the threat of personalities, shrugged and turned to thump Mostyn's elbow. 'Come on, Hugh. We want to get back to town before evening—'

'*Wait,*' he snarled.

'You'll have the rest of your *life* to look at the bloody thing—'

'Oh no he won't,' threw in Judy doggedly.

'I don't quite *get* this ...' Mostyn mumbled. '... Forgotten why I distorted the perspective here ... And *here* ...'

'You were in *depression,*' she snapped in his ear.

'I bloody wasn't. They *told* me I was. Like a fool I believed them. Look at this. Never got such spatial *density* since ... I was right. Right all along. Christ, if I'd stayed what they called *depressed* I'd have been a damn sight better painter. *Depressed*—'

'You tried to cut your throat. You've told me that often enough,' barked the woman, sidetracked.

'Chap cuts his throat, it's not because he's *depressed.* 'Sbecause he's done a rotten painting. —Most of this is lousy of course. Look at that Millais ivy on the trunk. But *that*—' He slapped the flat of his hand, almost jovially, against the focus of moon-blue light in the painting's background. '... Where *was* the place anyway?'

'God knows,' she said, losing interest again.

'... "Glebe Woods". Remember the woods ... but why was I trying to get this imbalance of shade ...'

Lydia, beside him, had drawn slowly close, and now had her elbows on the cabinet; the picture itself might have exerted the attraction. Now she looked up into the gnarled face above hers and said:

'It was somewhere near where the Mitchells lived.'

'Eh?'

She straightened and shouted at him: 'The Mitchells. They had a vicarage. You stayed near there one summer.'

'Hr'mmm ... Mitchell. Yes. I remember the Mitchells. M'hm. So that was it. But almighty God that was during the war. No wonder I was depressed,' he added as if tossing the idea aside. He narrowed his eyes at the picture again, tilting his head. '... S'pose I had battlefields in mind ... blasted, y'know ... Accounts for that bloody awful drawing of the transition-lines *here* ...'

Lydia plucked at the tweed sleeve. 'You were in love with their *daughter*,' she yelled. 'You gave her this picture.'

'Daughter? ... Was there a daughter—'

'Yes. Miss Mitchell.'

'Daresay. I was in love with everybody's daughter in those days.'

'Don't you *remember* her?' cried Lydia, clinging to his arm. Roused, he looked down at her quite kindly and said:

'No, m'dear. Never heard of her. Picture's beginning to come back, though. 'Stonishing. Thought I'd scrapped the lot.'

He shook her off and turned back to the painting, but Lydia caught his elbow and hauled him round again. He tottered and propped a hand on the wall, frowning at her, irritated. She shouted at the top of her voice:

'You'd better *have* the picture, then.'

There was a gasp of protest from Judy, but Dring with a wave of the hand checked her. He asked encouragingly:

'Why, Lyddie?'

'Because if he doesn't even remember Miss Mitchell he might as *well*.'

'Yes. I see.'

'—And anyway, he *gave* it to Miss Mitchell, and she *gave* it to me, so nobody paid for it ever, and so nobody can sell it.'

Lydia, planted there with hands on hips, marmalade on her cheek, her tummy bulging over her tartan trousers with their bust-off button, was laying down the law. Dring said again: 'I see.'

'What *I* don't see,' began Judy, 'is—'

'Let Lyddie have it her way,' Dring said sternly.

'He's old,' pointed out Lydia, with more contempt than

pity. 'He can't even remember who he was in love with—'

'He always was a dirty ram,' remarked the woman.

'Shut up,' said Lyddie to her, rather superbly. The woman, not apparently surprised by the impudence, shut up; probably she had had nothing else at the moment to say. Lyddie went on: 'He can't help it. But Miss Mitchell remembered *him*. And he remembers the picture. And he wants it. So he'd better have it.'

She had explained it all to her own satisfaction. She strode away and sat down on the stool by the Rayburn, quitting the stage.

Judy said: 'It isn't as easily decided as that, I'm afraid. The picture hasn't been valued yet, for one thing—'

'It's my picture,' asserted Lydia; for the last time.

'Lyddie *has* decided it, I'm afraid,' said Dring to Judy. 'Let's have no more wrangling.'

Judy tossed up her head in stupefaction and despair, but before she spoke, Deborah said:

'Shut up, Mummy. Lyddie's quite right.'

Judy's intended speech dissolved into a helpless sigh and: '... Oh God ... Are you quite *mad*, all of you?'

Lydia observed detachedly: 'Everybody in this house is a bit mad today.'

'That'll do,' Dring told her warningly. He added to the woman—whose name and status they were never to be told: 'It seems you may have the picture, then.'

Of course she uttered no word of thanks. In fact she turned to Judy and demanded several sheets of strong paper and a large polythene bag to carry the picture in.

When the visitors had gone, the atmosphere of the cottage was as interrupted as if a tornado—or Dring's anticipated 'doom'—had blown through. It was odd to see the breakfast plates still on the table.

Only Lydia watched from the window as the roof of the car, after some delay no doubt due to the bundling-in of the

[201]

old man, slid away down the lane. Her chin crumpled and big, hot tears fell: she'd never see the picture, the bears-that-were-trees, again.

The first of the family to comment was Judy: '*She'll* sell the thing as soon as he dies. *Someone's* going to get that money.' She had sat down again at the table, running her hands through her hair; with a deep sigh she summed up: 'What a *waste* it all is . . .'

'Oh,' said Dring, 'I don't know. It's given us something, you know. It's shown us that *one* member of this family has unblemished integrity.' He stretched an arm and turned Lydia round to face him.

'Who— Me? . . . Got what?' she asked warily, sniffing and fisting her nose.

'I simply mean, that you've been perfectly right all the time. One doesn't sell presents, for however much money, and one doesn't betray one's friends' intentions. And we were quite wrong to try to make you.'

Her eyes measured him suspiciously for one more moment before she dropped them, squirming a little, blushing; she couldn't help smiling. 'Heck,' she said, disclaiming and embarrassed. Her face had changed; even the blush was of a different shade—petal-pink instead of sullen crimson. Her nosetip had turned upwards cheerfully again. She shrugged away as if to go, but seeing the table, apparently remembered she hadn't finished her breakfast. She took an apple from the bowl and sat down, wiggling her behind comfortably, and began chomping.

Judy remarked: 'However, integrity won't *feed* her.'

Deborah said quickly: 'Daddy's right. You *shouldn't* have sold the picture.'

Lydia swallowed a lump of apple and admitted justly: 'All right. I'm sorry I bashed you last night.'

Correctly, Deb should then have said she was sorry she'd tried to pinch the picture. But Judy broke in on this sisterly reconciliation:

[202]

'Considering it was for *you* we wanted the money, Debby—'

'Why', exclaimed Deborah turning on her, 'do you keep on blaming *me* for everything?'

This was the fifth time in twelve hours that Deborah had uttered a thought as it came to her, without noticing that she had. Nor did Judy, since the thoughts had been on each occasion inimical to herself— 'Because', she retorted vigorously, 'it was you and your capers that started all this trouble in the *first* place.'

'*What* capers?'

'You've never explained *what*, yet. All those idiotic things you got up to in town—'

'They had nothing to do with you. They weren't idiotic, either—'

'Well if they weren't, that makes you *criminal*—'

'Me? *I* don't go pushing my own children downstairs—'

'Oh no— You just throw *bombs* at people—'

'With damn good reason. —Anyway it was only a *banger*—'

'There's no good reason for violence. You wouldn't have minded if you *had* killed that man—'

'You wouldn't have minded if you *had* killed Lyddie.'

Lydia, taking another bite of apple, turned her head, which had been going to and fro as if she were at Wimbledon, to see what her mother might reply to that; she appeared merely interested. Dring, leaning on the Rayburn, was listening intently.

'. . . There was no question of killing her,' returned Judy rather weakly after a short pause.

'Nor was there with me. At least I knew what I was doing—'

'That makes it worse. It was *calculated*—'

'It's better to be calculated than to give way to a crazy impulse—'

'Who', demanded Judy throwing her hands wide, 'is supposed to be the *crazy* one in this family?'

'I only know who *is*,' said Deborah coldly.

It wasn't surprising that Judy, in spite of her professions

and her guilt, nearly seized the nearest object from the table and flung it at Deborah. *That,* she would have explained, was all it meant when *she* hurled things about: superficial nervous reaction to extreme provocation. Anybody could suffer that; *anybody* couldn't be as cold-heartedly savage as Deborah. But that was by the way; squabbling with Debby was only a symptom of the plight into which Judy had been, she felt, betrayed.

After all she had done for them (and in fairness, that phrase was not all self-pity), she had been isolated by her family and put in the wrong. God knew quite how. Judy certainly didn't. Guilt, refracted by such ignorance, flashed up translated:

'From the way you've both—*all*—been carrying on lately it's a marvel I haven't been driven quite insane. And now, what's supposed to happen? Are we back to square one? I simply can't *face* that. I've had enough. —At least,' she said, as Lydia threw her apple core at the coke hod and missed, 'let's get the place tidied up before you make it a complete slum— Look at the *time* ...' She clattered two plates together, standing. 'Lyddie—pick that *up* ...'

Lydia obeyed. Dring, straightening, looked about as if he wished to be helpful, and noticed that the front door was still open, letting chilly air in through the passage. The visitors hadn't bothered to close the door behind them on departing, and certainly no one had bothered to see them off. He went to the door and stood looking out, attracted by the brightening morning.

'*Which* war', he called into the kitchen, 'was the old chap talking about? It must have been the first—the Kaiser's—surely, if you reckon it up ...'

No one answered, if anyone heard. No one was interested in reckoning the chronology of their late caller's life history. But to Dring, Hugh Mostyn was still very much present and significant. He lingered; he had entered Dring's life to lasting effect.

He was the answer to that obscure loneliness that had

[204]

plagued Dring for so long. He was what Dring had faithfully believed in, exemplified. Dring in his way had experienced that sense of 'presence', of personal reality, that every Christian church in its way depends on. Hugh Mostyn incarnate had shown that the world of imagination exceeds the actual. It was the breakthrough at last.

Not that Dring would necessarily, even with effort and grace, get there; but his centre of emphasis had shifted; now that he knew *that* world was real, *this* fell into place.

It's a question, he mused idly in the doorway, of values ... He should be able to discard, now, his anxious scruffy self that did (he could now admit) want to hide away from this cruel world, and was afraid of being second-rate, and saw itself only as other people did, so that the unwilling desire-to-please clogged every impulse. Judy had been quite right when she said he'd gained his freedom only by other people's giving. *Would* he ever have had the guts to chuck up his teaching job? He didn't suppose so. —Perhaps, guts wasn't what it took; spirit, rather; love of the work, like old Mostyn's for his picture though Mostyn himself didn't appear to think the picture a particularly good one. It wasn't the virtue of the work itself, but the virtue one put into it—

'Alan; have you finished with this *coffee*?'

Judy's voice was deliberately edgy; she was making an act of getting the house straight again, although, for what, it was doubtful that she herself knew. Dring closed the front door and came back into the kitchen.

'It must be stone cold,' he said, drinking it nevertheless.

'Shall I make some *more*, or may I start the washing-up?'

'Since when', he asked lightly, 'have I been incapable of making myself a cup of coffee?'

Poor Judy, now examining the wreck of the kettle, had experienced no illumination. She replied, predictably: 'Oh yes, you're quite good at *that*, if at nothing much else—'

'Let me have that; I'll chuck it in the bin.'

'How the hell did this *happen*? Who left it on?' Nobody

owned up; Deborah had genuinely forgotten that she'd even put the kettle on last night. Last night's events were a patchy nightmare, she could see in haphazard recollection Judy's face, could hear her shrieks and feel Lydia's bashing; tentatively now she was wondering what she herself had been doing in the middle of all that. It was as if her dream had sucked the other two into it. *Could* dreams do that...? She sat with tightly folded arms at the table corner.

Dring, not answering Judy, took the kettle from her. She hung on to it for a second, then relinquished it saying: '*Well?* What's wrong now— Am I not fit to be talked to?'

'You do seem rather overwrought,' he mentioned. He took the kettle to the back door.

'—But *you* aren't of course— As if those beastly people hadn't just walked off with our last hope—'

'My dear, it certainly wasn't that. In fact, I think this house is better off without that picture in it. In every way.' He opened the door but paused again as Judy pursued:

'As if it hadn't represented enough money to straighten us out—'

'It's time we straightened ourselves out under our own steam, don't you think? You said yourself, riches that come as a gift can weaken the character. Or something to that effect ... Is there any point in keeping a kettle lid, in case we happened to need a spare, any time?'

'No. —Yes. I don't know ... How precisely', she said, striding to the sink, 'do you intend to straighten *yourself* out now?'

'*Un moment,*' Dring excused himself, going out into the yard. As Judy turned on taps, the clatter and clank of the kettle being put in the dustbin sounded from outdoors. As soon as Dring reappeared she took up:

'... When are you going to get that book finished, for instance?'

'Oh, never,' he said cheerfully. 'I'd rather cut my throat, like old Mostyn.'

Judy's mouth tightened. Deborah looked up.

'What I'm probably going to do—' Dring went on, leaning again on the Rayburn, 'is—'

'So can you kindly explain what's to be done about poor Debby, and Dr Foster?'

'Yes; I've been thinking about that. We haven't been terribly practical about it—'

'We?'

'You,' amended Dring coolly. 'I might talk to the chap myself. Do we even know whether he has to be paid by the week or the month, or how much? Some of these places let you defer the fees. Or, for that matter, need it be that place? We might get her into a psychiatric unit under the National Health somewhere—'

'How absurd. Debby isn't a mental patient.'

'Why does she need the attentions of Dr Foster, then?' asked Dring equably.

'Oh God, what's the use. Stop meddling, and go and get on with your writing.' She crashed a pile of plates upside down on to the draining board.

'Not today. I think I might go out for some exercise—'

'What a time to choose. —Are you simply trying to madden me?'

'Certainly not. If anything I'd like to persuade you to be saner about all this. You're—'

'There's nothing insane about taking the situation seriously. —Why shouldn't you finish that book, for God's sake? Just because you're afraid of prostituting your *art*—'

'Something like that, yes. I should have known better—'

'You should have known better all along. If you had the slightest concern for Deb—*or* me—you wouldn't have let us get into *any* of this mess.'

Staring absently at Deborah, who was staring as absently at him, Dring mused: 'I had the wrong kind of concern. I was trying to play *your* game.'

[207]

'Mine?' echoed Deborah dimly. He didn't answer her; and Judy, swinging round, was saying:

'Yes, it's all a *game* to you. You admit it. Can you wonder I'm absolutely fed up with it all— Pinching and scraping and boosting your conceit and *mouldering* here ... It'd bloody well serve you right if I walked out.'

'That's an idea,' he agreed.

She started to say something, stopped on a gasp, and eyed him brilliantly. Dring, looking away from Deborah, said to Judy with new energy: 'Yes; if you hate it here, why martyrize yourself?'

'Well, I'd rather thought I had a duty to my family,' she said, uncertainly.

'You thought I had, too. But you feel I put myself first. Why don't you try that as well?'

This confused her. 'Not everybody's as selfish as you. What would I do, anyway, if I left here?'

'You might try earning your freedom. Just as you advised me to.'

'But that's entirely different. Marriage is a duty, too—'

'If that's all it is, why bother?'

'I didn't say it was *all* ...' But his quizzical, not unkindly gaze distracted her. Her own face emptied of expression as if she queried the unquestionable. For a silent interval they shared: What *is* our marriage to us? That it might be mortal shifted their world on its foundations.

This morning Dring was poised for such a shift. To Judy, it was giddily unsettling. Guilt, she could deflect; the sense of failure she could only fly from. Nothing had prepared her for this. She knew, *yes*, she passionately wanted to be free of this place and alive in the real world. With a now-or-never desperation she said:

'All *right*. I'll do just that. I'll clear out and go to London and make a decent life for myself. I'll get a job—even *teaching*. And you can stay here and sort everything out and good luck to you.'

[208]

'That's the spirit,' applauded Dring.

'Alan, for God's sake—I mean it.'

'I think you do—'

'You'll see I do. I'm going to leave you.'

Lydia said: 'Yes. You do that. And I'll stay here and keep house for Daddy.'

They had forgotten that she was still there. Uncharacteristically, she had been employing herself quietly, reading a *New Statesman* from the rubbish box and picking her nose. Now she sat up, slapped down the *New Statesman* and looked from one parent to the other as if she were settling their problems in the most practically helpful manner.

Dring smiled at her. 'That's a good offer, Lyddie.' Almost, he was tempted. At the moment he appreciated Lydia's worth. She would make an excellent daughter-at-home—independent, unsympathetic, reliable. But it wouldn't do. In any case, she was only a child—

'Don't be silly, Lyddie,' Judy was saying promptly.

'It's no sillier than *you* going away.'

'There's nothing silly about that,' threatened Judy. It didn't help, that Lydia's word for her mother's desertion was no more than 'silly'. 'You'd be sorry if I *did* go away.'

'Would she?' murmured Deborah.

Judy turned on her; but to ask: Well—wouldn't *you*? would be to risk altogether too much. She hesitated, then spun round to plunge her hands into the washing-up bowl— 'I can see when I'm not wanted— And for that matter, I can do very well without the *lot* of you—'

'I'm sure you can,' said Dring, pacifically. 'The trouble is, we all depend on each other in the wrong way. We prop each other up in our deficiencies. It's not a bad thing to review those, now and then. Well ...' As he read into Judy's back that further conversation was impracticable, 'I still intend to go on the fell while it's sunny. Deb, d'you want to come?'

'My boots are bust,' she remarked, which might have been her only objection.

'So they are,' he agreed, going to the cupboard for his own.

'Can *I* come?' asked Lydia.

This was quite unprecedented. It had always been accepted that Lydia was too young, too fat, too lazy, too busy for fell-walking.

'You haven't got any boots at all, have you,' Dring pointed out.

'Only gumboots.'

'I'd rather not take you in those. Not safe.'

'Okay,' said Lydia without resentment. 'I think I'll get on with my garden, then.' She found her gumboots, dragged them on, and set off out of doors with a skip and a jump over the back step. Crossing the yard, she paused to kick at a loose cobble, and to whistle back at a starling who was trying to perform Mozart on the byre roof. She looked a happy, rosy-faced little girl. Indeed, her world had, after some turmoil she was not competent to analyse, settled on its smooth course again, because she had found a new friend, Daddy, in place of Miss Mitchell. This recognition she did not dwell on either; picking up the rusty fork she began digging, careful not to impale the glossy worms, her mind full only of the smell of spring soil.

13

AFTER LYDDIE AND PA HAD GONE, Deborah, not wanting to be left alone with that madwoman who was crashing about the kitchen, went up to her room and lay on her bed to re-connect. Early this morning when the birds splintered the greyness with their din, Deborah had been almost sure she'd found a new way out; a trapdoor in the floor of the prison she didn't *think* she'd noticed before. It had seemed obvious, that the only way to live up to Miss Mitchell was to *die* up to her; to exceed her; if Miss Mitchell had died 'on purpose', Deborah could do so, but more quickly and positively. She'd wondered why she hadn't thought of it before; it *was* obvious.

... But, after the recent interruptions, she couldn't envisage suicide in those simple terms again. Some other idea was jarring on her, muddling her; she'd have to admit it ... Oh yes; Pa, saying he'd cut his throat ... She tried to forget that again, but couldn't. It had spoilt everything. Not only had somebody else spoken her idea aloud and so stolen it from her, but he'd said it as a kind of joke. —Yet in a sort of way, he had meant it. It puzzled her.

... So here she was, puzzling about Pa, distracted from her own destiny. She rolled on to her face, blacking out vision in the pillow, but even as she receded into the accustomed safety of her inner prison he was still *there*, somewhere in the dark, so that every time she made a circuit she might somewhere bump into him. Madly muddling, and it stopped her from remembering ... She couldn't even remember the *point* of looking for the trapdoor. Miss Mitchell...? The awful thing was, Miss Mitchell seemed to have eluded her.

With the removal of something else—the picture— Oh yes; the *picture*, Deborah did now remember—Miss Mitchell had disappeared too. Only Pa lurked solidly and silently; a presence.

Deborah had vacillated, particularly since the change in the family life when she was thirteen or so, between her two father-images: the hero-poet, the affectionate Daddy. She hadn't been able to decide which she wanted, so she had accepted him in neither rôle, and blamed him for fulfilling neither. That he had been even unconsciously aware of this she hadn't imagined; she had made nothing of his remark this morning that he had been 'playing her game'. This morning, though, she did feel things had changed. Instead of being useless, Pa had become an obstruction. He got in her way; he wouldn't leave her in peace. She couldn't even *die* with him looming there . . .

If Deborah were not naturally psychotic, she had by now frightened herself into a state not distinguishable from that.

Lydia burst open the door. 'D'you want any lunch?' she asked importantly. 'I'm making beans on toast for Daddy and me. Mum's gone out.'

'Go away,' sighed Deborah. Lydia did, banging the door. She was too busy to wait.

Judy had indeed gone out. Dring, coming back from the fell at one o'clock, had found her crying in the bedroom. He understood clearly enough that there was nothing he could usefully say to her at this juncture; it was he who had shattered her, flinging at her the freedom she wasn't yet sure she wanted. He was inclined to think she did, but it was for her to decide. Detachment has to measure up to its opportunities. These, offered, appear as their opposites; what drudge wants to be useless—what wife, free—what mother, unwanted? Judy didn't know what she wanted; that was her trouble. He suggested:

'Go out somewhere for a breather. Go and talk to somebody— Go and see Miss Dunn, for instance—'

Judy sat up and said furiously: 'Miss Dunn isn't the kind of person one just drops *in* on. Nobody round here is *that* kind of friend. That's just what I always *say* ...'

But she had gone out, taking the car, bucketing down the lane without farewell. Lydia, hearing the car, had come from her gardening to say: 'Gosh if she's only just going out, when'll we have lunch?'

'We needn't wait for her? I'll get us something. Or could you?'

'Yes, *I* will. I'll wash my hands first,' she added generously.

She even washed up afterwards. Dring dried for her. The day remained sunny. Lydia went down to see what Susan was doing. Dring sat at his table, surveying the gill in all its length, tearing up fussy little notes he had made for various half-conceived projects. Deborah lay on her bed. Judy did not return.

In her absence the house's afternoon silence solidified. Even when Lydia coming home switched on the radio in the sitting-room, the sound travelled up soothingly through the floor-boards to Deborah, who hadn't been asleep, but, now that she sat up to look out of the window, felt heavy, drugged by the ebbing of some general commotion ... We might all be in a trance, she thought, watching the stillness of Mellbreak beyond the unmoving, red-spangled larch twigs. We might stay like this for a hundred years and nobody would notice ...

But as if that were too much to expect, there approached an outsider, running down the slope of fellside that Deborah could see obliquely from her window. Some ruddy walker, wall-clamberer, knocker at doors. Instead of climbing the wall —much less looking for a gate, of course; they never did *that* —the figure came straight for the thorn hedge at the top corner of the garden. Optimist ... Deborah, watching, was reminded of the prince who hacked his way through to waken the Sleeping Beauty. She played with the fantasy that she was to be rescued ... In fact the knight-errant was attacking the hedge with great purpose and to some effect. He swiped with a stick, edged in a long sideways stride, twisted and finally made a dive and slid into the compost heap on his stomach, leaping up undaunted and turning out to be no armoured knight or prince but—Lesley. *Christ*.

Deborah shot away from the window and fell on to the bed. Lesley what's-her-name—Gibson. Popping out of the fellside when she was supposed to be in town and even if she weren't, lived at Yeovil—or Minehead— Somewhere, anyway, like that. How the hell had Lesley got *here*. The shock made Deborah's teeth actually chatter. At the same time she couldn't help seeing that it was just *like* Lesley to pop up simply anywhere at all. You'd never known where you had her ... She'd organized the squat and then at once moved out again, with—what was his name—Chris. She'd opposed the demo but dragooned everybody into the library sit-in. She'd taken Deborah in hand at the time of the Vincent flap and dragged her to the VD clinic. —All these memories, collapsing upon Deborah as if a ceiling had given way, left her stunned. She couldn't cope with Lesley. Not now. Not *here* ... It was too much to hope that Lesley merely was a trespassing walker and didn't know Deborah lived here. Lesley always knew exactly where she was going. Deborah could only burrow into her pillow, paralysed, and wait for what all too soon happened—

Bang-wallop at the bedroom door. 'Hullo. Your Papa said I could come up and find you—'

He *would*.

Deborah, peeping under her elbow, found the undeniable intrusion of Lesley—bouncing, smelling of fresh air, carroty hair on end, a scratch on her forehead—alarming and reassuring. It was, after all, only Lesley ... And there was no need to make an effort; Lesley did all the talking, meanwhile pulling off her anorak and attending to her toilet with Deborah's comb:

'... Walked all the way from Mosser over the tops ... John's gone to see some friend of his in Seascale ... Can stay the night with you if that's okay ... Stayed last night at Barrow House ... Did Skiddaw in the morning ...' And at last, perching on the bed: '... And how are you, kid?'

'Okay,' managed Deborah, faintly.

'You look fine. —Who've you been hearing from? You knew Mike'd been moved to an open place? Celia's buggered off somewhere— She always was a clot. They'll pick her up before she gets to Katmandu or wherever she thinks she's going ... Got a bog in this house?'

Forced, up to a point, to act as hostess, Deborah up to a point responded. Lesley's observation that she looked 'fine' had flattened her; couldn't Lesley *see* ... What Lesley did see was that Deborah was altogether different in appearance from the shrivelled waif she had last seen in town. Catching sight of herself in the bathroom glass as she ushered Lesley in there, Deborah was forced too to see what Lesley meant. She didn't know whether to be pleased.

Lydia had taken Lesley's arrival with much less dismay. This was, she saw, just unexpected-visitor day. Rising to the occasion she went obligingly down to Martins' to borrow some eggs. While Dring scrambled these she made raspberry Instant Mousse with a pint of milk she had borrowed on her own initiative, after laying the table with a set of melamine mats she had dug out of some forgotten drawer; they depicted English cathedrals and were one of Fiona's presents. Also she had tied back her hair with orange ribbon that looked as if it came off a chocolate box.

Deborah, too numb to escape, followed Lesley to the table. Any encounter between Lesley and Pa would normally have boded nothing but calamity. Unable to cope, Deborah discovered that she need not. She need say nothing; Lesley and Pa did all the talking; they argued, apparently, the place of art in modern society; once or twice Lesley flashed at Deborah an applauding glance; God, Lesley *admired* him ... It was turning out to be a friendly meal, and Deborah couldn't yet see the snag in it—

The telephone rang. Lyddie, still obliging, went. She came back to announce: 'It's Uncle Michael.'

'... Excuse me,' said Pa, rising.

'Hullo, old son,' said Michael. 'I've been thinking over your problems and I'll tell you what you'd better do. In the first place—'

'Save it,' said Dring.

'—'Mwhat...? I only wanted to suggest—'

'That's slightly better expressed. But, thanks, we're coping.'

'I'll bet. —You never *would* take advice, would you.'

'People so rarely do. Are you all all right, at your end?'

'... Oh; yes. Fine. What's happening, then, about Deb? Are you managing to send her to Foster?'

'That's still to be decided.'

'Good Lord, you're taking your time about it. If it were my daughter I'd have settled it ages ago. What's the hitch now—apart from money?'

'I might know when I've seen the man tomorrow.'

'... *You're* seeing him? Can't see that'll do much good ...'

'I,' said Dring quite amiably, 'am in the middle of a meal.'

'Okay, okay. I just do wish you'd let me help.'

'Well, I did ask you to lend me some money, didn't I. I suppose it's no use asking you again?'

Michael's silence was cautious; he suspected mockery. 'Well, I daresay it *could* be arranged, but it always makes things so damned awkward in the long run—'

'It might make *me* if anything less awkward than usual. Try me.'

'You bastard. —Look, why don't we talk the whole thing over reasonably? What I wanted to say: Okay if we pop up for a night, just Fiona and myself, right after Easter? I don't want to come at the holiday weekend; everywhere's so beastly crowded. Next week the kids are both going to Granny's for a day or two so it'd fit in.' He added, aware that his suggestion was not being leapt at: '—Fiona wants to see Judy. She could maybe give her a bit of womanly chat—'

'Then how', said Dring, 'if Judy pops down to you, for a night? She could do with a break.'

'... Ye .. es ... But I thought, you know, the countryside, and all that—I mean, Judy'd miss it?'

'Not for one night. In any case, you're constantly telling us that your place is as good as in the country?'

'Oh, of course. —But we aren't madly gay here, you know. There'd be nothing much going on, to amuse Judy—'

'There's less here.'

'Oh. M'm. Well ...'

'I haven't put this to Judy yet; she may not care for the idea. As a matter of fact, at present she's thinking of leaving me altogether.'

'Good Lord.' A pause. '—Well I can't say I blame her.'

'She'll be grateful for that.'

'—No, there's no need to be shirty. I'd no idea things were as bad as that. Of course we'll have her here if they are— Only hasn't she got ... friends, you know ... who'd be more use to her?'

'Let's hope so.'

'Good Lord,' repeated Michael, inattentive to that, 'I'd no idea ... No wonder you don't want us to come. Lord, you *have* made a muck of things, haven't you.'

'It might lead to improvements—'

'It can't do that. —I must say you sound pretty bloody cheerful, considering.'

'Yes; I am.'

'I must say, I don't understand you in the least,' said Michael with satisfaction. 'I've been feeling rather sorry for you lately, but *now* I think you're just dippy.'

Judy, coming into the house soon after eleven, felt her way upstairs, hoping not to wake anyone. Her bedroom light was on. From the doorway she watched Alan, reading. He lowered his book to say:

'I should warn you, there's a friend of Deb's sleeping in the sitting-room.'

She hadn't expected—or wanted?—an open-armed welcome, but now she felt he had laid in reinforcements to make her the stranger. Not replying, she moved back into the passage and stood there, nowhere. But there *must* be comfort ... She looked into Lydia's room. Lydia was a rumbling heap in the bed. At its foot, the floor seemed to be strewn with pale fragments—was the wall collapsing? Judy went to inspect what seemed to be a jagged hole in it—

'Hullo,' said Lydia drowsily.

Caught between door and bed—between 'I didn't mean to wake you' and 'Whatever happened to the wall?'—Judy took a step forward and knelt, laying her face against Lydia's on the pillow. She said softly: 'I've been in Carlisle.'

Somebody must want to know ...

Lydia said: 'Did you buy a new kettle?'

'... I forgot. I tried on coats. But none of them fitted. Then I saw a film.'

Lydia stirred, hot sleepiness wafting over Judy. 'We had beans on toast for lunch,' she said. 'And then scrambled eggs for supper. Deb and Daddy and thingummy ... What colour?'

'What colour what?'

'—Coat, did you get?'

'I told you: They didn't fit.'

'Oh. What colour,' persisted Lydia, her head rolling away, '*didn't* you get then?'

So like Lyddie; she liked to have even the blanks filled in ... Judy put her arms round her and admitted: 'There was a rather nice blue one.' Just right for London in April.

'Oh,' on a fading note. She was asleep again. —No; suddenly she fought her arms free of the covers and they slung round Judy's neck. 'Night-night,' she said, hugging.

That was the devil of it: if Lyddie forgave her, there was no real reason to stay here.

*   *   *

[218]

'If I took on every case regardless, just because it was interesting ...' said Dougal Foster.

'I suppose so,' Dring allowed.

They were both pacing the office, not so much restlessly as intently. Foster came to a halt by the far window and said: 'You couldn't conceive what the overheads are nowadays in a place like this.'

Dring didn't imagine he could. The Hollies was the kind of elaborate late-Victorian mansion that by now would anyway be falling to pieces. From the other window he looked out at roughly cut sloping lawns and a high crumbling wall—mortared—that must stretch for a good half-mile round the property. Foster's tone had been confidential rather than querulous. He looked just now not the brilliant doctor but the suffering householder, haunted rather than harassed by the struggle. 'Haven't you', said Dring, impatient on Foster's behalf, 'someone to worry about all that side of things *for* you?'

'My accountant worries *me*. When problems mount, they usually come home to roost. —I shouldn't really have launched out here.'

'But you'd be cramped in any institution,' reflected Dring aloud.

They both turned from their windows, eyes crossing as they paced again. Foster recollected that it was not his own case history they were discussing; he did not suspect Dring of entering into that to further his own cause; simply, the man was taking a fair, all-round view. 'You do see, I can't make any promise about length of stay here.'

'In either direction.' That, Foster took at face value. Short of money he might be, but so was everyone; he was scrupulous about discharging patients as soon as he was satisfied. He nodded.

'... Still,' harked back Dring, 'Deborah *is* interesting.'

'They all are.'

'M'm. —She's got real originality.'

[219]

Foster conceded: 'I thought so. —You know, I have *pared* these damned fees—'

'I know. —There's a possibility', said Dring, 'that her mother may be taking a job. Which might bring in enough to be going on with.'

'A sign of the times,' said Foster, smiling a little, 'when a man can send his wife out to earn ... Her mother', he resumed, serious again, 'appeared more personally involved with the girl than you are.'

'Naturally,' said Dring, forgetting that he was speaking to someone better qualified than he to assess the naturalness of relationships. '... I think she's felt she had to make up to Deb for my lack of interest.'

'You aren't interested in your daughter?'

'Well, at heart I've been envious of her ... originality.'

Foster's pacing had brought him back to his desk. He perched on a corner of it, watching Dring thoughtfully. 'You're a writer, Mrs ... Dring told me. Haven't you made the success of that that you'd hoped to?'

'No,' said Dring simply.

He had arrived at the far window. Gazing out into a shaggy yew hedge, surprised by darkness, he forgot Foster as the sub-visual mechanism sprang into action and Wenzel Weinberg was there again, as large as super-life, waiting in the wings ... '—Sorry; what did you say?' he asked Foster, turning, annoyed at the interruption.

'We'll have to sort something out, somehow ...' said Foster; but that was not, Dring was pretty sure, what he'd said just then; if he'd said something about his writing, the man could save it; Dring hadn't come here for a free consultation about himself.

What Dougal Foster had said, he saw no point in repeating. It had been only a piece of jargon, and obviously the man hadn't heard it because he had no need to. If he hadn't succeeded as a writer it had been his own fault and according to Dougal's guess, Dring knew that as well as anybody.

'Let me know,' he said sliding off the desk, 'as soon as you can, about Deborah.'

Later that afternoon Deborah came out to the garden where Dring was making a sustained effort to rebuild a stretch of fallen wall. He knew the principles well enough. The footing stones were still in place and he'd filled in the hearting up to the first set of throughs. He knew too that, once you picked a stone up, you must not put it down again except to set it in the wall. Consequently, he had been standing here a full five minutes with a stone in each hand, determined not to give way.

'Hullo,' said Deborah, sitting down on a spare stone and wrapping her arms round her knees.

'Has Lesley gone?'

'Yes. That was John's car, if you heard it.'

'I heard it. I hope it gets them back to wherever it is.'

'They're going on to Scotland ... Daddy?'

'M'm?' Pondering his stones, he betrayed no surprise at that appellation.

She hesitated for a while, then asked: 'Would you really put me in a bin? —A proper one...?'

'Does that', he countered after a moment, 'put a different complexion on your insanity?'

'I just wondered.' As he looked at her she smiled, wryly. 'Well, I expect, in a way, it does ... But, Daddy?'

'M'm?' These stones were getting heavy; he rested one hand on the wall.

'You see, Lesley was talking to me this morning and telling me what she's going to do next. Actually it's what she really came here to tell me about. It's Lesley, and Morgan Wallis— he's a bloke who's just finished his degree in chemistry— Anyway, you see, there's this man who's running a kind of relief operation in the north region of Wezanda. Africa, you know. I forget what its old name was—'

'So do I. Go on...?'

'Well, this man—Brian Potter—was born there. His parents were missionaries. They must have been awfully good ones because even after independence the people still liked them—I mean, they're dead now, but Brian Potter, because of that, he still has the "in" to the place. Nobody else has. It's a frightfully poor country and they need help badly but their government won't allow any foreigners in. Except Brian Potter's lot. You see, it's a marvellous chance, isn't it.'

'For Lesley and her John?'

'Not John, he's a bit of a go-getter—Morgan. They need people just to be general dog's-bodies at the moment. Distributing supplies and mending buildings and teaching elementary hygiene. Brian Potter doesn't want to work too fast, in a way, because he's got to establish goodwill and lay the foundations for more advanced work. It's not a religious thing—Brian Potter's not actually religious, in spite of his parents. But he loves the people there, and that's as good, really, isn't it?'

Dring rested both hands on the wall, hanging on patiently to his stones. Deborah's flow of speech—even if it were mostly quotation of Lesley—amazed and warmed him. 'I think I catch your drift. You'd like to go and work for Brian Potter in Africa yourself, wouldn't you?'

'Oh yes. It would be *just* the thing. It'd be valuable and useful and I'd learn far more than I would at a university about the real life of the world— Anyhow, it would only be for about a year. After that, I could maybe start again ...'

'I see. We'll have to think about it.'

'Yes, because, you see, the only thing is ... Well, Brian Potter can't afford to *pay* his helpers. They don't need money at all, really, when they're there. But there's the fare, there and back, and things ... Lesley's got some money because her grandmother died.'

'Unfortunately, one of yours has had her fortune squandered, and the other is in rude health.'

'Oh yes. I only meant ...' She picked at the lichen on

her stone, sighing. 'I just thought I'd tell you about it. I know quite well, if we haven't got enough money for Dr Foster we haven't got enough for this either, have we?'

'We'll try to work something out.' This nutty idea of Africa reassured him that she was recovering sanity.

Deborah nodded, as if accepting that. Then she said:

'Everything comes down to money, doesn't it?'

He glanced at her suspiciously. He was about to say: Don't *you* start. But she was smiling faintly at her scrap of lichen; her tone had been ironical.

And then she showed that her values were sound after all, because suddenly pointing into the roots of the sycamore a little way up the garden she cried in a different, joyful voice:

'Oh *look*—the first primrose!'

He tossed down his stones, and they went together to admire it.